ETIVE

ETIVE

best wishes

Ronald D Morgan

Ronald D Morgan

Matador
Unit E2 Airfield Business Park,
Harrison Road, Market Harborough,
Leicestershire. LE16 7UL
Tel: 0116 279 2299
Email: books@troubador.co.uk
Web: www.troubador.co.uk/matador
Twitter: @matadorbooks

ISBN 978 1803135 212

British Library Cataloguing in Publication Data.
A catalogue record for this book is available from the British Library.

Printed and bound in Great Britain by 4edge Limited
Typeset in 12pt Minion Pro by Troubador Publishing Ltd, Leicester, UK

Matador is an imprint of Troubador Publishing Ltd

To the brave men and women who gave their lives
so that the rest of us could have our freedom and to
those who returned but suffered so much with PTSD.
War had changed their lives and those around them
forever!

As Laurence Binyon, the English poet, wrote in his
First World War poem, *For the Fallen:*

'They shall grow not old, as we that are left grow old:
Age shall not weary them, nor the years condemn.
At the going down of the sun and in the morning,
We will remember them.'

One

The nightmare

Laura cried out, begging her. "I want to see my baby." Through her tears, Laura could barely make out the blurred vision of the lady in her room, her matronly presence enforced by her staid sense of dress.

Laura was bereft. She felt her heart had been torn out. Her head pounded, her eyes swollen from the constant crying. The lady sitting on her bed stood, before walking to the table by the small window. She poured a glass of water from a ceramic jug, her back to Laura all the time. She kept talking to Laura, calmly but firmly, then returning to the bedside, she placed the water on the bedside cabinet.

Taking hold of Laura's hand, she said softly, "I am sorry, I am so sorry, but it was for the best!" Then, without emotion, she dropped a bombshell, sharing the shattering news, "Your baby didn't live."

With that, Laura's staring eyes were wide and wild with fear, disbelief and anger, before she screamed, "Noooooooooooo."

Laura restlessly tossed and turned in her bed, her blonde curls, damp with perspiration, pressed against her forehead. "Noooooo," she screamed, as if in great pain and with that, awoke startled and disorientated as she sat up in bed and was relieved to see she was in her own small room at the Scottish boutique hotel where she worked. Her heartbeat gradually slowed as she looked around at the comfortable, familiar room. She was alone; her breathing eased. "Thank God," she said out loud, finally realising it was all just a nightmare.

Laura shuffled into the bathroom, splashing cold water onto her face, her tall frame bent to witness her stressed visage in the mirror, her blue eyes positively bloodshot as she reflected on the content of her very real terrors of the night.

Flashes of the unsettling dream came back to her. Laura could still see the lady, recalling she wore a mustard-coloured twin set of a matching jumper and cardigan, offset by a string of pearls, a brown tweed pencil skirt and brogues. She was probably in her mid-forties. Her short brown hair gave her a stern look and her manner was matter-of-fact, almost officious, a little like a headmistress.

Still rattled, she reflected on her dream. She searched the corners of her mind for any little morsel of information, but all she seemed to keep hearing was the mystery lady repeating softly, "Your baby didn't live."

Laura could not remember any more of the dream, no matter how hard she tried.

Showered and dressed, Laura headed downstairs to reception, but still her nocturnal picture show perturbed her. For some reason, she kept thinking about the lady in her room and especially her brown laced-up shoes, something from a bygone age which an older lady, perhaps a grandmother, may have worn.

"Good morning, Mrs Draper," said Laura to a guest who was heading for the breakfast room. Laura settled behind her desk at reception, shuffled some papers and tried to put her disturbing night behind her.

Arisaig House was set in the West Highlands and could be reached by rail and road. Many used the road to the Highlands from Fort William at the end of the glens and headed for Mallaig, a ferry gateway to the Isle of Skye and the Western Isles.

Surrounded by ancient woodland and beautiful coastline with lots of scope for scenic walks and punctuated by idyllic beaches, Arisaig House had terraced gardens and a tennis court. Arisaig House was quite simply in a very tranquil and secluded spot.

Arisaig House and the area had a fabulous history which Laura was well aware of, as her job was also to help market and extol the virtues of this fine house, which had been refurbished to a high standard but sympathetically so.

History was all around. On 20th September 1746, following the failure of the 1745 Jacobite rising and the defeat at Culloden, Bonnie Prince Charlie left Scotland for the Isle of Skye and ultimately France from Borrodale

Beach, sometimes referred to as 'Prince's Beach', just below the house, which could be approached over boggy land. The cave in which the Prince took refuge on his last night in Scotland could be found within a stone's throw of where Arisaig House was now. Just to the west, across the meadow at Borrodale House, which the English troops searched without finding him, the original home of the Macdonalds, who gave haven to Bonnie Prince Charlie, was razed to the ground in 1746, but its splendid, much bigger, replacement was still imposing and dated from the 19th century.

Over one hundred years later than the original Borrodale, in 1863, FDP Astley, a wealthy industrialist from the Midlands, commissioned Philip Webb, the 'Father of the Arts and Crafts Movement', to build a shooting lodge amid this spectacular West Highland scenery and to include terraced gardens, which gave birth to Arisaig House.

But it was the knowledge that during the Second World War, Arisaig House became the headquarters to the Special Operations Executive, who took over the area to run paramilitary training to prepare agents for missions in Occupied Europe, that was troubling Laura's mind this morning and kept bringing her back to her dream, almost as if she had been transported back in time. Arisaig and its environs were a draw for many tourists, especially those with an interest in WWII, and a dwindling number of returnees who were once associated with Arisaig House and other houses and lodges like Garramor, Traigh House, Camusdarach Lodge in the area, having served here.

The remoteness and wild nature of the Lochaber peninsula and the neighbouring islands and many lochs no doubt brought it to the attention of the Special Operations Executive and the desire for training their operatives on tough terrain, with the benefits of its seclusion from prying eyes. It was soon closed off to all but military and authorised personnel and the few locals who lived in the area.

Laura had worked at Arisaig House for a few years now, following her university degree in hotel management and a few other jobs where she had gained experience. Laura tended to live in when she was working. The three-hour drive each way to her home in Comrie, where she still lived with her mother, Elise, was a bit too much, given the vagaries of the Scottish weather. It was springtime and the tourists would soon be descending on Scotland in their droves as Easter approached.

Not that it mattered for Arisaig House, as even though it was very expensive to stay here, it always managed to have a high occupancy rate all year round; a credit to the owners and Laura.

This somewhat understated property was in a glorious setting, and people liked the seclusion and comfort of Arisaig House. Not far down the road, the pretty village of Arisaig was a real tourist honey pot, sat on the shore of the sheltered Loch nan Ceall, not far from the port of Mallaig and gateway to the Isle of Skye, Inner Hebrides and other Western Isles, or going east, not far to the highest mountain in Scotland, Ben Nevis, and the little town of Fort William, gateway to the glens and lochs and everywhere boasting majestic scenery. The house was cocooned by trees and linked to a small road by a now thickly lined rhododendron hedge, ending up in a dead end in front of the house. All conveniently not far from a small rail halt at Beasdale.

Arisaig's collection of largely white-painted buildings dotted between the harbour and the line of the road to Morar was situated on an inlet on the Morar peninsula at the western end of the legendary 'Road to the Isles'.

The rocky coast bordering cool blue seas and white sand all added to making the village a great base for exploring the incredibly scenic surrounding countryside. The views out to the islands of Rhum and Eigg were amazing, and the beautiful sunsets were a photographer's dream.

Laura felt blessed but then contemplated it would not be long before the midges became a darn nuisance, but that was not what was bothering her; she could not help but feel her dream, whilst disconcerting, was related to her in some way. As if disturbed by a sixth sense, she was perturbed.

Whilst Laura was happy to be here and enjoyed her job, she yearned for a change. After all, she was approaching thirty years of age.

Due a weekend off, the next morning, Laura headed back to her home in Perthshire. She enjoyed her drive home and listened to a Celine Dion album, singing along to *The Power of Love*. As she came beside Loch Earn, she smiled to herself. Not long until she was home now in the little village of Comrie, a picturesque little village which sits in the middle of Glen Lednock and Glen Artney on the River Lednock. It was once famous for weaving and as a town used by drovers as a staging point to cross the river and utilise some refreshment and rest at the local hostelries, before driving their cattle and sheep onwards to market. Comrie is a combination of Gaelic words, meaning *coming* or *running together*. Its population is barely over 2,000 and it feels like everyone knows everyone and their business! Laura loved it!

Before long, Laura was entering through the door of her childhood home. Her mother came down the hallway to meet her, hands in yellow rubber gloves as she was doing a little spring-cleaning. After they had hugged each other, Laura dropped her holdall in the hall and they retired to the kitchen for the obligatory cup of tea.

"How is work?" enquired her mum.

Somewhat distant, Laura said, "Yes, fine. Busy, of course."

"What's bothering you, Laura?"

Laura looked at her mum without replying.

"I am your mam. I can tell something's not right."

Laura smiled knowingly. "It's just a couple of nights ago, I had this dream."

After Laura had explained what she could remember, her mother, head on one side, just said, "It's just a bad dream, probably something you have read or seen on the television mixed up with lots of other images."

Plaintively, Laura said, "It is more than that, Mam. It seemed very much like it really was me or something and someone very personal to me. Mam, it got me thinking. I never met my grandparents. What were they like?"

"Well, I never met your father's parents, they had passed on, but my parents were very caring. They had me late in life and always seemed old to me. Don't get me wrong. They did what they could for me and loved me, and I wish they could have met you." Smiling, she sat with her hands wrapped around her teacup, exuding a love that invisibly enveloped Laura and comforted her.

"Where were they from?"

"From the Isle of Skye, where I was born, at Neist Point."

"Why didn't you have any brothers and sisters?" enquired Laura.

Turning her back on Laura, Elise boiled the kettle again. "Another tea?"

Laura nodded. "Yes, please."

Sitting back at the table, Elise took her daughter's hand. "I was adopted, Laura, way back in 1943. Things were tough back then, but my parents, Tam and Mary Macrae, were salt of the earth and took me in and gave me a wonderful life. They couldn't have children, so for me, I guess I was a blessing and they doted on me."

"That's nice to hear how much they cared for you, Mam. I didn't know you had been adopted, which makes their care and love even more special. I know they died before I was born so, after their departure, did you stay on the Isle of Skye?"

"After my parents passed, I did for a short while, staying with my dad's sister, but soon I moved to the mainland and got a job in a house as a scullery maid here in Comrie."

"Were you ever told who your biological parents were, Mam?"

"Alas, no. It is so long ago now, a lot of water has gone under the bridge."

"Aren't you curious to know if your real mam and dad might be alive?"

"Yes, I am, lassie, or I was, but why rake up the past and perhaps open old wounds?" said Elise with resignation and a sigh.

"Did my dad know you were adopted?"

"I do believe I shared that with him. Your father was such a good man, Laura."

"I know, Mam, I miss him dreadfully. I cannot believe he is gone, taken so young. Where did you meet Dad?"

"Oh! I am not sure, maybe a ceilidh in Comrie one Christmas."

"Was it love at first sight?" said Laura, raising her eyebrows and smiling.

Elise hesitated. "Shall we say your dad grew on me."

"That's not very romantic," jibed Laura with a smile. "As you say, he was a good man.

"Do you mind if I make some enquiries about who your real mam and pa may have been?" said Laura, returning to her interest in her family ancestry.

"Feel free. I doubt if you will find anything out," said Elise with a shrug.

"Do you still have any relatives anywhere?" said Laura, all excited.

"As far as I know, my pop's sister is still alive, and last I heard still living in Glendale, a few miles inland from Neist Point, but I have lost touch with her over the years."

"That's great, Mam. Let me have her last address and next day off I have, I will drive onto Skye and try and find her."

Elise nodded and, waving her hand dismissively, said, "Come on, go and unpack. I will make some lunch!" Elise began clearing the cups away.

Two

In search of a grandmother

A week later, Laura took the famous 'Road to the Isles' and caught the CalMac ferry from Mallaig for the short thirty-minute crossing to Armadale on the Isle of Skye. She had pondered driving further north to Kyle of Lochalsh and driving across to Skye via the bridge, but it was a lengthy detour and she didn't want to waste time. She just wanted to relax and let the sea breeze blow through her hair and fill her lungs, full of excited trepidation for what she might find out in Glendale, assuming her great-aunt was still alive, or, if this sister to her Grandfather Tam was not around, if anyone else knew anything of Tam and Mary Macrae, her mother's adoptive parents.

As close as Skye was to her place of work, this was only the second time Laura had been, and she had never been to her mother's birthplace on the far west tip of the island. Laura anticipated it would take about seventy-five minutes to drive the winding road from Armadale where the CalMac ferry had docked. It was a cool and clear day, as spring comes a little later to these northerly latitudes of the British Isles, and she had a great view of the awesome Cuillins, the mountain range with peaks approaching 1,000 metres. The roads were quiet and she wished she had time to go walking in this area but comforted herself with the thought, *Maybe another day.*

Right now, her focus was on Janet Macrae, a spinster she had never met. Laura decided to take a break for a cup of tea and a snack in the large village of Dunvegan to gather her thoughts. Seeing the sign on the wall '*Skye's oldest bakery*', how could Laura not take advantage of this temptation? Even better, the Dunvegan Bakery had its own little café, which was old-fashioned and bijou but where the bakery goods were all freshly made. An older lady took Laura's order. She couldn't resist the carrot cake, which she justified as a treat and decided to forget her waistline. She needed the sugar rush, as she was full of trepidation. Would she indeed find her great-aunt? What might she discover? Lots of 'what ifs', and somehow that made her fatigued.

Before long, Laura was back on the road, sustained by the delicious piece of cake and with a takeaway beef pie in her hand, which she had persuaded herself would be lunch and dinner.

Shortly, she took the turn onto a single-track road and headed into Glendale. Laura's mother had explained this was an *area,* an estate of land owned by the community. It wasn't a village as such, and Glendale's shops, restaurant and community hall were all located in the small hamlet of Lephin, a couple of miles from where Great-Aunt Janet's last letter came from. Her mother, Elise, had said it was just all so parochial, and as a young lady she had felt boxed in and wanted to explore the wider world beyond Skye.

It took another thirty minutes to reach her destination, regularly pulling in to let vehicles pass and tooting her horn to encourage the occasional obstinate sheep or cow to move from blocking the narrow road, where they would stand in defiance of any oncoming vehicle.

In truth, Laura barely noticed as she waited each time.

As Laura approached Waterstein, another community of dwellings spread around the locality, she marvelled at the remoteness and soon found herself turning up a slightly inclined drive off the road before stopping in front of a detached cottage, reassuringly built in the traditional island style, typified by its whitewashed stone walls and corrugated tin roof with a low doorway and black painted door. It looked positively chocolate box.

Above Laura, billowing clouds like smoke signals were peppered across the blue sky, reflecting her own confused state of mind. Her recent disturbing dream was constantly streaming through her head like some tantalising code which needed deciphering, but she could make little sense of it.

Laura mused that at least it was close to Lephin for supplies, and wondered what lay on the other side of this croft door as she hesitated, then knocked. As she did so, she turned around and took in the glorious vistas of Loch Mor. *Absolutely idyllic*, thought Laura, as she figured this was not far from Neist Point, where she understood her grandparents had lived.

This cottage looked like it was on a working croft, as there were sheep grazing on the verdant emerald green land all around.

As there was still no answer to her knock, Laura walked around the side and up the path. She walked through the free-range hens, who clucked in warning and parted, allowing Laura to enter a small garden that boasted enough produce for market but more likely was for personal use to sustain her great-aunt, smiling to herself at the thought. It was a rather peaceful and tranquil location. Before Laura could knock on the back door, it creaked open and a little old grey-haired lady stood a step below her, balancing on a stick. She suspiciously asked, "What d'ye want, lassie?"

It was a rather abrupt welcome. "I am looking for a Janet Macrae."

The lady looked over her oval-rimmed glasses and replied, "Who wants to know?"

Laura smiled at the clearly strong-minded and cautious woman. "Well, I am her great-niece."

The lady stepped up towards Laura and looked closer. Sharp as a whip, she quizzed, "Are you Elise's bairn?"

"Yes! I am indeed."

"Umm…" She turned and said as she walked away, "You had better come in. It's fair jeelit outside, lassie, and shut that door."

Laura entered the low-ceilinged croft. A smell of peat fire assaulted her senses as she followed the stooped back of the arthritis-plagued lady – who, she noted, was wearing a well-worn paisley pinafore. Its mooted washed-out colours had seen better days – before they shortly entered a cosy living room with a welcoming open fire.

"Now let me see. So you are, Laura, aye, I can see a bit of your mother in ye."

Laura smiled.

"So, what brings you up here in tae the back of beyond, lassie?"

"It's beautiful here, Great-Aunt Janet – oh! May I call you Janet?"

"Aye, ye dinnae need to add Great-Aunt, it makes me sound old," she said with a grin as she peered over her glasses as the atmosphere thawed.

"Well, I have been thinking recently about my ancestors and realised I knew little or nothing about them, and my mam, Elise that is, gave me your address in the hope you might still be here and that you could help me with some of my family tree," said Laura hopefully.

"Well, as you can see, us Macraes dinnae go far. I have been farming here for many a year. This is our home and we don't know any other way of life."

Nodding, Laura went straight into her mission. "I would really like to know about my grandparents, Tam and Mary Macrae, and am intrigued to know the story of how they managed to adopt my mam."

"Do ye now? Well, you had better boil the kettle whilst I warm up some scones, as this could be a long chat, Laura. You know, your grandparents and your mother lived very close to the lighthouse at Neist Point. Their home is still there, about a fifteen-minute walk from here. Actually, we have a little beach just ten minutes from here. Perhaps we can go for a walk and I can show you."

Laura smiled as she lowered her lofty frame to avoid banging her head on the thick, slightly skew-whiff old wooden beam lintel that seemed to slope in line with the kitchen floor. As she entered the small and homely kitchen, she said, "So my grandparents lived nearby, close to the lighthouse?"

"Aye, they did. Tam was the lighthouse keeper after the war," said Janet as she pulled on the cupboard handle of an old-fashioned metal and glass 'Kitchen Maid' cabinet painted in a pale eggshell blue that had seen better days. Conveniently, the panel dropped down to provide a work surface. The interior sported a sliding glass door cupboard marked 'Bread', from which Janet extracted a tin once used for shortbread biscuits, but the scratched and dented tartan-emblazed container was now filled with home-made scones.

Soon settled back in the living room, Janet watched as Laura took a dainty bite of her scone (not wanting to admit she had just had a large slice of carrot cake in Dunvegan), before having a sip of the steaming hot tea. "Very tasty, Great-Aunt, sorry, Janet," said Laura as she juggled to keep a crumb of scone from leaving her mouth.

"I am glad you like them. It's a pleasure to share them with you, it will save my waistline," she said with a knowing look. "I dinnae see too many folk around here so have no one to bake for."

Laura cupped her hands around her blue-and-white-hooped patterned mug of tea, and looked expectantly at Janet.

"Tam and Mary died when your mam was just sixteen years old. Sadly, they had a car accident, leaving the road, resulting in the vehicle being upside down in a gully. Both must have been killed instantly. The police figured, as it was at night, that an animal must have caused them to swerve off the road with tragic consequences, but Sergeant McCormick told me they had been witnessed having a wee dram or two in Dunvegan with friends, and he left it at that." Janet took a sip of her tea, her eyes not leaving Laura's shocked expression.

"Oh my gosh! My mam hadn't told me anything about them dying or that she was only sixteen years old when they passed. Perhaps she is still traumatised by the memory of that event."

"Maybe," said Janet wistfully. "Your mam was staying with me that evening. When her folks did not arrive home, we were worried.

"Eventually, I had a call from Sergeant McCormick and he told us the awful news. We were dreadfully upset and, of course, your mother was beside herself. She went even more quiet than she normally was.

The wee bairn withdrew into herself for a long time. Anyway, it was decided she would come and live with me and help on the smallholding.

"Your mother always seemed in a dream. I knew she was restless; I just thought she was still grieving, as I was. I had allowed her to spend a week with an old school friend in Portree during the summer. She had taken the bus over to Portree. What I didn't know was that whilst she was there, she had managed to get a job as a servant in a big house in Perthshire, Comrie, in fact."

"So, Mam has not moved very far since then," said Laura, smiling and stating the obvious. "Why did you lose touch?" questioned Laura.

"The lassie was young and confused. Elise was bitter and angry. She had lost her parents, and perhaps my old-fashioned ways were a bit restrictive for her, and in many ways, she just wanted to run away. She had a rebellious streak, let's leave it at that."

Laura nodded and understood.

"Very sad for you all, Janet," said Laura timidly. "Do you know who my mam's real parents were?"

"Well, ah dinnae ken who they were. That's a mystery and I suspect that it will stay so. Tam had been helping with the war effort and had gone to help out between here and the mainland. He was a good seaman and I believe he helped with boats and transferring military folk around. He did mention ferrying people from Morar train station, perhaps to somewhere on Loch Morar or up to Arisaig or sometimes to the Inner Hebrides, who knows. One day, he came home with a bairn wrapped in a blanket. Your grandmother couldn't believe it.

"At first, she thought Tam had abducted her, and certainly was not prepared for having a newborn bairn. Tam told the story that a mother from the Arisaig area had gone into labour on the ferry and by the time they transferred her to the mainland, the mother had been very ill in childbirth but they had managed to save the baby. Somehow, Tam persuaded the doctor that he and his wife, Mary, would temporarily look after the bairn, which was born short of term and quite weak. He presumed the mother had died.

"His wife, Mary, had always wanted a bairn, but the shock of one arriving was a little difficult to handle at first but she soon accepted the situation, as it would only be short term until its future could be decided. So, instead of the child heading to an institution on the mainland, it went with Tam. For some reason, he got it in his head to bring it home and believed Mary would love the chance to look after the child, or at least be okay with it.

"Mary at first was very tentative, cautious indeed, as she didn't want to get attached to the bairn and then have it taken away from her, but time passed by, days turned into weeks. For whatever reason, no paperwork was filed, nothing official done, and your mam stayed with them. Mary and Tam were very taken by her and now it would have been hard to let her go. Nevertheless, she feared the knock on the door to say a new home or relative had been found for the wee one.

"Weeks turned into months. It was almost as if, in the fog of war, she had been forgotten.

"Mary and Tam doted on your mam, and as far as they were concerned, after a year, she was their daughter. Mary enjoyed playing piano and was very good at it. Tam particularly loved a piece by Beethoven, *Für Elise*, so your mother became Elise Macrae and eventually her birth was registered as such." Janet closed her eyes as if she wanted to rest.

Allowed the opportunity to examine her great-aunt's lived-in face, complete with wrinkles around the eyes yet a very smooth skin and structured high cheekbones, Laura thought Janet must once have been quite an attractive lady.

Bursting back into life as if recharged, Janet firmly told Laura, "Och! I never found out who the mother was or indeed if the father was a local. I dinnae ken if Tam knew, and if he did, he kept it to himself."

Again, Janet closed her eyes and just as Laura was thinking she should leave for the journey back to Arisaig, Janet opened up again.

"A number of years later, Tam did speak to me one evening that Elise was tinn – very ill – with scarlet fever. He was having a wee dram and then another one and became a little maudlin. He was worried Elise was not going to make it.

"It was then he told me what he said was the whole story. He had returned to Loch Morar to act as a boatman for transporting some men on military exercise. He went into Arisaig to drop men off at Borrodale Beach and they invited him up to Arisaig

House. It was then he met a lady wearing a uniform, and she was accompanied by an older lady carrying a baby.

"He said, 'I had no idea what a bairn was doing there. I was astonished and started to chat. As I opened the door for the woman with the bairn, as she walked to an awaiting car, I asked who the baby belonged to.' To his utter disdain, she said, 'The child is unwanted. I am taking it to a home for orphans down in London.' He couldn't bear that and on a whim of caring responsibility, he somehow managed to persuade this lady that he could provide a loving home for the little one, and he and his wife had always wanted children, but his wife could not have children.

"After initially saying this was out of the question, something struck a chord and she softened. She returned to the house whilst asking Tam to hold the youngster and beckoning him to follow her into Arisaig House.

"She then disappeared before returning with the officer, who asked a few curt but direct questions about the type of life Tam and Mary could give the child. Tam waxed lyrical about the Isle of Skye and the beautiful location and environment the little one would be welcomed into, and it was decided there and then that Tam could take her into temporary care. Which nowadays would be incredulous to believe!

"Tam learned from the woman, who he remembers was from Arisaig, that the mother was in the military when she became pregnant and had been taken to a camp at Inverlair near Inverness, but she absconded and somehow travelled all the way across the country through Fort William. Where she was going, he was not sure, but she was on the ferry to the Knoydart Peninsula, or possibly Inverie, when she went into labour."

"Wow!" said Laura. "That is almost unbelievable," as Janet nodded with raised eyebrows.

Janet just smiled. "So, take your pick, maybe nah'body knows, lassie. Ah dinnae ken an' ah dinnae care. Neither story may be accurate or true, as Tam could weave a tale, but it was wartime and strange things happened."

"Do you remember the woman from Arisaig's name?" asked Laura as she tried to collect as many pieces of her ancestry jigsaw as possible. She was soon to learn that getting the pieces to fit together would prove a lot tougher.

"Aye, it was Mctavish. Mary, I think, no, Lizzie, that's it," said Janet with conviction.

Laura went on to say that not only was the whole story fascinating, but the coincidence that she worked in this very house, now a boutique hotel, was unbelievable.

It had started to get colder and Laura had a good long drive back yet and wanted to make a start before it became dark. Saying her goodbyes and taking Janet's phone number, she promised to ring, keep in touch and ask her mother to do so too.

"Come and see me again," said Janet as she watched Laura walk away from her home. Laura waved as she turned to see her great-aunt framed in the small doorway. Laura jumped in the car and headed back to the mainland.

On her drive back to Armadale, Laura pondered many scenarios as they scurried through her mind. *How would a lady be pregnant in the military? Why was she in Inverness? Why wasn't she sent on leave or discharged from the Army?* Tam's story, as recanted by Great-Aunt Janet, didn't quite stack up.

Three

Discovering S.O.E.

Laura wanted to learn more about this wartime era. Over the next few weeks, Laura spoke to local people, like Harry, an enthusiastic local historian who was intrigued by WWII and in particular the military occupation of the area which involved the Special Operations Executive.

Harry entered the hotel lobby from the courtyard and felt as if he was on a pilgrimage and that he had reached the holy grail of his S.O.E. journey. He had been here before, but each time was special and a privilege as he thought of those who had come here in wartime with one goal: to train and ultimately use their training to harass and defeat the enemy.

"Hello, you must be Harry," greeted Laura, who had been loitering in the foyer, awaiting his arrival. She appreciated his punctuality for their meeting, which fitted with her morning off.

"Hello, dear, lovely to meet you. Fine morning for once!"

"Indeed, would you care for a tea or coffee?"

Over a cup of coffee on the delightful terrace at Arisaig House, Laura briefly shared the reasons for her interest in Arisaig House but stopped short of talking about the circumstances, just saying she believed her grandmother was here during the war, circa 1943/44.

Laura recognised the small wiry character with a beard and wispy ginger hair, perhaps about mid to late fifties. She had seen him around on many an occasion in Arisaig and Mallaig.

Laura was soon captivated by his enthusiastically rapid speech as he explained and effused about the wartime history of Arisaig and the whole Lochaber area as he pointed out that a number of parts of Scotland and the United Kingdom in general became restricted areas, some because of army manoeuvres, but in this location, it was kept secret primarily because of the Special Operations Executive and commando training.

Arisaig House was the hub of the physical side of the training that the secret agents had to undergo. Arisaig House, like many places, had been requisitioned for military use, and even today most official details were still kept from the public under the guidance of the Official Secrets Act.

"So, what was the Special Operations Executive, Harry? Can you explain it in lay terms?"

"Ah, I am sorry, my dear. In a nutshell, Churchill

wanted a sabotage organisation putting together to slow the Germans up, or as Churchill put it, 'to set Europe ablaze', so around July 1940, the S.O.E. was formed under a chap called Hugh Dalton. It essentially planned to train agents and send them into Europe and later other parts of the world's theatre of war to cause the Germans problems, and also to report back information that would be helpful to the Allied war effort. In time, this idea morphed to raising secret armies to rise up against the Germans as and when the allies could raise an invasion force, but we are getting ahead of ourselves. Let me tell you how they operated and why they were here.

"Arisaig House was requisitioned by the British Army in 1941 to help form the base of the Special Operations Executive following Winston Churchill's concept of forming an elite corps trained for the express purpose of undertaking covert operations on the ground in occupied Europe, and for Churchill's desire to 'set Europe ablaze' and fight back against the Nazis! This area was ideal for secrecy for the clandestine training needed."

Harry gave Laura the background to the four-stage plan in the training of prospective agents of the British Special Operations Executive. At preliminary school, the agents' characters and potential were assessed. This was first at Wanborough, a large private and relatively isolated property in Surrey, without revealing to them what the S.O.E. did.

Those candidates not deemed suitable were soon sent to the 'cooler', where they were ensconced for most of the war, as the powers that be feared they may give away secrets of the organisation and what they had learned about the S.O.E., whilst those who passed the preliminary stage were sent to paramilitary schools, referred to as the group A schools. These were based mainly in Scotland, where the courses were as gruelling as the unforgiving terrain. It was the same course for men and women and they learned to kill with their bare hands or more likely the famous FS knife.

The trainee agents were then introduced to parachuting at Ringway, Manchester, and finally their spy craft techniques were polished up at the S.O.E.'s own finishing schools for spies, the group B schools, based at Beaulieu in the New Forest. Not until all these stages had been successfully completed were the agents sent to a holding flat, or residence, where they awaited their final briefing before being dropped into 'the field'.

The preliminary school's syllabus included physical training, weapons handling, unarmed combat, elementary demolitions, map reading, field craft and basic signalling (use of radio communications). Agents who fell at this initial hurdle would also likely be sent to the 'cooler' at Inverlair in Inverness-shire.

Laura found this all very interesting but wanted to learn more about Arisaig House and its wartime occupants.

"Is anyone from the second world war at Arisaig House still alive?"

Without losing his flow, Harry answered, "Oh yes, a good number," before continuing with great enthusiasm to detail their weapons training and unarmed combat, which equipped agents for close combat only. William Fairbairn and Eric Anthony Sykes – two ex-Shanghai municipal police officers – taught unarmed combat, or silent killing. The pair gave their name to the FS fighting knife – a small knife used mainly by the Commandos – and their Fairbairn Fighting System was subsequently taught to members of the FBI and CIA.

Weapons training introduced these brave men and women to weapons such as the Colt .45 and .38, and to the fabled favourite, the Sten gun, which was considered unreliable by some. Just ask the guys who tried to kill Heydrich.

"Aah! So, women were trained here too," interjected Laura.

"Indeed, they were," said Harry. "In fact, the agents were taught to fire by 'pointing' the gun and tucking their firing arm into their hip, rather than by the more orthodox method of taking aim, and they always fired two shots to be certain of their target. This system was known as the Double Tap system and it was specific to S.O.E. agents. Some ladies were excellent shots. One of the inventions used to help the students with target practice was a life-sized figure on a winch, set to come at the agents at speed.

"Demolition and explosives training was essential, as sabotage was high on the S.O.E.'s remit. Using dummy explosives, rail sabotage was carried out with the co-operation of the West Highland Line, who also supplied the school with a train and crew. Agents were taught how to lay dummy charges and fog signals, then quickly hide to observe the havoc they hoped to wreak. There is evidence of some explosive and target practice on Borrodale Beach." Harry showed some cartridges and detonators he had found in the location, displaying them with relish, his raised eyebrows inviting Laura to be amazed, as if she was witnessing a handful of gold dust!

"At first, it was just men, but it soon became clear that women had a much better chance of travelling around any occupied country unsuspected by the Germans because of the lack of men due to incarceration or being transported elsewhere to work, so women were enrolled and trained.

"Arisaig was an ideal base to challenge the agents in paramilitary activities and was also perfect, as it was so secluded." Standing, he walked to the edge of the terrace. "See those two small brick-built outhouses, they are important and left from wartime days. Shall we take a walk in the grounds?" said Harry, drawing breath.

After passing through the orchard and walking across the dew-soaked meadow, they stopped at the two small huts in the lea of a line of trees, on the path down to Borrodale Beach. "The hut on the left was probably where munitions were kept, but the one on the right is reputed to be where they would perform mock interrogations. See the small windows with bars on them?"

Something dawned on Laura. She started to wonder about her real grandmother; could she be one of the ladies being trained?

Harry let Laura survey the buildings before adding, "It was rumoured there was a subterranean firing range too, situated perhaps in the basement of the house."

"Indeed," said Laura, "I believe there are still bullet casements and markings in a fireplace on the lower ground floor – a reminder of the room being used as a firing range, albeit for indoor short-distance target shooting by the S.O.E., or so I have been told by my employer. I must show you them sometime. I will just need to get permission, Harry."

"Yes, please!" beamed Harry.

Harry continued. "After Arisaig, assuming all was well with the conduct and progress of the agent, they would head south to the Manchester area around Altrincham, undergoing parachute training at Ringway, which is now Manchester Airport. Students did at least two jumps, one from a plane and one from a static balloon. They were all equipped with a little spade attached to their leg, for the purpose of burying their parachute and S.O.E. jumpsuit after they had landed. In the 'field', they had to jump from altitudes as low as 300 to 400 feet, and would hit the ground within ten to fifteen seconds. The plane's pilot was compelled to drop them at such low altitudes in order to avoid enemy radar detection.

"Finally, they invariably headed for near the south coast, what is now more renowned as a tourist attraction. Beaulieu formed part of the group B agent training schools. It was based in the New Forest on Lord Montague's estate, where eventually there were eleven schools. Within each school, there were five departments covering topics such as agent technique, clandestine life, personal security, communication in the field, how to maintain a cover story and how to act under police surveillance.

"There were also specialist subjects, such as burglary and picking of locks. One department dealt with the recognition of enemy forces, whilst others dealt with the dissemination of white overt propaganda and black covert propaganda, and with codes and the use of invisible inks.

"One famed instructor was 'Killer' Green, who had learned his skills from master figures of the underworld. One of the first lessons that the agents learned was that you didn't pick a lock – instead, you manipulated or pushed the lock back, using a protractor. Taking impressions of keys was also a simple matter. For this, agents would carry a matchbox full of Plasticine, which could take an impression of a key. It was easy then to make a copy."

Laura was incredibly thankful to Harry, and it helped her understand a lot about Arisaig House and areas and indeed the S.O.E., but what she really needed was information on her grandmother. Was she barking up the wrong tree? Time would tell.

Interrupting, Laura asked, "Well, that's all fascinating and a great help to me, but one other thing, Harry, have you heard of a Liz or Annie Mctavish that worked at Arisaig House during the war?"

"Sorry, that name doesn't ring a bell. Well, the surname is associated with a family that used to own a lot of property in the vicinity if I remember rightly, but they all pretty well emigrated to Canada many, many years ago, before the Second World War even. I will keep my ear to the ground, though, and bear the name in mind when I speak to people. There was a Duncan Mctavish at Rhu Farm not far away, but he died and the property was sold, I believe."

"Thank you so much for all your wonderful information. You are really knowledgeable on the wartime happenings of this area, it has been very interesting. I just wish I could find out more about the people here during that time."

Harry smiled and replied, "My pleasure. I know I go on but it is so intriguing to me that this little corner of Scotland played such an important part in World War Two. You might want to try Vera Atkins, you know. She knew all the F section agents."

Laura frowned. "F Section? What is that, Harry?"

"Yes, the F stood for France. Of course, the person you are looking for may not have gone into France but possibly one of the other occupied countries or even not been an agent, but if you can get to speak to her, Vera, that is, she can rule that in or out for you, and that would be a good place to start."

"How do I find her?"

"I will call you this afternoon with the number of a former serviceman who may know." With that, Harry said his goodbyes and, with a spring in his step, departed.

Four

A secret agent?

It took a bit of doing but after a few phone calls and knock-backs, Laura had obtained the addresses and telephone contacts of Vera Atkins and her boss, Maurice Buckmaster the former head of the S.O.E., now deceased. His son had been able to help, as Maurice, Vera's former boss, had kept in touch. He also supplied the number of the S.O.E.'s code master, Leo Marks. Tim Buckmaster suggested he may be helpful and at the very least informative.

Much to her surprise, a few weeks later, after an initial rather curt and dismissive telephone conversation with Miss Atkins, when Laura tried again, this time she was granted an audience and duly set off south, travelling by rail on a few days' leave.

Laura had established from Harry and some

official records that now Vera would be eighty-seven, and she lived in a house on the South Sussex coast called 'Chapel Platt'. It sat amidst a group of white clapperboard houses perched on top of a hill close to the Church of St Thomas. At the bottom of the hill was Winchelsea Rail Station.

It was a fine day with blue skies and a few clouds; she felt the light onshore breeze playing with her hair as she ascended the hill. Laura walked up the hill from Winchelsea Rail Station, resting every now and then to look back as she climbed the lengthy incline to take in the view. At the top, she was about to turn right into Chapel Platt but realised she was a little early, and suspected that could be almost as bad as being late to a stickler for detail like Vera Atkins. She suspected correctly.

So, seeing the churchyard of St Thomas' at the top of the hill from Winchelsea, she decided to have a few minutes browsing around the gravestones and composing herself for what she felt may be a rather testing experience ahead. She spotted the New Inn over the road from the graveyard and pondered having a stiff drink to galvanise her for the coming meeting but decided against it.

Twenty minutes later, Laura pressed the buzzer on the intercom at Chapel Platt, which also had a camera allowing Vera to see who was there from the safety of her own home. Shortly, a stooped but once tall, elegant lady, still displaying attractive facial features, opened the door and said, "Laura," before turning, leaving the door open. She walked aided by a stick, a roll of white/

grey hair tucked under, exposing the nape of her long neck.

As Laura followed her, she noticed a portrait of Vera on the wall. Vera turned and saw Laura looking at the portrait.

"It was painted by a former S.O.E. agent and P.O.W., a chap called Brian Stonehouse, one of my agents, a talented chap."

Laura thought it looked recent, as Vera was clearly shown in old age and not too different from today.

Vera sat on a chair, pressed a button and slowly the lift ascended up to the next floor. Laura took the stairs to the first floor.

As she reached that level, Laura paused a moment to survey the view through the window, as she saw that Vera's house looked out to the sea beyond.

"Come and sit down. Do you like that view to the sea and over to the Dungeness Lighthouse?"

Laura turned and nodded. "From up here it gives you a feeling of space and freedom, a bird's eye view. Is that why you chose to move here?"

Vera didn't respond.

Laura surveyed her host. She noted her face was dabbed with face powder, a modest lipstick, and a silk floral scarf was draped around her shoulders. Three rings with large diamonds sparkled on her hands.

Though slightly stooped now, Laura estimated Vera had in her prime probably been a similar height to her.

"Please take a seat."

Settling in a winged green velour armchair, Laura veered from her task, perhaps overawed by Vera's presence.

She so wanted to ask what Vera might be able to do to help her find her grandmother, but for some strange reason she started asking about Miss Atkins.

"So how did you get involved with the S.O.E.?"

Not losing eye contact, Vera drew on her cigarette and blew the smoke skywards towards the nicotine-stained ceiling.

"In 1941, after living in Chelsea for a while since arriving in the UK, I became an Intelligence Officer with the S.O.E. F Section, but it's not me you need to know about, is it?" she said impatiently.

"No, no, you are right," said Laura, feeling chastised. Before she knew it, Laura had told the whole story of her search for her grandmother and how this lady had given birth to her mother, and she wondered if Vera remembered this incident, and ultimately if she knew the identity of her grandmother.

"Look," said Vera, "I dealt with over 400 girls as agents and, after all, your grandmother may not even have come through F section. You don't know her name or seem to even be sure if she was with the S.O.E. If dear old Evelyn Balchin was still around, she might have been helpful, as she dealt with a lot of recruits, whether they ended up being administration staff, potential agents or secretaries like herself.

"Over one hundred of my agents did not return when the war ended, so I made it my personal mission to go to Europe and find out what had happened to them, as I couldn't accept the agents were missing in action presumed dead. I needed answers.

"I wanted to track down any Germans responsible

for the demise of my 'girls.'" With that, Vera drew sharply on her cigarette and puffed the smoke almost immediately from the corner of her mouth, squinting her eyes to avoid the cloud of exhaled burning tobacco.

Dejected and realising the futility of her question, Laura's eyes took in the pale green carpet as they spoke, and scanning the surrounding space, she noticed there were lots of vases with flowers in dotted around the room, a few pots of flowers growing too. A *Daily Telegraph* lay open at the stocks and shares pages on a coffee table in front of a very long, faded and worn pink couch.

Laura had noticed on arrival when Vera returned to her chair that she had a magnifying glass which she removed before seating herself. An open letter, coaster and ornamental paper knife lay on a side table.

The walls of the room were adorned with landscape paintings, but there were no shelves full of books, which for some reason surprised Laura.

Laura was taken by how when addressing you, this confident lady spoke surprisingly softly and calmly, albeit in deep tones, perhaps because of her fondness for smoking. She seemed to be permanently in a cloud of smoke, as she didn't appear to inhale. Vera extracted her untipped cigarettes at regular intervals from their elegant silver box in which they were contained. She placed the cigarette quite deliberately between her first and second finger and struck a match, and Laura felt like she had momentarily lost her in a scene from the wartime film *Brief Encounter*, with railway engine steam enveloping her on the station platform.

Laura listened to Vera talk of the bravery of her girls.

"They were full of self-confidence, which encapsulated all of them, partly from their attractive presentation and appearance," said Vera. "They all had an uncommon trait of self-reliance I knew I could depend on."

As she twisted the matchbox round and round in her free hand whilst narrowing her eyes, puffing on her cigarette held in the other, she seemed to slip into the ether of time as she recalled the regular missions of her girls.

"I recall an occasion on a perfect June day as I picked up the scent of dog roses through the car windows as we approached the aerodrome at Tangmere. Sometimes, I went to Tempsford if a parachute drop was in order, usually from a converted Halifax bomber. I remember having met the agents at a rambling old chocolate-box cottage, Tangmere Cottage, talking about inconsequential everyday things, before heading the short distance to the departure hut and going through the agents' belongings to make sure nothing would give them away to the Boche should they be captured, perhaps an English lipstick, a matchbox, a perfume, a label."

Vera didn't say but Laura was sure Vera must have wondered if she might ever see those agents again.

Laura put her shoulders back and tried again.

"Miss Atkins, do you have any recollection of any agents who went to Arisaig, Morar, Inverie or any of the training establishments who you heard might have become pregnant whilst there?"

All of a sudden, Vera Atkins' face seemed to harden, almost a blank stare.

Stubbing out her cigarette, she said dismissively, "I am tired, it was a long time ago. As I have mentioned, I went to Germany after the war finished to find my girls alive and dead and seek the perpetrators who caused the deaths of any who were indeed dead."

"Were there any you didn't find?" said Laura.

This question seemed to sting Vera momentarily.

"I was given the rank of Squadron Officer as a reward for my services and to help me succeed in this post-war mission. I arrived in Berlin in the allied sector and transferred to a place called Bad Oeynhausen, where I insisted on speaking to the man in command, who turned out to be a chap called Somerhough.

"Somerhough confirmed he had the concentration camp Kommandants of both Sachsenhausen and Ravensbrück, concentration camps both north of Berlin, and allowed me to interview them after mocking my chances of getting anything out of them. I believe they were surprised by the outcome. It was a very tough and emotionally charged journey, but I stayed in Germany until I had traced everyone.

"I have to add that a lot of this was with the help of, and in conjunction with, a doughty fellow from Yorkshire called Major Bill Barkworth, who I believe was establishing what had happened to some S.A.S. troops dropped behind enemy lines in 1944 as an advance party. Many of them were executed after being tortured, as were four of my girls we tracked down to Natzweiler Concentration Camp in the same area around the Vosges Mountains between Nancy and Lyon in France, not far from the German border. It made sense we joined forces and shared information."

Vera Atkins was a strong and tenacious lady, for sure. Laura had confidence in her that she must have instilled in those around her during WWII. Laura learned from others over the coming weeks that Vera Atkins was proficient in languages, notably French, German, English and a little Romanian. Vera was very well spoken and Laura felt she had an air of confidence, almost superiority, but also that she didn't suffer fools gladly.

Lots of thoughts were going through Laura's mind. *Who was my grandmother? Could Vera Atkins actually know who my grandmother was and therefore is being economical with the truth, perhaps for reasons of protecting me and my family from the truth, or does she genuinely not know? After all, I could not give her a name, yet in another breath she inferred she remembered all her agents, so clearly and logically. She does not have an inkling about my grandmother's identity. Or just perhaps my grandmother was not active in the French theatre of war. Maybe not even an agent or military-related.*

Other somewhat random things Vera recalled needed factoring into Laura's findings. She had said the first agents were ready to be deployed around April/May 1941, but these were all men. In fact, Basil Street in London, where they were living, was bombed, killing and injuring a couple of the agents. She recalled that a chap called George Noble was the first agent dropped into unoccupied France. His code name was 'Bombproof'.

Vera recalled in early 1942 that a chap called Selwyn Jepson joined the S.O.E. and he took over the role of recruitment from Lewis Gielgud (brother to John, who later became a famous actor). It was about this time that ladies were recruited for the first time, perhaps because the resistance in France had realised that women were less scrutinised. Men were often stopped and grilled. Or possibly it was Selwyn Jepson's idea? She wasn't sure. Then Vera reiterated that she remembered all her girls and their personal stories, so this led Laura to believe her grandmother was not one of her girls. This took the wind out of Laura's sails.

Miss Atkins mentioned that after recruitment she often met them in a brief interview to establish some background and family information.

Vera confirmed women enjoyed far more success and all her girls were confident, courageous, effective and prepared to take risks. Vera looked at Laura and said, "Be assured, we made them very aware of the risks!"

Briefing her agents then seeing them off at departure points such as Tangmere or Tempsford was very clear in Vera's mind. She said she found this time most stressful on top of her already busy schedule and this involved often being out until 4am in the morning and being back at the office later that morning, and often working until between 7pm and 9pm, waiting for the BBC news when they sent coded messages to agents in the field.

Laura asked Miss Atkins what briefings involved. Miss Atkins habitually pulled on her cigarette, looked to the window as if recalling her agents then looked back at Laura or, more accurately, past her and said, "We gave them topical information on the region they were going to, providing documents such as they would be expected to carry, like an identity card. Of course, this was a new identity in which they had been schooled, a military history card and of course ration cards. All this was kept updated with information they received from interrogating arriving refugees and from newspapers brought back to the UK. We had invariably spoken to these agents in the S.O.E., Flat number 6, Orchard Court in Portman Square.

"I felt for the pilots and their crews too. Sometimes, the agents parachuted out of Halifax bombers, although often the Lysanders – little three-seater planes – took agents in and landed and picked up passengers. The pilot flew in difficult circumstances, with a map on his knees, doing his own navigation, often finding a river and following above that then as he neared his drop point, looking in the dark for a small field somewhere in France, trying to make out a V of electric torch lights being held by the welcome committee of the resistance. There was no room for a navigator, you see, when passengers had to be brought back.

"Sometimes the Gestapo were there to ambush them or arrived just as an allied airplane was taking off. There were many alarming close shaves like that which I was told about."

Vera then reiterated that all volunteers were self-starters, full of courage and prepared to take risks. They had to be, as the estimated survival rate was one in two. About 25–30 per cent of them were arrested. Out of about one hundred agents, around forty returned.

"I am getting rather tired now." Vera stood as she said this, as if to dismiss Laura.

Slightly dispirited by her failure to get anything that might lead to discovering the identity of her grandmother, she thanked Vera and said her goodbyes. As she was just going out of the door, Vera said to try some of the other sections. Maybe Balkans 133 or Far East 136 may be worth exploring.

As she was leaving, Laura turned and said, "Could I contact Selwyn Jepson? Where does he live now?"

"Alas, poor old Selwyn passed away in 1989, I am afraid," said Vera, puffing again on yet another cigarette. "Selwyn was an author pre-war and turned his hand to screenplays and directing after the war, you know.

"Leo Marks may still be around. He was a codebreaker. He joined the S.O.E. in June 1942, if I remember correctly, and used to come up with original poems that were used as codes by the agents, as Leo was a very capable cryptographer. He promoted the use of original poems in preference to widely known ones, forcing an enemy cryptanalyst to work it out the hard way for each message. Using a well-known verse would have led to the enemy quickly establishing an agent's entire set of keys after breaking the key to a single message, or possibly just part of the key.

"Marks wrote many poems, later used by agents, the most famous being one he gave to the agent Violette Szabo, *The Life That I Have,* which gained popularity when it was used in the 1958 film about her, *Carve Her Name With Pride.* Apparently, Marks wrote the poem in Christmas 1943 about a girlfriend, Ruth, who had recently died in an air crash in Canada; supposedly the goddaughter of the head of the S.O.E., Sir Charles Jocelyn Hambro."

With that, Vera recited the poem:

"'The life that I have
Is all that I have
And the life that I have
Is yours.

The love that I have
Of the life that I have
Is yours and yours and yours.

A sleep I shall have
A rest I shall have
Yet death will be but a pause.

For the peace of my years
In the long green grass
Will be yours and yours and yours.'

"Delightful, don't you think?
"Not sure Leo would know anything, though."
Laura smiled, made a mental note, thanked Vera

profusely and said her goodbyes. As Laura headed back down to Winchelsea Rail Station, the wind off the sea had picked up and the sound of seagulls distracted her. As she sat on the train heading home, she ran the afternoon's conversation through her mind and made copious notes to herself whilst everything was fresh in her mind.

Laura never met Miss Atkins again, although they did speak on the phone.

Five

More questions than answers

Laura felt the visit to Vera, whilst compelling and interesting, had been fruitless but was not going to let this go. As frustrating as it was to be stalled by the apparent reticence of Vera to share information, she reflected it may be the Official Secrets Act all these people had signed that was making them appear reluctant to help. But there is always another way. Gradually, a Plan B started to emerge and by the time Laura reached Comrie, she had decided on her next move.

She would ring Maurice Buckmaster's relative again, his son Michael, who everyone knew as Tim, to see if he had any ideas. She would speak to Leo Marks. Laura also decided to make a newspaper appeal but pondered which paper. She thought it had to be a national publication, although maybe a local newspaper in Scotland might jog someone's memory over this child being born, but then as she pondered this course of action it seemed this would be a long shot, given the secrecy around at the time.

Laura arrived late into Comrie and wearily told her mother of all her investigations and how well Aunt Janet was and how impressive but vexing Vera Atkins had been.

"Well, I'm off away to bed," said Laura. "I am very tired, emotionally and physically."

The next morning, she packed ready to head back to work a day earlier than she had planned. Elise was cooking breakfast as Laura's nose twitched at the smell of bacon wafting up the stairs. Entering the kitchen, she said, "That smells delicious, Mam."

"Aye, well, I thought you could do with a fry-up before your long journey back to Arisaig." Laura didn't answer, as her focus had been drawn elsewhere.

"What's this?" said Laura, her attention attracted by an old chocolate box wrapped in an emerald green ribbon, which was sitting on the pine kitchen table.

"Oh, that's a few photos, letters, diaries and whatnot I found in the attic when I went ferreting after your last visit. I knew I had them there somewhere," she said, carrying on frying some eggs.

"Are these yours then, Mam?"

"No, they are my mam and dad's."

"Wow! Can I open it and take a look?"

"Oh well, let's have breakfast first then we can settle down and have a good gander at them."

Laura could not hold back her excitement. "There might be a clue or two to my true grandmother's identity, Mam!" she said as she hurriedly sipped her tea and wolfed down her breakfast.

Seeing Laura's impatience, Elise smiled. "Okay, away with yoursel', lassie. Go and have a look, I will be with you in a minute. I will just wash up. Shall I make another pot of tea?"

Laura had not heard; she was already sliding the ribbon off the box and removing the scenic lid, which displayed a faded Highland crofter's cottage with views towards a loch in the distance, some highland cattle in the foreground.

Inside, a treasure trove of postcards and other memorabilia stared back at Laura. As she sifted the contents, some black-and-white and sepia photographs emerged in her hands; one of a couple, the lady carrying a young girl on her hip. The girl had long hair in ringleted curls.

Elise had quietly followed her daughter into the lounge and rested herself on the back of the settee, looking over Laura's shoulder.

"I believe that is me when I was, oh, I suppose about three years old," said Elise, hesitatingly.

"What a lovely picture, Mam. Is this Mr and Mrs Macrae, your mam and dad?"

"Aye, it is, I know what you're thinking. They look quite old, well, I guess folk did in those days, but they were probably only in their late forties."

Laura was like a child in a sweet shop, trying to take everything in but not knowing what to look at first.

"Have you had a good look at these, Mam?"

"Not really, Laura. I did take a brief look at them when I was much younger after Maw and Da passed. I had left the few belongings they had with Janet, but I did keep this boxful of memories with me, although some of the pictures, well, I do not know who they are. Perhaps Janet could help."

Laura focused on an envelope. She thought the handwriting was beautiful, as if written by a practised calligrapher. Drawing out the thin blue notepaper from its similarly blue vellum envelope, she immediately felt a connection, as if this was important.

Dear Mr and Mrs Macrae,

I hope you are well and life is treating you kindly.

It has been a while since I have been in touch but I just wanted to check if your daughter, Elise, is well and in fine fettle. How is her schooling going?

It seems an age since we last corresponded and I apologise for not writing sooner. It has just been so hectic since the war ended and, well, everything has seemed like a whirl!

Since I last wrote, I have moved back home to the south coast, having been demobbed, and I was just thinking about you all.

I do hope this rationing is not on for much longer and we can start to get some more produce, although I suspect wonderful people like you are self-sufficient, having your own small croft.

Well, that's all for now. If I am ever in your neck of the woods again, I will be sure to look in.
Best wishes,
Marjorie Spencer
25 Shore Road
Poole
Dorset

Laura looked up at her mum who had by now sat opposite in her comfortable green velour armchair. She sat nursing her cup and saucer and inclined her head. "What is it, Laura?"

"Mam, I think this might be a letter from your real mother."

As she handed it over, Elise reached for her glasses case on the coffee table. Perching her spectacles on her nose, she read and looked at Laura. "Well, it might be, but I would have thought it would have been a bit more inquisitive and asked more questions about my well-being, don't you think? Perhaps even been more intimate and said something like 'give my love to my darling daughter.'"

"Perhaps, Mam, but we need to find out if this lady is still alive, whoever she is, as I am sure she will have some information that might help us discover who your mam is."

A few minutes later, Elise was speaking on the telephone to Janet, her aunt.

"Well, hello, Elise. Long time no hear. It was great to meet your daughter. She is a pretty wee lass and bright too."

"Aye, thank you, Janet. I am so sorry I havenie been in touch in all these years, but Laura has brought me up to speed. I am so pleased you are doing well."

There was a slight pause. "I have the feeling you need to ask me something, Elise."

"You are still as perceptive as ever, Aunt Janet. Do you remember that chocolate box full of letters, photos and other small mementos my maw kept and which you gave to me?"

"Aye, that I do!"

"Well, there is a letter in there." Elise went on to explain the content and then hesitated.

"And ye want to know who this might be, is that it?"

"Do you know, Aunt Janet?"

"No, not really. I do vaguely remember a woman calling by the house, and I had been out and stopped by to drop a few provisions off for your maw and pa. You were sitting on this lady's knee; she had brought you a woollen bonnet. Perhaps she had knitted it herself.

"Look, Elise, I dinnae think this was your real mam, if that's what you are asking."

"Well, who could the letter writer have been? Was it a distant relative? After all, this address is in the south of England."

"All I can remember is I seem to think she was something to do with one of the services. It might have been the First Aid Nursing Yeomanry or the Women's Auxiliary Air Force or something like that, and the only reason I have that inkling is something your da Tam said once, that she wouldn't be coming to see us anymore, as she had been demobbed.

"She was in civvies when I saw her, so I might be confused. Sorry I cannot be more helpful. I know that's not what you want to hear."

"Thank you, Aunty. That is very helpful, though I think we will still try and find her. You never know."

"No, you don't, but don't go getting your hopes up. Tam and Mary were your folk. They were very good to you, treated you as if you were their own."

Elise felt a little guilty. "I know, Aunt, I couldn't have wished for better parents. I have missed them every day of my life since they..." Elise struggled to control her emotions. It was a huge wound from the past, which was being opened slightly and was sore, as the memories bled into the here and now, albeit a trickle.

"I know, well, let me know if you find anything out, and come and see me with Laura. It has been so long since I last saw you."

"I will, I promise. Cheerio for now!" With that, Elise hung up.

Laura and Elise discussed Aunt Janet's thoughts and sifted through the rest of the box, enjoying the snaps but learning nothing new. In fact, the box of intrigue had brought more questions than answers.

Laura put her arm around her mum. "It must have been so tough to lose your parents so young, and of course losing Dad too. I wish I had known Dad."

Elise looked dotingly at Laura. Holding her hand, she said, "I am so proud of you and thankful I am blessed with such a caring, respectful, loving daughter, even if she is a bit too inquisitive sometimes," smiling as she did so.

"Well," said Elise, composing herself and changing the subject rapidly, "Marjorie Spencer!"

"Yes, Mam, first thing tomorrow, I will set about seeing if I can find a telephone contact or confirm the address for Marjorie. I believe I can get that from Directory Enquiries, or, if not, an electoral roll, and failing that I will go and visit her, assuming she still lives there."

"Listen to you, quite the detective. I think you should have joined the police. Perhaps I should call you Agatha! Well, try and find something out before you go to the expense of making a long and possibly fruitless journey. Right, I am tired. I am off to bed," said Elise, kissing the seated Laura on the head. "Sweet dreams!"

So much for heading back to work a day ahead of time, thought Laura as she took a cup of Horlicks to bed. This popular malt wheat and barley drink was like comfort for the soul. It took her back to her childhood days when her mum used to do the same. She used to say it helped her sleep.

That night, Laura could not sleep; she was too excited.

*

Over the next few weeks, work was as busy as ever, and occasionally one or two people would visit who had wartime memories or ties to Arisaig House, and Laura did due diligence, asking them as many questions as she could, building up more of a picture of the time back then. One was a daughter of a former man in charge at Arisaig House during the war, a Lieutenant Colonel AD Balden, but she knew less than Laura and indeed she herself was looking for information and answers to questions.

Laura had been stymied in her efforts to find out if Marjorie Spencer was still at the Poole address. She had written to the address but no reply had been forthcoming until, one day, Laura received a telephone call out of the blue.

"Yes! This is Laura Dewar, how can I help you?"

"Hello, you will not know me," said a voice with a very English accent. "My name is June Maurice. I believe you wrote to my mother, Marjorie, and asked her some questions about someone who lived on the Isle of Skye?"

Laura's heart skipped a beat. "I did indeed." There was a silence as Laura feared she might soon be hearing that Marjorie Spencer was no longer alive.

"We are so sorry to take a long time to reply, but my mother has been in hospital. Unfortunately, she has broken her hip, but we do hope she will be home tomorrow. She asked me to give you a ring to apologise for not replying earlier."

"I am so sorry your mother has had a fall, but very pleased she is on the mend. Might I be able to ring her or even pop and see her sometime in the near future?"

"I am sure Mum would like that, but she is not sure how much she can help you. She is quite good but she has slight dementia, and her memory is not as good as it once was. It's age, I am sure you understand."

Laura took down the home number and also her daughter's contact details and said she would ring in a few days, allowing her mum time to settle back in.

Sure enough, keen not to waste time, Laura called Marjorie Spencer three days later.

"Hello, sorry to bother you, is that Marjorie Spencer?"

"No, it is her neighbour. Hold on."

Laura could hear a lot of rustling and commotion before someone else came on the phone, and a very weak voice, cracking as she spoke, entered the conversation. "Hello, who is it?"

"Hello, Mrs Spencer. It is so good to hear your voice. Are you feeling better?"

"Who is this?" said the voice, becoming stronger and somewhat disgruntled.

"Oh! I am sorry." Speaking more slowly and louder, she continued. "This is Laura Dewar. I sent you a letter from Scotland and spoke to your daughter June a few days ago. Is this a good time to talk?"

"My hearing is not too good, so please speak up!"

Laura repeated the message, louder still.

"Oh yes, I do recall my daughter telling me she had spoken to you. How can I help?" she declared. Laura was surprised this elderly lady's voice bore such authority even now.

Laura briefly ran through her finding the letter signed by Marjorie and her efforts to find out who her mother was, asking Marjorie how she knew Mr and Mrs Macrae. "Mrs Spencer, I would like to know especially if you could shed any light on the name of my real grandmother." She waited with bated breath.

"My married name is Marjorie Spencer Dorricott but everyone calls me Madge. Yes! I do remember coming to see Mr and Mrs Macrae. It's a long time ago now and I have lost touch with them. How are they?"

"I am afraid they have both passed away." Laura explained briefly about their tragic early demise.

"How very sad. So, you must therefore be Elise's daughter?" said Marjorie, sounding as if she was interrogating Laura.

"Yes! I am indeed."

"Laura, I hope you don't mind but I am rather tired. If I may, I have your address, I will write to you and tell you what I know. I am not sure how helpful it will be but I will rack my brains to see what I can do to help. How is Arisaig House? I had happy days there, even though it was the war."

Laura described the house as it was now and that much was unchanged. "Perhaps one day, Marjorie, you would care to visit. I would love to show you around."

"That would be nice, dear, but I am afraid I am a little too frail for travelling so far now."

"What did you do at Arisaig House and in the war in general?"

There was a brief stillness, and Laura thought Marjorie had hung up.

Marjorie looked out of the window as if conjuring up her memories.

"I was an officer in the F.A.N.Y., the First Aid Nursing Yeomanry, and I was what was called a 'Conducting Officer', a sort of facilitator, coach and pastoral guardian and many things rolled into one.

"I am sorry, I really am exhausted, Laura. It has been very good talking to you. Give me a little while to gather my thoughts and I will drop you a line. I have your address, I believe."

"That is so kind of you. I hope I have not worn you out."

"Thank you, dear, toodle-pip!" With that, Marjorie hung the phone up.

Laura was full of trepidation as to what Marjorie may be able to share with her, but also had slight doubts and fears in her mind that perhaps Marjorie was trying to avoid telling her something and wondered if she would indeed send a letter or even if she could remember much at all as her memory faded.

Madge Dorricott said goodnight to her neighbour and walked slowly back to her living room, using her stick as support. She poured herself a glass of sherry from the decanter on a tray near her armchair and thought back to 1944 and her time in Arisaig.

A week later, she wrote a short note to Laura, inviting her to visit.

Six

A link to the past?

Yet again, Laura made the long journey south, but this time she had taken a week's holiday, thinking she might like to head into London after visiting Madge Dorricott in Dorset. To give her more freedom and flexibility, she had decided to drive.

As Laura dropped down the bank of Haven Road, she turned left onto Shore Road and followed the shallow bay, with its busy waters full of pleasure craft on a highway of brine to and from the harbour at Poole, and various marinas and moorings which dotted the approach.

It was wonderful to be by the coast, but she felt it was not as dramatic as the coastline she worked near at Arisaig and appreciated how lucky she was to be living in this fabulous, indeed stunning, part of the Scottish coast.

Before long, Laura entered Panorama Road and found the address she had been looking for. Large gates blocked the entrance and once the intercom was pressed, she was summoned up the drive to the characterful property, past pine trees and shrubbery, all very well maintained. Laura was very surprised at the size of the house.

As she pulled up in front of the house, the door opened and a middle-aged lady stood on the doorstep.

"Good to meet you, Laura. I am June. We spoke on the telephone!"

"Yes indeed! Great to meet you."

Laura followed June through the hallway into a reception room and on into a lounge, which had large picture windows looking out onto the harbour.

Almost speechless, Laura looked at the view and at June and before she could say anything, the voice she recognised as Madge Dorricott spoke from the wing-backed chair, which had its back to her.

"Come and sit down, Laura. Let's take a look at you whilst June makes us some tea." June raised her eyebrows and smiled wistfully.

Laura came around the side of Madge's chair and put out her hand.

One hand on her stick, the other gnarled and motionless in her lap, Madge just nodded. "Take a seat, dear, you have had a long drive."

"Yes indeed, but it is so good of you to invite me and such a privilege to meet you."

"Poppycock," retorted Madge. "I thought it best you come and see me. It was difficult for me to write a letter and say all I wanted to. I felt I wanted to see you face to face. I do not get many visitors and certainly not any that wish to rake up the war again!"

At first, Laura didn't quite know what to make of Madge.

Returning with a tray of tea, biscuits and a slab of madeira cake, June said, "Don't mind Mum. Her bark is worse than her bite," as she deposited the refreshments on the low wooden coffee table in front of the window, feeling the scowl from her mother burning an imprint on her back.

Madge tutted.

Laura told Madge and June of the dream she had had. At this, she noticed Madge become a little pale and her hands seemed to tremble a little, but she soon recovered her composure.

Puzzled, Laura continued. "I had conversations with my mother, Elise, that led to the perusal of some family pictures and documents, including the letter I mentioned to you, Madge, on the telephone.

"I just wondered how you knew Elise, my mother, and why you kept in touch with Mr and Mrs Macrae, who were my mam's—"

"Adoptive parents," interrupted Madge.

Laura sat back, surprised by Madge's candour and knowledge. Finally, she was getting somewhere.

"Yes! I knew Elise as a little one, because I knew her real mother. That is what you want to know, isn't it?"

Laura just nodded. Her heart skipped a beat as she took in this revelation, confirming what she had hoped for. All this was beyond her wildest dreams.

"Did you think I was her mother?" said Madge.

"It had crossed my mind," said Laura, smiling.

During the following hour, Laura listened, spellbound, interrupted only by refills of tea.

Madge stared out of the large picture window as if mesmerised by the bright spring sunshine playing on the shimmering expanse of water beyond her lawned garden, which led down to a small dock. In the distance, Brownsea Castle, taking its name from the largest island in Poole Harbour, stood resplendent in the afternoon sun.

A reel of cinematic memories, seemingly forgotten in the archives of Madge's mind, now opened like a vault of the forgotten past and unwound in a somewhat staccato and disjointed format. Some were very hazy recollections, which Madge hoped would gradually become clearer.

"I was a conducting officer in the S.O.E. and I shared my role at first with 'Alice' – real name, Simone – a returning secret agent for the S.O.E. herself. Having been in France behind enemy lines, Simone was considered ideal to be assigned to a group of agents. Simone and I followed the agents throughout the various facets of their training course until Simone was posted overseas again, and that is why I came to overlap and take over monitoring your grandmother. Alice – Simone – was needed urgently behind enemy lines.

"I was there to offer advice and to give encouragement whilst keeping the agents afoot of changes that were happening in the country of their likely deployment. France was a country I had grown fond of and that was going to be their destination.

"I nurtured and supervised their progress and reported to the commanding officer on this progression and indeed the agents' suitability for the likely tasks in hand. We tried to pick up on any problems that may have arisen, so I highlighted positives and negatives that I knew may be a bonus or a detriment if the agent was posted in the field.

"As well as looking at how well the agents achieved or went about their tasks and challenges, I was there to listen to their problems and concerns, a sort of pastoral care, one might say.

"These agents knew little about what they were going into, for the most part. We did emphasise that it was going to be very dangerous and they had a life expectancy of six weeks, but somehow it did not deter them. Perhaps they did not grasp the enormity of the threat the German security, and indeed the French Milice, could be to their very survival.

"People were from all walks of life, differing backgrounds, and men and women trained together and no quarter was given. Both genders were treated the same. A number who didn't make it through training for whatever reason were sent to Inverlair, near Inverness, as we couldn't risk letting them back into society with all they now knew. Remember Inverlair; we will come back to that.

"Your grandmother had been on one of the last courses at Wanborough Manor in Surrey around June or July 1943 and then headed for Arisaig, as this was the paramilitary training where it toughened them and sorted them out. She was on to phase two."

Laura sat beguiled by the unfolding missive. She had planned to make notes but all was being committed to memory, as she was spellbound.

"I, of course, was with my girls throughout their training and then after reports and hopefully their acceptance for active duty, I would move on to my next group of unsuspecting sacrificial lambs!

"Your grandmother was a studious and intelligent lady. Her French was excellent, probably because of her schooling and holidays with family in France and finishing school in Switzerland, but her German was just as impeccable. Not only this but her ability and understanding of her situation seemed more acute than most of her fellow students. She was also probably the best shot of her group.

"But I must tell you that it was only after finishing her course at Wanborough Manor in Surrey and starting at Arisaig that a few weeks into the course she was taken ill, or should I say that is what we thought. When she became very sick, we feared food poisoning then when it continued, we were worried she had contracted something more infectious.

"It transpired she was pregnant. There was nothing for it but for her position on the training course to be terminated. As I mentioned before, we could not just let people go back into society, although your grandmother was a special case, so we sent her to Inverlair, a sort of cooler for those agents who could not finish training for one reason or another. She was kept busy there, initially doing some admin and other light duties, but stayed off base with a local family, as she insisted on having the child. She also insisted the father was not to be told. We understood, as she was not married and her family would not be told anyway, as they were likely still in Austria if they had managed to escape deportation to the death camps, all except her brother, that is, but that is another story."

"In Austria," said a shocked Laura.

"Yes! Vienna, I believe. In December 1943, to our surprise, it had been decided that 'Etive' could rejoin the course and complete the course again. I can only think it was because she was a valuable asset with her multiple languages and her resolute determination, not forgetting Etive was a crack shot on the range when it came to weapons. I cannot remember the specific dates."

"Was Etive her Christian name?" said Laura, intrigued to finally learn an identity for her grandmother.

"No! Etive was her designated agent name.

"It was at this stage, one evening in her room, that I spent a number of hours with her, as she was fretting. She was distraught her baby had been taken from her, as was her wish. She was no doubt confused and scared. Perhaps she didn't believe the father was alive or perhaps would want a child and anyway she wanted to continue the course, but she was very upset for a while. She naturally felt she had abandoned her child and everything was her fault.

"She bounced back from this and her excellent performance on the course showed why an exception had been made to reinstate her to the war effort.

"But the powers that be obviously still had some

reservations, and it was decided, I believe, not to send her into Europe immediately but to use her as one of the 'honey trap' girls at Winterfold, which had largely replaced Wanborough Manor as the preliminary training school. I suspect she was rather disappointed, as I am sure she felt she wanted to get back onto Europe and give the Boche a bloody nose for what her family had no doubt endured."

"What was a honey trap?"

"Aaah! My dear, a honey trap was where a planted agent was used in social downtime, often at the end of the course when the relief of knowing that stage of training was over. A few drinks and a little flirting in getting to know a fellow agent ensued and perhaps some information was given away, even their real name or something they should have kept to themselves. Unwittingly ending the likely chances of their own future as a courier or wireless operator for the Special Agents Executive! As Alice used to say, as she had performed this very position as a temptress, 'Loose lips cost lives.' Another well-known exponent of the honey trap was Agent Rose.

"Very soon, though, I believe your Etive was called upon to train as a wireless operator.

"It is then a bit vague as to where she went. She may have joined one of the other sections, possibly the Résistance Française B.C.R.A. section, de Gaulle's crowd. I don't really know, I am afraid, it really is all just speculation. It was war, so much happening and so much hush-hush; a need-to-know basis was adopted by all the security forces.

"So, there we are," she said, turning to Laura.

"I liked her, very much, but we could not afford to get emotional in wartime. We lost too many friends and fellow service personnel."

"So, my grandmother was called 'Agent Etive', but what was her surname?"

Madge took a sip of her tea, replaced the cup in the saucer and looked Laura in the eyes as she inclined her head. "Etive was her code name, her real name I only recall knowing as Marta or Martha, but this again may not be her true name. This was the Secret Operations Executive, and not all was as it seemed."

"Why did you go and see my mother when she was an infant?"

Madge filled up and her hand started to shake as she put the cup and saucer down on the coffee table.

"Eventually, rightly or wrongly, after giving her baby up for adoption, I had been ordered to tell your grandmother her baby had died. It was not my idea but one my senior officers felt we had to go through with this plan of action, so that your mother was as focused as she could be on the task ahead, and in spite of her initial grief, she became stronger and resolute. I always felt bad about it, but it was an order from above which I obeyed.

"I didn't have to, but I made it my personal duty to make sure your mother was well cared for and all was well. That is why I stayed in touch with Mary and Tam Macrae, well, at least for a while. She seemed to be flourishing. I am just so sorry to hear she lost her adoptive parents at such a young age!"

Laura was still trying to come to terms with what she had learned.

"I would still like to find out what happened to my grandmother and more about her life. You mentioned Austria. Can you help me with this or point me in the right direction?" Laura just kept babbling.

"Whatever happened to Etive, I can tell you she had that ability to compartmentalise her emotions, which I had hoped would help her survive whatever was to befall her. I like to think if she was ever in the field and captured, that she would escape and find her way back to Austria and be reunited with her family," said Madge, trying to give Laura something positive to hold on to.

"So many questions I still have. Who was my grandfather and could he still be alive? Did he ever find out he had a daughter? Did my grandmother have any friends, perhaps other agents?"

"I cannot give you any concrete information about what happened to Etive beyond what I have already shared. Perhaps Vera Atkins could help you find out. She has many contacts, although of course time has passed, and many who served are no longer with us. You could always try to get hold of your grandmother's personal file, but this may not be possible because of the Official Secrets Act. Many files are still embargoed from release and I heard some were destroyed in a fire."

Laura sighed. "I have spoken to Vera Atkins and I feel as though she was reluctant to help. She said she had traced all her girls and found out what their fate was, yet she claimed not to be aware of my grandmother, surely if—"

Madge interrupted. "I would try her again now you know the name Etive. Vera can be a tough cookie, to use an Americanism, but nothing ventured nothing gained. She may recall something. Of course, Vera may be right. Perhaps Etive worked with the French at RF Section, de Gaulle's secret agents, who knows?"

"Thank you so much," said Laura. "I will try Ms Atkins again. I have nothing to lose."

"The only other recollection I have is that I am sure your grandmother's paramour was called Dennis, as all she kept saying when I told her that her baby had passed away, was, 'Poor Dennis, I wish he could have known, or indeed could have met her.'"

Enthralled and surprised by this nugget of information, Laura's eyes lit up. "Do you remember if he was in the military and which unit? What nationality was he?"

"Sadly, that is all I can recall, Laura, I am sorry."

"I understand. It was a long time ago! You have been so helpful. I know it cannot have been easy for you thinking about those who you have lost, and I suspect you find it hard talking about such a traumatic time."

Madge opened her hands and raised her shoulders. "*Comme ci, comme ça.*

"I believe Etive did have an affinity to a fellow agent, indeed, my fellow conducting officer who I mentioned before.

"Throughout the course whilst I was there at the same time, I was aware they seemed to have something in common, some camaraderie beyond that of the group. This officer's code name was my fellow conducting officer for a short while, 'Alice'. Her real name as I said before was Simone Dubon or Dubois or something like that. I remember her name because I had a good friend in France with a similar surname. My friend Yvette was tragically killed by the Boche. Etive and Alice were always laughing and chatting together, which made me feel uneasy, as we were instructed as conducting officers not to become too familiar with the agents, but for Alice, having been under the pressures of being in the field, who was I to criticise? I am sure she just wanted to get back to some sort of normality. If she is still alive and you can find her, she might be able to help."

After a long afternoon, Laura knelt in front of Madge, took her hand and said a heartfelt thank you.

"You are truly amazing, Madge, and like all the special agents of the executive, very brave. Thank you so much for being considerate to my adoptive grandparents and especially my mother."

"Tosh, I was certainly not brave. I did my duty and was fortunate to survive the war. Many didn't. I feel ashamed I had to lie to your grandmother but I understand why."

"I do too," said Laura.

With that, Laura stood and said her goodbyes, but as Laura was leaving the lounge, she saw a picture of a lady in uniform on the sideboard, a candlestick sat each side of the frame. She was drawn to it. Picking it up, she turned. "Was this you, Madge?"

Madge smiled and nodded. "A long time ago, Laura, a long time ago!"

The image was strangely familiar to Laura.

As Laura commenced her onward journey towards London, she reflected on her day. She was thrilled she now knew her real grandmother's identity, or at least her code name, and that was somewhere to start. *What of Simone? Could she still be alive, and who was Dennis?*

Then it came to her; the photograph she had just seen of Madge was the lady in her dream.

Seven

On a mission

Laura had toyed with the idea of driving on to Winchelsea to see Vera Atkins again but as the phone rang out, she pondered the reception she would get from Vera today. After some time, the deep tone of Vera's voice answered.

"Yes! I do recall vaguely an Etive. Aah yes! So, her name was Martha. That was her real name or at least her anglicised name then. So was that your grandmother indeed?" said Vera rhetorically.

There was a silence, punctuated by the familiar sound of a draw on a cigarette. "Sadly, I lost track of Etive, as she was not S.O.E. F section. She was seconded, I believe, to de Gaulle's jurisdiction, the Résistance Française B.C.R.A. section, this was the French Bureau Central de Renseignements et d'Action, and I vaguely recall she also worked with OSS, the Americans, or quite possibly the SIS, Secret Intelligence Service, though no one would ever know that, as they kept things very close to their chests. We didn't really see eye to eye with de Gaulle's crowd at the best of times, you see.

"Therefore, I didn't really get to know your grandmother Martha. I just remember the name Etive. Such a pretty and unusual code name. You see, de Gaulle's organisation was only nominally part of the S.O.E., as they were staffed almost entirely by the French and were just as secretive and exclusive by de Gaulle's decree. Sometimes, I wondered what his motives for this lack of liaison were. That all became clear at the end of the war. He wanted power and to do that he had to manufacture the credit to get him this.

"One other thing… many S.O.E. records were destroyed in a fire, so it may be impossible to find out any information from historical records."

Disappointed, Laura probed further. "Do you remember a Simone Dubon or Dubois or a similar name?"

Laura recognised the long pause again as Vera took a drag on her cigarette, a ritual that was almost part of her thinking time. "Simone Dubois, yes! I remember Simone was our agent 'Alice' and also referred to as 'Michelle', or at least they were two of her field names. She married a Peter Stanley after the war. I am not sure what she could tell you, as agents were discouraged from sharing any personal information with one another."

"Really?" said Laura. "Is this Alice still alive?"

"She was at the Valençay S.O.E. Memorial event in 1991. There is a monument in Valençay, France, commemorating the members of the Special Operations Executive F Section who lost their lives working to liberate the country during World War Two. The memorial was unveiled in the town of Valençay, on the 6th of May 1991, marking the fiftieth anniversary of the despatch of F Section's first agent to France. So quite possibly. Hold on a minute, I may have an address."

A few minutes later, Laura heard the rumbling of the phone receiver being picked up from the table and Vera's voice returned. "Yes, she lives in an old mill in Pontwgan near Conwy in North Wales. I have a telephone number for her, or at least the last one I had, and incidentally she is now not known as Simone Dubois. Her married name is Alice Stanley. I presume she grew used to the name Alice. Her husband has passed away. I believe he was a Royal Army Medical Corps Major."

"Thank you, Ms Atkins, that has been most helpful."

"Let me warn you before you go barging in. Alice was at Ravensbrück Concentration Camp and had a pretty rough time until she was liberated. I do believe that's when she met her husband, as he was on the medical staff of the army units liberating the camp."

Duly warned, Laura thanked Vera once more.

"One more thing, I do not remember Etive being on the memorial, but then not all agents were on this memorial. In fact, only thirteen female agents are remembered here, a third of the female agents the

S.O.E. sent into the field, but that is because they did not return and were all F section, which makes it even more likely that your grandmother was RF section with the French, and beware… she may have been known by another code name in addition to Etive, and then you have to establish her real name. I advise it might be worth finding these things out to move forward."

"Thank you."

"There is another thought. It could be that Etive was trained and never made it into action, or should I say was never used as an agent in France or anywhere in Europe. I know of others who were excellent, like Noreen Riols, alias Agent Baxter, who spent much of her time in London on various duties helping the S.O.E. war effort, such as preparing and seeing agents off at Tempsford or Tangmere, so make sure she definitely was a fully-fledged agent before wasting much more time."

"Oh! I am sure she was, but thank you for the caution and advice," said Laura, somewhat indignantly.

"You really ought to visit Valençay one day. It is a fabulous memorial, very symbolic, and was dedicated by Queen Elizabeth the Queen Mother and some French dignitaries.

"It symbolises the working relationship between the S.O.E. and the resistance in France, by using two columns: the black column representing the night and the secrecy essential for many resistance and their clandestine activities; the white column the shining spirit that eventually triumphed over the evil of the German invaders. What I really liked was that the moon is used to link the two columns, as it was primarily under a full moon that our agents were landed or parachuted into France and supplies and ammunition were dropped.

"It does not stop there. The sculptor Elizabeth Harrison uses three floodlights at the bottom of the monument to represent the L-shaped path of flares laid out by each reception committee for the agents so that the pilots, especially the Lysanders and Hudsons that landed, were able to touch down as safely as possible on the improvised landing strips. It really is a well-thought-out and meaningful memorial sculpture, or should I say monument."

"Wonderful. I would like to see that memorial and pay my respects one day."

Appearing much more supportive but pragmatic, Vera ended the call with "*Bonne chance.*"

As she put down the phone, Laura didn't quite know what to make of her grandmother not being on the memorial at Valençay, other than the possibility she may have been with the French-run B.R.C.A. rather than the British-controlled S.O.E. Maybe there was another memorial somewhere in France if she was indeed deceased, or maybe she was alive and well somewhere. Maybe she did have other noms de plume and maybe, just maybe, no one had ever told her story. Lots to figure out, but for now Laura contemplated another journey instead of London. *I must head to North Wales,* she thought.

Laura called the number she had been given for Alice Stanley. Frustratingly, the phone number did not connect. A message of '*Please try again*' was greeted by the same monotonous tone that an incorrect number indicated. Not to be daunted, Laura had the gut feeling that she must just make the journey and call unannounced.

Abandoning her London plans, Laura took her time and after a long day's drive from the south across country, it was getting late, so she decided to overnight at the small Welsh town of Llangollen situated on the River Dee, a pleasant little market town famous for its annual Eisteddfod. Laura was happy to lay her head on a pillow and in spite of her excitement, she slept well that night.

Next morning, after a hearty Welsh breakfast, Laura enjoyed a scenic drive along the busy and winding A5 towards Snowdonia. She found the countryside had similarities with Perthshire. At Betws-y-Coed, she headed north and by late morning she was turning off the A470 and along a narrow road. In just a few minutes, she had reached the small hamlet of Pontwgan, just to the south of Conway on the North Wales coast.

She became a little apprehensive. Just as she entered Pontwgan, she passed a house on the left, so she decided to stop and ask directions.

There was a vehicle outside, and she could hear the fast flow of water nearby so thought she couldn't be far away from an old mill. Straightening her appearance, she knocked on the door and shortly a smartly dressed elderly lady answered.

"Hello, I am sorry to bother you. I am looking for Alice Stanley."

"Ah, Alice, of course. Are you a friend?" questioned the lady, who Laura could feel was weighing her up like a Neighbourhood Watch gatekeeper.

"No, not as such, but a mutual friend told me she lived in Pontwgan and I believe she knew my grandmother."

The lady nodded. "You are almost there. She lives in Pontwgan Mill. Take a first left and she is just across the bridge on the left-hand side. I think she is in, I could see smoke from her chimney this morning. After all, it has been rather damp and chilly these last few days."

Laura thanked the neighbour and took the road left just before a small row of terraced houses.

As she crossed the bridge, she almost missed the small slate house plaque sign on the left saying *Pontwgan Mill*. Laura drove past the sign and pulled into the side of the narrow road to allow space for people to pass. Walking back, she dropped down the few slate-topped steps to the front door. She was taken by the immense noise the rush of nearby water created and couldn't help but get nearer to the river and see the water being forced through the narrow arch of the bridge, and mused to herself that it was a perfect place to build a mill powered by a water wheel.

The river below the house was powerful and recharged by the previous night's heavy rain. As she knocked on the door, she suddenly became aware of the stillness, punctuated by a chorus of birdsong echoing from the surrounding trees. What a magical dell Alice Stanley lived in.

A few minutes elapsed before she heard the latch

being raised and an immaculately coiffured grey-haired lady of diminutive stature stood before her.

She surveyed Laura and, her accent evident but with perfect English, she asked, "Can I help you?"

"Hello. Am I speaking to Mrs Stanley?" said Laura, in a hopeful but tentative voice.

"Yes! I am Alice Stanley," she said cautiously whilst holding the collar of a beautiful black Labrador who was moving his head excitedly from side to side.

"My name is Laura Dewar. I believe you may have known my grandmother, Etive."

Alice seemed momentarily stunned. For a second or two, nothing was said. Alice just looked at Laura.

"I was given your contact by Vera Atkins. I am so sorry just to drop in on you, but the telephone number I had greeted me with an unobtainable tone so I drove all the way from Dorset on the off chance."

"*Mon dieu*! Come in, that is a long journey," responded Alice, regaining her composure. "Come, Nero," she called to her Lab as she pulled him away from the open door.

Both Nero and Laura followed Alice into an open wooden-floored room with a sunken area leading to a fireplace. "You must take me as you find me," she said, tidying up some papers she had strewn on the dining-room table. "I was just replying to some correspondence."

"Gosh, this is much bigger than it looks from outside. It's beautiful and quirky all at once," Laura said as she took in the winding apparatus of the old mill, which acted as a beam above her!

"It is of course an old mill which has been redeveloped into what some people call an 'upside-down house', as the bedrooms are downstairs," explained Alice.

"Come, let me take your coat. Would you like a tea or a coffee?"

"Yes, please, a coffee, black," replied Laura. "Oh! Here is a small gift," said Laura, extracting a loaf of *bara brith* from her bag, which she had picked up from a bakery before leaving Llangollen.

"Ah, *merci*, a weakness of mine. How did you know?"

Laura smiled and opened her hands, intimating it was just luck!

"Please take a seat," said Alice as she took Laura's jacket and hung it in the hall cupboard. Alice was trailed by Nero.

In the living room, Laura was drawn towards the grand piano, its polished black veneer showing it was a treasured possession. In one corner of the room was a right angle of bookshelves, with books ranging from local wildlife, geology and treks to classical books of Shakespeare and timeless novels like Charles Dickens' *Oliver Twist*. One shelf was populated with a number of books on the Second World War, but before Laura could peruse them properly, the kitchen door opened.

Returning with a tray of coffee and buttered *bara brith*, Alice struggled to tackle the two steps into the sunken living room and Laura assisted, placing the tray on top of the low newspaper-strewn coffee table.

"*Merci*, my dear, I am not as nimble as I once was," she

said, her green eyes twinkling. Alice was still an attractive lady, even in her old age. Laura loved her French accent.

Coffee poured and *bara brith* placed on the side plates, Alice sat straight-backed in an armchair and looked at Laura. "I do believe there is something of your grandmother in you. That said, it is over fifty years since I have seen her."

A shiver overcame Laura as a frisson of excitement encompassed her body, hearing a woman who knew her grandmother. Taken aback, Laura replied, "That is lovely to know. I have no photographs of her. I do not know much about her."

Alice nodded. "Of course! Why would you? Alas, nor do I. Maybe her service file has more details, although I suspect this is still embargoed. Tell me, how did you find out Etive was your grandmother? What do you know about her?"

"I know very little, Mrs Stanley."

"Please! Call me Alice."

Laura went on to explain her journey so far, starting with her dream, followed by the pursuit of information, her conversations with Vera Atkins and Madge Dorricott.

"How is the redoubtable Vera Atkins? Is she still smoking those awful untipped Senior Service cigarettes?"

"I believe she is smoking untipped cigarettes, probably Senior Service, and she is indeed a formidable lady, if indeed a little less mobile than when younger.

"Alice, I would dearly love to find out who my biological grandfather was too. It would be wonderful to be able to share this with my mother, who knows nothing of her real parents."

"I understand, of course, I would want to know too. Wartime was a very difficult time. It was not all horror, though. There was a chance for love and lighter moments, you know, Laura. In fact, we lived each day as if it was our last. I loved Etive, as she became known. The name I knew her by was Martha. She told me her real name, the one she had before she came to England as a refugee, was Marta, but my mind is hazy, as my memory fails me on facts more and more."

Laura now hoped she could find a possible surname. "A refugee? Did she say where she was from?" quizzed Laura. "What was her surname?"

"Look, we were not supposed to discuss our backgrounds, but Martha and I became very close, that is, until one day when we were in Arisaig House and I saw her being ushered through the reception area to a waiting car. She was with my fellow conducting officer, the lady you met, Madge. They were accompanied by two orderlies.

"I knew she was pregnant. She had recently confided in me and agonised about what to do. She so wanted to do something profound to help the war effort but she was torn. She wanted this child, it meant so much to her." Alice inclined her head, reached over and touched Laura's hand reassuringly.

Laura was fighting back the tears.

"I never found out her surname. I was being sent back into the field and was about to leave for London and then Surrey to fly back to France.

"I have to tell you, Laura, I never saw her again and she has never been in touch. I was told after the war that she may have returned to the S.O.E. to complete her training, and likely ended up in Europe, possibly being flown into France, but it was hearsay and much is said without verification. During war, you never quite know who did what and why."

"My conversation with Madge Dorricott – sorry, you would remember her as your fellow conducting officer, Marjorie 'Madge' Spencer – did tell me a little more, but she knew no more about what happened to her and why she did not return.

"She was never listed as missing in action as far as I can find out. Ms Atkins said if agents were arrested, they may have been interrogated and sent to a prisoner of war camp, or worse, a concentration camp, although she pointed out they all had a cyanide pill to take their own life if that was their choice."

Digressing, Alice continued. "It is a tragedy, of course, your grandmother and grandfather couldn't have stayed together and brought your mother up, but war changes so much," said Alice, sipping her coffee and taking a small bite of her *bara brith*.

"I wonder what you know about my grandmother's man, the father of my mother."

"What is your mother's name?" enquired Alice.

"Elise."

"Aah, Elise, such a beautiful name."

"Indeed!" confirmed Laura.

"He was a good-looking man. I never met him, of course, but it was clear your grandmother really loved him. I did see a photograph of him that Etive kept in the lining of her beret, so that he was always with her. He was a handsome fellow. I know his name was Dennis. He was in the British Army."

Laura was over the moon to hear her grandfather's Christian name, which appeared to corroborate Madge's recollection, so it looked like Dennis really was her grandfather's name.

"Etive told me she had met him by chance where she had been living down south. She talked of others, as we girls do. She did meet another fellow on the train to Beasdale – that is the railway halt near Arisaig House on her journey up from the south – a Frenchman, I believe, who engaged her in conversation, and then one evening she attended a dance at Astley Hall, a community hall in Arisaig, and this same Frenchman asked her to dance. I recall Etive saying they had a pleasant evening and I am sure if she had not previously met Dennis… well, who knows. However, it was clear your grandmother was besotted with Dennis."

Alice shared another story with Laura.

"I suspect Etive had lots of admirers; she was a very attractive lady. She told me that one day early in her training, totally out of the blue after a rather hectic but enjoyable initial course at Wanborough Manor, a young chap called Jimmy Bland approached her – she was talking to one of her fellow female students at the time – and asked if they would care to join him for a spot of lunch the next day, now they had completed the course.

"Céline declined, making some excuse, but Etive

said he was rather surprised when she said, 'Might as well whilst we wait for our assessment, as long as I drive.' Taken aback, Jimmy was a little stuck for words momentarily before quite happily agreeing.

"The next day, Etive had borrowed a motorbike and Jimmy was rather speechless when a helmeted and goggled Etive turned up on a Royal Enfield 350 CC motorbike and said, 'Well, hop on, Jimmy, and hold tight. Where are we going?'

"A little while later, they were at the Plough Inn in Cold Harbour above Dorking in Surrey.

"You see, Laura, your grandmother had a great sense of humour and was very confident."

Alice continued: "Etive said on arrival they strolled into the Plough and Jimmy asked a perfectly innocent question to the barmaid as she poured his beer: 'Do you live far away?' Just making small talk, as apparently red-headed Jimmy was quite clearly admiring the barmaid's hair. The brunette's hair was set in rolls and curls as was the popular style of the day, inspired by pictures in magazines and popularised by film stars like Rita Hayworth and Betty Grable.

"'My name is Rose, what's yours?'

"Stuttering a little, he replied, 'Jimmy.'

"Rose continued: 'I live almost next door at number 2 The Nest, here in Cold Harbour. Pop in for a cup of tea anytime, handsome,' adding a wink as she placed his pint of beer on the bar. 'Say, soldier, do you ever go to the dances in Dorking? Better still, you should go up to the smoke and do some dancing to Glenn Miller and all those fabulous tunes the Yanks have brought over with them at the Hammersmith Palais. Beats the pants off Victor Silvester, as the Yanks say.

"'The Palais has a fab maple wood dance floor there, soldier. I bet you can jive with the best of them, honey!' Etive smiled at Rose whilst Jimmy blushed, becoming rather red-faced at Rose's response, choosing to focus on the frothy pint of beer that he had in front of him.

"'What can I get you, love?' said Rose to Etive.

"'A soda water and can we have two ploughman's lunches please?' said Etive, realising Rose enjoyed playing games and flirting with the clients.

"Etive said, drinks in hand, that they had taken a small table outside the pub.

"Embarrassing Jimmy further, Etive commented, 'Rose certainly has the hots for you, soldier,' her smile more a smirk.

"Jimmy was defensive, replying, 'I think she probably talks to every service man like that,' as he regained his composure.

"Etive said she loved the quintessentially British setting of the pub as they looked towards a signpost across the road where the road diverged and the patch of green behind sported a red telephone box. It was a pleasant summer's day so they made the best of it.

"After lunch, Etive, goggles on, revved up the peppy Royal Enfield motorcycle and set off to the viewpoint on Leith Hill, deep in the Surrey Hills. Following a steepish climb to the top, they were afforded fabulous views of the surrounding areas. She recalled it was an incredibly clear day, not a cloud in the surreally beautiful blue sky.

"Etive turned to Jimmy and said, 'Look, Jimmy, you can see London over there. In fact, I think I can make out the Hammersmith Palais.'

"Etive said Jimmy seemed rather mooted and she sensed he would be happy to return back to base, which they duly did. After returning to the Manor, she thanked him for lunch and Jimmy went his own way and she never saw him again, not in training or socially. It appears her sense of humour and a sarcasm more indicative of the British than someone brought up in Austria was a bit too much for him.

"That's one thing I always admired about Martha. She was like a chameleon and could adapt almost instantly to whatever situation. I suspect that is one of the qualities the S.O.E. saw as a huge benefit for an agent behind enemy lines, as Martha could easily become Etive.

"You see, Etive had arrived from Vienna as a refugee just before the war started, because I must tell you she was an Austrian Jew and feared for her life and had to escape Austria.

"Etive was first in Deal in Kent, where she had been taken to a camp for displaced persons, but soon she was fortunate enough to find work at a large house near the camp.

"She got on really well with the family. However, the family became increasingly concerned and frightened by the bombardments happening daily, as the Nazi warplanes were on regular sorties across the Channel and constantly attacking settlements on the coast and, of course, around London.

"So, the family all moved to Shropshire to stay with relatives and took Etive with them. They were living at a big house in the country. She told me it was a sort of smallholding. The house she talked about had orchards and chickens, ducks, pigs, and so on.

"Martha had a lucky escape, but her parents were not so lucky. It transpires they had been transported to a concentration camp not long after Etive left Austria. I am sure Etive never knew what happened to them, but for sure she wanted to make Hitler pay.

"More coffee, dear?"

Putting her hand up and declining, Laura was too entranced to stop.

"Do you know what Dennis' surname was?"

"Greaves," came back the answer, swifter than an arrow.

Laura was so elated that she now knew her likely grandfather's surname.

"Dennis Greaves. He had been in the Royal Engineers, I believe. Etive said he was very bright, a great linguist. He could speak German, French and Classical Greek as well as some Arabic, as his father had been based in Alexandria in Egypt. Frankly, Etive could not stop talking about him, then she found out she was pregnant and everything changed for her.

"I had no idea what happened with the pregnancy, whether she had the baby or... Well, now I know. I am sure your mother being born made her so happy, but it must have been difficult for Etive to part with her baby, your mother." Laura didn't tell Alice what Madge had shared with her. "But what became of Dennis, I do not know. I wish I had met him, for sure. I feel like I knew him," said Alice, smiling.

"I wish Etive had been able to tell him about the baby." Alice looked through the window and then back at Laura, her eyes misted. "Etive was a lovely girl!"

"So, did you go straight back to France, Alice?"

"I did indeed. My brother Gilbert was still out there. We had both flown back from the Bordeaux area when things became a little hot, as we had a traitor in our midst, which almost led to our capture. Gilbert did some wireless training, I believe, back in the UK. I, of course, was involved at Arisaig House and Wanborough Manor before that."

"How old were you? Sorry, that sounds rather impertinent."

"At the start of the war, I was thirty years old, so in my thirties. As you see, I am not very big. We would say *petite*. My hair was once jet-black, would you believe?"

"Were you married?"

"No, my fiancé, Pierre, was killed early in the war."

"I am so sorry to hear that. What was it like being undercover?"

"Frankly, a lot of the time, it was lonely and boring, but as D Day approached, it became busier, for sure. Sometimes, I had to cycle a long way, taking messages as a courier for Gilbert. When we came to German checkpoints and road blocks where they asked for your *papiers*, it could be nerve-racking, but I found a little flirting always helped." A twinkle in her eye, Alice smiled.

"Sometimes, if I had missed curfew, I would sleep

in some woods, or even a ditch. As sabotage activities were called for to hinder the Boche, we would lay mines on roads or be blowing up railway lines."

"Were you ever arrested or did you have any close shaves?" queried Laura, spellbound at being privy to such first-hand accounts of the war.

"*Oui*! One time, I was arrested with a fellow agent. She had some radio parts with her, some valves, as I recall. They were inserted in loaves of bread wrapped in her basket. We pretended we were not together, but were nevertheless both taken to the nearest town and I feared interrogation.

"I was put in a cell. Whilst my friend Mary was taken for interrogation, a short while later, I was escorted out of the cell up some stairs into a small office and asked my name, address, what I was doing on the road to Poitiers, and so on. Softly, at first, even offering me a cigarette, then they would get louder and more angry. Then they would ask me the same questions to which, of course, I gave the same answers.

"Then the S.S. officer standing at the back of the room came behind me and said 'Stand up', which I did.

"'Take your jacket off', he said calmly.

"As I did so, he said, 'Now your blouse.'

"I did as I was told and started shaking. I covered myself with my hands, as the man in front of me had stopped writing and was leering at my breasts, protected just by a silk slip.

"Then suddenly the door burst open and some sharp words were exchanged and the Gestapo officer disappeared.

"Almost apologetically, the seated officer who had been asking my details and calmly interviewing me until the SS officer intervened said, 'Please dress, *Mademoiselle,*' as he looked down at the paperwork, somewhat embarrassed.

"Then he left the room.

"A short while later, he came back and I was told I was free to go.

"It is clear my friend had confessed or at least persuaded them she did not know me. I cycled back to Gilbert so quickly that I can barely remember the journey. I had been fortunate."

"What happened to Mary?" asked Laura.

"We never found out. We can only assume she was taken to a concentration or labour camp or maybe murdered, but she never gave anyone up. She just disappeared. *Nacht* and *Nebel*, dear girl. *Nacht* and *Nebel.*"

Laura looked at her, puzzled.

"Night and fog! A German policy for eradicating opposition and making them disappear, taking away their identity and whereabouts before murdering them, basically."

Laura grimaced at Alice's description.

"I don't know if Vera told you but, eventually, I was captured and, long story short, I ended up in a dreadful place called 'Ravensbrück' in Northern Germany."

Alice seemed to shiver and become a little morose when she said, "I remember my journey from Fresnes Prison in Paris. We were crammed into cattle trucks, maybe eighty or ninety of us. People fought to be near a ventilation crack or near the door. Our only latrine was a 10lb jam tin by the door, but if you were wedged at the end of the carriage, you had to urinate in a small can and pass this to be emptied out of the ventilation windows, some blowing back, of course, as the train steamed on.

"Windows were four narrow slit-like openings high in the carriage, so there was little light that was getting in, let alone fresh air. The place was so hot and the foul stink of bodies and air made some pass out.

"We had no water, no food, and were in there for hours on end. Occasionally, we stopped and we banged on the side of the carriage for the door to be opened so we could breathe more easily or even get out and stretch our legs, but then the train would start up again and the nightmare continued.

"We were all in such a poor state of health that our minds were beginning to play tricks on us. Each day was about survival. Then Ravensbrück, which was like hell on earth.

"By August, the allies had broken through and we reverted to wearing our uniforms to greet the troops. I still have my F.A.N.Y. uniform somewhere in the attic."

Alice indicated she was weary; it was clear the audience was over.

"It has been wonderful meeting you, but I must away," sighed Laura. "I cannot tell you how thankful I am to have met you and received a real insight into who my grandmother was, not just her name but to have it fascinatingly confirmed that she was Austrian!"

"Etive was well educated, Laura. She spoke Italian,

German, French and English. I felt she was from a quite wealthy family, at least well off, anyway. She always talked about her parents... mama this, papa that, but no mention of siblings."

"Thank you. I guess I need to find Dennis Greaves, or at least what may have happened to him!" smiled Laura with a winsome smile. "Thank you, Alice, for being so brave."

"Good luck," said Alice, "and please let me know how you get on. Keep in touch." She walked slowly behind Laura to the front door and waved goodbye.

She heard Nero scratching at the back door. "Where have you been, boy? Your paws and snout are all dirty." Wiping them off, she put out some dog food in Nero's bowl and returned to the pile of papers on her living-room table, which she used as a desk. Sifting through them, she found the envelope she was looking for and extracted a letter.

Picking up her fountain pen, she wrote:

Dear Vicky,

Thank you for your recent letter. I was very interested to hear that Leo came to stay with you. How is he?

I too had a visitor today, quite a surprise, you will never guess who.

I had a visit from a young lady called Laura. She claims to be Martha Swanson's granddaughter.

I don't have to tell you what that probably means. It's a pity Dennis isn't alive to meet her.

But needless to say, the fears you have had all these years may well have been correct.

You may well have been right in believing Martha was more than just a friend to Dennis. This could well be the evidence that he had been intimate with her, or so it seems on the face of it. Give me a ring.

Alice completed her letter with some general chit-chat and what the weather had been doing before sealing the envelope, addressing it to: *Mrs Victoria Greaves, Pharoah's Cottage, The Bog, near Shelve, Shropshire.*

Eight

Past meets present

Vicky Greaves could not believe what she was reading. After all these years, Martha was still managing to mess her life up.

Vicky took her black spaniel Ali for a walk up to the Stiperstones and the infamous Devil's Chair, which perches on a rugged ridge made up of large jagged stones. A number are large outcrops of rock, weathered and foreboding in the brooding winter weather. Their exposed position on the top of the ridge allows myths and legends to abound, especially when silhouetted against the skyline. It is rumoured that covens of witches meet even to this day whilst the Devil sits on his chair, which has been perfectly shaped by the elements, atop a substantial rocky mass where he supposedly surveys all around him.

Skylarks can be seen and heard, and the very

different call of the grouse is distinct. Whinberries are collected for a delicious local pie offering from the bushes that proliferate amongst the rocks!

Vicky loved the wildness; it helped her think. The light but cool breeze made her tighten her scarf and pull her hood up as the faintest raindrops fell. The heather-lined rock-strewn path slowed her progress. As she reached the ridge, she looked down past her house nestled in the lea of the hill, surveying all in the panoramic undulations of the patchwork quilt of land with its fields of sheep, some cattle grazing and hilly outcrops. She took in Corndon Hill, rising 1,683 feet from across the border in Powys. She loved the isolation here but now and again craved a little company. Red kites circled above, looking for the faintest movement from a small mammal.

A million and one thoughts passed through her mind as she walked a circuitous route up to Nipstone Rock and back home.

It was early evening as she lit the fire and dusk descended on this idyllic Shropshire wilderness. Vicky picked up the telephone, a glass of red wine in hand – not her first. The phone rang out.

"*Allo*," came the familiar French accent.

"Hi, sweetie," said Vicky.

In her familiar, comforting French accent, Alice replied, "Aah, Vicky, how are you?"

"A little agitated, to tell the truth, Alice. I wish you had kept the visit you had to yourself."

"*Ma chérie*, I thought you would want to know," said Alice, somewhat indignantly.

There was a silence. "Are you still there?" queried Alice.

"Yes! I need to deal with this, Alice, and finally put this to bed. Perhaps I am being paranoid and maybe not. As you infer, I may well have had just reason to always feel Martha was part of my short marriage to Dennis."

"Men! What do you expect?" chided Alice, dismissively.

"I just knew when I met him, he was the one. From that first time we danced at the summer charity ball in Shropshire at Trench Hall," reflected Victoria, her mind drifting back.

Alice started to retreat. "Maybe he was faithful, I do not know."

"In fairness, Alice, I had no hold on him. We were not engaged, or married. We merely had an enjoyable weekend or two together when he visited Shropshire on leave. I lost touch with him, as you know."

"Such was war," philosophised Alice. "We lived for the moment, did we not?"

"Until, of course, we met again overseas." Vicky paused in reflection. "Alice, I think I need to speak to this girl. I feel I owe Dennis that, or he would be turning in his grave."

"I have an address and telephone number. She is working at Arisaig House, where both Martha and I were based for paramilitary training during the war. It is apparently a hotel now, rather smart one, too, I gather."

"Strange how fate conspires to unlock the past

and taint the future," said Vicky bitterly whilst sipping her wine. "It seems a long time since I was part of your debrief when you returned from France and we became friends."

"Half a century, *mon amie*!" sighed Alice.

After a little more tittle-tattle on Leo Marks and his life and the local communities they both lived in, Victoria hung up. She poured herself another large glass of wine and looked at the Scottish address and number she was now in possession of.

Should I open this can of worms? she thought. A few glasses later, she fell asleep on the couch.

*

As the first light filtered into the room and warm fingers of the new day touched Victoria's inert being, she shivered, stirred and woke to another day. Her head thumped as if the blood needed to escape in a hurry, as she pushed herself up to sit and stare through fogged eyes at the now quenched embers of the log fire.

The wall clock came in and out of focus as she squinted. She pulled the throw off the back of the settee, covered herself and fell asleep again.

A few hours later, Ali's cold, wet nose was nuzzling her, asking to be fed and to be taken for a walk.

Victoria's mouth felt like the bottom of a budgerigar's cage, as if she had been chewing sawdust. As she stood unsteadily, she unwittingly kicked the empty wine bottle across the wooden oak floor as she shuffled towards the kitchen, causing it to roll up to the skirting board. Victoria helped herself to a glass of water and put the kettle on the Aga. She felt so thirsty but enjoyed the warmth of the faithful stove as she leaned against it until the kettle whistled.

As she scooped out the dried dog food, Ali, short for Alison, watched and waited patiently then consumed the contents of her bowl speedily. Victoria opened the back door and a chill morning wind made her pull her cardigan around her. Ali scooted past her, desperate to meet the call of nature.

Victoria ran a hot bath and lowered herself into the luxuriant foam of bath salt-perfumed water. Her mind went back to her telephone conversation with Alice then drifted back to Dennis and the time she spent with him in Egypt. A smile came across her face.

A piece of toast and another cup of tea later, the phone she called was ringing out.

"Arisaig House, how may I help you?" said the broad Scottish brogue.

"Good morning, may I speak to Laura Dewar?"

"Yes, certainly, who may I say is calling?"

"Victoria Greaves."

"May I ask what it is with regard to?"

"Laura will not know me but she will want to speak to me."

A few moments elapsed.

"Hello, this is Laura. Can I help?"

Victoria hesitated, her mouth becoming very dry again.

"Hello."

Victoria put the phone down; her hand was shaking.

She just couldn't bear to think that a granddaughter of Martha was a product of a relationship with Dennis.

Laura was puzzled. Victoria Greaves – was this just coincidence or could this be a relative of Dennis Greaves?

Laura returned to her meeting and hoped the lady would call back.

*

A few days elapsed and Laura couldn't bear it any longer. She felt she needed to ring Alice, as the question burning her soul was just who is Victoria Greaves, and Alice just might know the answer. But she didn't call.

The next morning, a letter arrived for Laura, sent recorded delivery.

Laura had dealt with all the expected departures from the hotel and wasn't expecting any new guests until later that afternoon.

She saw the postmark was from Shropshire. She asked her colleague Moira to listen out for the phones and watch the reception area as she headed for the kitchen, made herself a mug of coffee and took a seat on the terrace with its view across the open land towards Borrodale Beach. It was unusually a blissfully warm day, so she removed her suit jacket and relaxed, pondering the content of the letter before her.

Dear Laura,
I am so sorry for the other day. I had hesitated
to call you at all; I never like to look back. On

reflection, I felt it was wise to contact you for a number of reasons.

It is such a small world. I have heard on the grapevine you are interested in finding out more about Dennis Greaves, as I am led to believe there is some sort of association with your grandmother.

I am coming up to Scotland, perhaps, to do some walking, and a change of scenery would do me good. Would it be possible to meet and I can then perhaps share what information I have, which may or may not help you?

I have made a reservation at the Arisaig Hotel down in Arisaig itself. I could not get a reservation at Arisaig House through the tourist information centre. I will be staying a few days. I am arriving by train a few days from now, this coming Friday, in fact. I may even be there by the time you have received this letter.

I do hope this is convenient. I will make contact with you after my arrival and hope you can find time for a drink and a chat.

Looking forward to meeting you,
Victoria Greaves

Laura stared at the letter and reread it before folding it and replacing it in the envelope.

She was bemused as she wondered how Victoria Greaves had heard of Laura's search for her grandmother and Dennis.

It could only be from one person: Alice Stanley.

She had intimated she had never met Dennis Greaves, so how would she know Victoria Greaves?

"Good morning, Laura, penny for them," said David Harrison.

"Mr Harrison, so good to see you on this fine morning. I hope you slept well. What are your plans today?"

For now, Laura's curiosity could not be sated; she had a hotel to run.

*

Friday arrived; morning and afternoon passed as clients departed and new ones took their place, most staying for the weekend.

At 6pm, the hall clock chimed and Laura tidied her desk, entered the reception area and checked on the bar and restaurant to make sure all was well, before departing for the evening.

After a quick shower and change of clothes, she left the seclusion of Arisaig House. Laura drove the 2 miles or so to Arisaig Hotel in the small settlement of Arisaig. As she stepped out of the car, a stiff cool evening breeze whipped off Loch nan Ceall. Laura wrapped her tan leather jacket around her and mused to herself, *Well, at least the midges have not descended yet.*

"Hello, stranger," said Rory behind reception. "To what do we owe this pleasure?"

"Hi, Rory, you are looking as well fed as ever," jested Laura sarcastically.

Rory smiled. "Aye, all bought and paid for, Laura!" he said, patting his ample belly.

"I just wanted to find out if a guest of yours has checked in, as I am due to meet her this weekend. A lady named Victoria Greaves."

"Aye, she has indeed. I believe she is around the corner in the Crofters' Bar, Laura!" It's going to be a lively one tonight. There is a band playing, as it's the weekend."

Laura thanked Rory and gave him a wink, at which the big brawny laddie blushed and laughed nervously.

As Laura entered the bar, she could make out Victoria Greaves rather easily. It wasn't difficult; she was the only woman in there.

As she approached the bar, Victoria downed the remains of her glass of red wine and slid from the bar stool. Picking up her handbag, she ran her hand through her grey-haired bob and came face to face with Laura.

"I am so sorry," she said, apologising for almost bumping into her.

"No harm done. You must be Victoria, I am Laura!"

Victoria frowned. "Sorry, should I know you?"

"Laura Dewar, we spoke on the telephone briefly and you sent me a letter," said Laura, proffering her hand.

"Oh yes! My mind is not as good as it once was. I am a little tired from the journey!"

"Would now be a good time to catch up, as I have the evening free?" invited Laura.

"Why not? Have you eaten?"

"No, but…"

"Well, perhaps we can chat over dinner. I plan to eat around 8pm. Do you have any recommendations other than here?"

Laura looked at the musicians unpacking their instruments – guitar, bagpipe, fiddle – and then turned back to Victoria. "It may be a little noisy to talk in here. The menu here is good for bar food, but shall we go and have a coffee in the Residents' Lounge and have a chat there? Meanwhile, I can ask Rory if he can book you a table nearby if you prefer a more upmarket offering."

Victoria was starting to realise Laura was a very to-the-point, organised and determined young woman. She reminded her of herself when she was younger. There was also something else she couldn't quite put her finger on.

"That would be very kind of you, lead the way," said Victoria as she moved slowly, feeling the effects of the wine she had been imbibing for the last hour or two.

The evening had become a little cooler and a roaring log fire greeted them in the Residents' Lounge. It was quiet; they were the first ones in that evening.

A pot of coffee arranged through Rory at the front desk soon arrived with a side plate of Scottish shortbread, which Victoria quickly helped herself to.

"So, Dennis Greaves, are you related to him?" said Laura, wasting no time.

"I suppose you could say that," said Victoria, somewhat smirking as she settled back into her chosen armchair.

Laura waited a few seconds as she poured the coffee. "White with?" she enquired.

"Absolutely, not too much milk, though," cautioned Victoria.

Laura sat opposite Victoria and weighed up this once attractive lady. Her face was a little rosy but perfectly heart-shaped. A substantial heart-shaped silver locket was dangling from around her neck, drawing attention as it plunged to the open green chartreuse silk blouse displaying her ample cleavage.

Immaculately dressed, yet Laura felt something almost melancholy about Victoria. Her skin was still good considering her venerable age. After all, she must be well into her seventies, but the odd face wrinkle and sagging skin of her neck were evidence of the march of time.

Victoria took a sip of her coffee and replaced it in the saucer.

"Dennis Greaves was my husband."

Laura immediately processed this information, not showing any emotion at first.

Then she raised her eyebrows, inclined her head and enquired, "You said 'was'. Are you divorced or…?" Laura hesitated to finish her sentence.

"Dennis is dead, I am afraid. Well, actually, it's a more complicated story than that. Look, you no doubt want to know about how Dennis may have known your grandmother. Perhaps I should start at the beginning."

Laura was entranced as a fascinating chapter of history unfolded from this well-spoken lady.

"I was also in the S.O.E. but as a cryptographer

or cipher operator, like the Bletchley Park girls, you know?" Victoria's clipped and rather proper high society-type accent announced. Victoria could see a slight lack of comprehension from Laura but continued nevertheless.

"It all started when I replied to a newspaper request for photographs of France, especially the coastal ports. I used to spend many summer holidays in France. It was so different to my home county of Shropshire. I loved it and guess what? I had lots of snaps so I replied to the Ministry of Economic Warfare.

"My father, Major Atkinson, had also suggested I register at the Ministry of Labour, which I did, saying I was willing to serve at home or abroad for the war effort.

"Actually, when I was younger, I spent some school holidays with a good friend, Janey Kenyon Slaney, another Shropshire girl, who I was at St James School with in Malvern. I lost touch with her. I read she was a debutante pre-war and amazingly I finally met up with her again, as we both signed up as Auxiliary Nursing Service personnel.

"Another rather surprising coincidence is that I saw her again at 64 Baker Street, as we were both interviewed there, ostensibly as providers of overseas holiday snaps our families had taken on the French coast and in Paris. The place where we were interviewed was the Inter Services Research Bureau, which was the name used as a front for the S.O.E., and we shared some of the ensuing training together for this organisation completely on a need-to-know basis. We were not allowed to share what we did with friends and family. As far as they were concerned, we were secretaries.

"Janey was very charismatic and attractive. Do you know, she was very friendly with Kathleen Kennedy, the eldest daughter of Joe Kennedy, the American Ambassador? Kathleen was known to her friends as 'Kick'. Janey told me of a meeting with Kathleen's brother J.F.K., who was three years older than Janey, having been born in May 1917, whilst Janey was born on the 15th of January 1920. She was staying with the Kennedys in the South of France when war was declared. I still remember her birthday now. Apparently, she had an affair with and was unofficially engaged to David Niven, the debonair actor. I haven't seen Janey for a long time. I believe she lives in Yorkshire now. Anyway, I digress.

"I was duly invited to a follow-up interview in London at the Inter Services Research Bureau before being taken to an apartment nearby, all rather clandestine really.

"There, I was asked rather basic questions at first, like about whether I was married, what languages I spoke fluently, and so on, then about my visits to and familiarity with European places. I had brought photographs of France and spoke fondly and knowledgeably about them. I was asked how long I was there generally, all in polite, rather convivial, conversation.

"I happened to mention I had spent a lot of time in Africa, as I was born there because my father's family owned a mining company, which seemed to intrigue the rather pleasant major interviewing me.

"I pointed out that I went to Cheltenham Ladies' College and finishing school in Switzerland. He was interested to know that for the first two years of the war, Cheltenham Ladies' College was moved to Shrewsbury.

"Actually, Laura, that was the very first time I met Dennis, as he had attended Shrewsbury Public School and had come back for a reunion or something. Well, that is not strictly true, as I was aware of him rather than met him.

"It was a friend of his, Harry something, who my father knew somehow in military circles, I presumed. My father had invited Harry to a soirée at our home in Shropshire and also bid Harry to bring a friend.

"Digressing, I know, but, you see, the college being moved to Shrewsbury was all rather convenient for me, as I stayed at home before my war service. I actually met Dennis formally because he was the friend who joined Harry at the party-cum-soirée. Dennis was a little older than me but very handsome, and we seemed to get on rather well."

"More coffee?" said Laura.

"Thank you, but you don't think we could get a bottle of red wine, do you?"

A few minutes later, Laura returned with a bottle of Bordeaux and two glasses.

"Splendid," said Victoria, quaffing immediately. "Umm, very good, now that is what I call a proper libation," approved Victoria.

"Now, where was I? Aah yes, Dennis. I rather fancied the fellow, well, who wouldn't have? He was a

6-feet-tall, athletic fellow with a shock of light brown hair and dreamy blue eyes. Who wouldn't swoon?

"Well, that was that, I thought, with the war and all, and he was apparently off on some training, all hush-hush, you know. So, I thought I may not see him again."

Taking another slurp of her wine, Victoria took a breath as Rory came in with a plate of canapés and nodded at them both before winking at Laura.

"Oh! Jolly good! I was getting rather peckish, how timely. I think that boy fancies you," grinned Victoria with a knowing glance as Rory walked away.

Without waiting for a reply, Victoria continued enthusiastically. "Well, to cut a long story short, I was sent off for some basic training, which did include some rather exertive physical exercise at a manor in Surrey before heading for telegraphy and cipher training at a number of places, like Thame Park, also in Surrey. A number of the other students seemed to be heading up north somewhere, such as Marjorie Lewis, a friend I made in training at Fawley Court near Henley when we were doing some learning about ciphers and codes. She was really bright and quick. I vaguely knew her from Cheltenham Ladies' College. She was a whizz when it came to the high-speed Morse code transmissions, which had to be at least twenty words per minute.

"Before I knew it, I was called for interview again, which was a bit more personal. Did I have children? and so on. A few days later, I received a letter to be told to prepare for relocation to a warm climate and take suitable clothing. By the end of the year, after a rather tortuous journey south from Liverpool, albeit on a converted cruise liner, I was back in Africa, not where I used to live, but Egypt. I heard Janey had joined Mountbatten's staff and was posted to Sri Lanka Hill Country, Kandy, I believe. Marjorie Lewis headed to Italy via Algiers. I believe that's where she met her future husband, Bob Clark. Top man; went on to be a director at the Bank of England, and I seem to recall he was something to do with the *Daily Mirror* too. He was an agent but was caught and ended up a POW. Poor old Marjorie fretted so much, but fortunately all came good at the end of the war.

"This wine really is splendid," said Victoria, topping up her glass.

Laura smiled and nodded. She could tell she had found Victoria's weakness.

"I hope you do not mind me making a few notes," said Laura, extracting the notebook from her handbag.

"Knock yourself out, kiddo. I am just happy to set the record straight."

Laura studied Victoria and wondered what she had been like when she was younger. Her blue eyes still sparkled in her visage, albeit they were getting a little bloodshot. She had noticed in the bar that she was a little shorter than Laura's 5 feet 9 inches, but even at a few inches shorter, Victoria still stood quite erect and was still slim, no sign of that spread of old age. It was evident she had been a good-looking lady in her day. There was a presence and confidence about Victoria Greaves but something was missing.

Turning her notepad to a clean page, Laura sat poised with pen in hand.

"Fire away, Victoria."

"Vicky, please. All my friends call me Vicky.

"After the harsh and rationed life in wartime Britain, Egypt was the place of plenty. It just didn't feel like there was a war on. There was a lot of dancing and eating out going on, all aided by an exotic surreal feel and the very warm climate.

"We now understood why we were told to bring a warm-weather wardrobe. Also, why we needed long skirts and eveningwear, very important for Cairo where we were heading, with soirées and dinner parties and clubs, like the Auberge des Pyramids.

"We arrived at Port Said and travelled by train, following the Suez Canal. Little Egyptian boys would jump on at stations where we stopped and try and sell us all sorts of strange fruits and trinkets. Some would assail us with a vigorous assault of enthusiastic chatter and a cheeky grin and say things like, 'Cigarettes, Vera Lynn?' which made us all laugh.

"When we got to Cairo, we were initially put up at Shepheard's Hotel for a night, which was fabulous, then strangely we were taken the next day after breakfast to the Nile and our home for our time in Cairo. Exotic green palm, almond and olive trees bordered the wide boulevards, swaying gently in the breeze, as if welcoming us to our new home.

"We were quite pleasantly surprised when we found out we were to be billeted on the Nile in a vessel which was rather grand and like a Mississippi steamer, complete with a paddle wheel midships – shades of Mark Twain. This houseboat, amongst others, had been requisitioned by the British Government from Thomas Cook. It was called the *SS Sudan* and do you know... it still exists today or so I am told!

"It really was rather a treat. We had a servant between two of us. They wore a long *galabeya*, like a long loose shirt, with a red sash and red *topi* hat – all very traditional Egyptian garb, you understand. The servants tended to be Sudanese. Mine was called Alim. He took great pleasure in telling us that it meant 'wise man', to which I replied, 'So it is you we will need to consult for wisdom.' He would smile and become a little shy!

"Alim sat at the end of our corridor all day, waiting to serve and be useful.

"It took me a while to get used to having a personal servant and calling for him. He would appear in a trice and nothing seemed a bother, you know, Laura!"

Victoria refilled her glass. "If we called him or clapped our hands loudly, he would appear at once. Clapping was a common form of getting attention, even in restaurants, so sometimes we would do this. I found it amusing at first but felt somewhat guilty after a while as we got to know Alim. He was such a charming little chap, and Mary Blythe, who also had Alim as her servant, felt very guilty about bothering Alim.

"The first few days were spent settling in and on general leave, but very quickly duty called.

"At first, everything was novel, but a very exciting routine soon ensued.

"Every day, we were picked up from the houseboat by Jeep, usually a soldier driving. To start with, it was every morning, heading for Rustum Buildings, a large house on the side of the Nile, and they picked us up after our shift every evening and drove us back.

"During the war, this was the hub of the secret operations plotting insurrection and sabotage across the Mediterranean, in particular, the Balkans, from the supposedly secret Rustum Buildings on Sharia Rustum. When I went back to visit Cairo years later, the name had changed to Sharia Mohammed Fahmy.

"Such was security in my time in wartime Cairo that if you took a taxi and said, 'Take me to Rustum Buildings,' the driver would invariably smile and say, 'Oh yes, Secret Building.'"

Laura chuckled.

"I remember going with some SAS officers for some outrageous knees-ups at 13 Sharia Naguib Pasha, where the novelist Olivia Manning also lived. There were a number of apartments in the building.

"We had a great time in Cairo. As soon as the translucent dusk settled over Cairo, we would head for a good night out if we were not on duty, maybe the raucous Sweet Melody Club or the Gezira Sporting Club, which was a popular venue for the 'fishing fleet' as they were called – debutantes looking for an eligible husband. It was an elegant club with swimming pools, polo club, restaurants and, of course, lots of handsome men!

"Of course, our shifts varied, especially as the war progressed and we were more on the offensive.

"There was no peace for the wicked, Laura. We worked day and night, decoding and coding messages. It became the norm that we alternated a week of day duty with a week of night duty.

"I remember, in the middle of the night, we took turns in having an hour's rest because it was so intense trying to perform to our best. The constant hum of transmissions and your eyes so focused in a room of subdued light really started to get to you. We would often go up and sleep on the roof, or just relax. It was so warm; I can almost feel the warm zephyr on my body now." Victoria seemed to drift off into her past momentarily, before returning to the room and Laura and pouring another drink.

"At first, it was difficult to sleep, whether at the office or on the houseboat. Hundreds of bullfrogs would bring a chorus of noise from down by the river. This went on until first light. After a month, it was like living near traffic noise from a busy road. You became used to it.

"You see, life was pretty good in Egypt, so much so that when I wrote home, I couldn't bring myself to tell my mother how much fun, good food and drink we had when we were not working, whilst knowing the hardships they were likely enduring back home.

"Sometimes, I thought of home after a long time of blackouts. It was a shock to see the twilight of Cairo turn to darkness, and lights start to come on in the mixture of city buildings as families enjoyed their evenings and neon signs flickered into life, some flashing messages and names. The skyline seemed to be ablaze in an amber tint as the scarlet sky made everywhere look so magical, minarets pointing skywards towards heaven. It was surreal compared to the deprivation of wartime England, where even if you lit a match outside after dark it was an offence.

"Things were developing apace in the Balkans in places like Yugoslavia, Greece and Serbia. Agents went from Cairo to these parts to endeavour to harness and work with anyone in opposition to the Nazi war machine.

"The S.O.E. in Cairo consisted of a group of smart and brave young soldiers who were dropped by parachute or taken by *caiques*, which were small boats, to the shores of Yugoslavia and Greece, including the islands, like Crete, where they would join various anti-German native groups hiding out in the mountains of those countries.

"Our work as 'cipherines' – occasionally referred to as 'codists' – was to keep in touch with them and pass on messages from General Head Quarters.

"If we were going to send a 'drop' of men, supplies or money, we would usually send a message to say 'light fires in the shape of a cross' or some such instruction at such and such a time, and wait for the drop.

"Money always had to be in gold sovereigns in wartime, the only way to… listen to me going on.

"Sometimes, especially when agents in the field were under duress, the main cipher room could not decipher codes because of mistakes in the messages sent to them. In this case, they were sent to a small office with just two decoders in it. I worked in one such duo.

"With my fellow coder, I battled against time to break the faulty codes. We usually succeeded, though.

"We knew most of the young men engaged in these operations, and a number of us had boyfriends amongst them, as indeed had I, so we needed no encouragement to work hard.

"One evening, we were just settling down for an aperitif on the terrace at Shepheard's prior to dinner when a despatch rider came gambolling into our midst with orders for us to return to Rustum Buildings immediately so some emergency could be dealt with. We knew what this meant.

"After a long evening, we had finally broken the code of one agent's message, which resulted in him being rescued from a tricky predicament, and I was a few days later invited to his debrief.

"He came to our tiny office. I can still see him so clearly now. He sat on my table, legs swinging, and he recounted the story of the whole operation, how it was planned and how it went.

"It was a fascinating story. All the time, I seemed to think this chap is familiar. I didn't recognise him at first. His hair was unkempt and he had a really unruly beard, but it was his eyes, so clear and blue, you cannot believe how fate deals you a hand. Incredulously and fortuitously, it was Dennis. He was the S.O.E. agent I had taken the S.O.S. evacuation message from, but I just knew him by his code name, 'Hercules'.

"Laura, I cannot tell you how wonderful it was to see Dennis again. I fell for him all over again. He said he remembered me but I am not sure he did, but who cares? He invited me out for dinner, ostensibly to say thank you, but what came next was a fairy tale.

"We had a whirlwind romance. It was just dreamy. It seemed so strange after what he had been through and what a lot of the world was experiencing, as the Germans, Japanese and their allies seemed to be winning on all fronts. I was lucky.

"Life was just perfect. Dennis lived in a villa on Gezira Island, set in the Nile. I think it was called 'Tara'. There was no rationing like back home, so our well-appointed dining room on our houseboat was the site of many a soirée, entertaining friends. We met up with one or two from back home who, of course, were now in the army, and met with all sorts of people from high-ranking officers and their wives, or shall we say partners, to Egyptian royalty and other dignitaries.

"Dennis, of course, would bring some of his fellow agents and, boy, would they let their hair down. Not all were men, some women. A Polish woman, Krystyna, I believe, used to come. Dennis said she was a countess or princess or something.

"Cairo was a bustling, busy metropolis with a fantastic marketplace stretching over many streets and alleys.

"Casra Nil was probably the best known. It was quite an experience, crowds of babbling Egyptians all around. Occasionally, there were beggars, some with no arms or missing legs. They would come right up to you and make you quite uncomfortable, shouting, '*Baksheesh, baksheesh*' – Money, money.

"At first, the sight was horrifying, but after seeing it each day you become anaesthetised to it.

"There were lots of pedlars on the crowded busy streets in those days, and even dentists and barbers, amongst other professions, just on the side of the street. There were water sellers, knife sharpeners, fruit sellers, and so on. The mango was my favourite fruit. The little Arab would cut the mango in half and produce a wooden spoon so that one could prise out its fragrant flesh to consume. I can almost taste it now.

"Dennis and I had lunch at Mena House, a wonderful hotel. We dined on the terrace with views of the pyramids." Victoria bit her bottom lip a little and paused, evidently finding the memory painful too.

"One day, we had been to the Casra Nil, and to escape the hustle and bustle and cacophony of chaos, Dennis found a *gharry* and we headed to Groppi's for lunch. Dennis seemed distracted, almost melancholy. I thought perhaps he was tiring of me. The clip-clop of the horse-pulled *gharry* seemed to beat like drums in my head.

Then in Groppi's, out of the blue, he reached across the table, put his hand on mine and with those cornflower blue eyes, bewitched me as he said, 'Let's get married, Vicky.'

"I was dumbfounded yet exhilarated all at the same time. Life is too short, we always used to say, so we married within the week and I was ecstatic. Heady times indeed.

"We were able to travel to Alexandria, as I had been granted two days' special leave. We sat under huge umbrellas on the beach and relaxed, and later enjoyed the evening sea breezes, helping to cool the day down. The sun set upon us as we walked the Corniche, the waterfront promenade. We stayed at the fabulous Hotel Cecil in front of the Corniche. It was just so romantic.

"One night, we sat outside on the terrace of a splendid beachside restaurant listening to the waves on the shore. We held hands across the table as a gibbous moon illuminated the magical night sky above. I wanted time to stand still.

"Sadly, the joy didn't last. Dennis told me he had to go on another mission, but he promised me we would have a really special honeymoon when this was all over.

"He headed down to Haifa, I believe, for some more training and to rendezvous and assimilate into a unit due to be dropped into Greece. I didn't know this at the time. I only found out afterwards when I…" She hesitated and looked away, brushing her hair from her face.

"Well, I never saw him again. He was reported missing in action in early 1944. The radio messages his unit were supposed to send were fine at first. He had landed and made contact with the ELAS partisans. They were communists, you know, but then from early January 1944, nothing."

Victoria was quite red in the face; her eyes welled up. "Sorry, Laura, it's tough to remember such hopes and dreams and for them to all be dashed by fate, to be so real then cruelly snatched away."

"What happened to him, Vicky? Where did he die?" said Laura.

"That is just it, he was listed as missing in action and his body or remains were never found; no one ever knew, such is the horror of war, probably killed with his fellow agents and partisans, perhaps buried in a grave with no memorial stone to remember him by.

"It was tough, Laura. I couldn't concentrate on my work, I was just so upset. By the time September 1944 came, Europe had been invaded by the allies and all was improving for the allies, but Greece was falling apart, not so much because of the Germans, who had been forced out of Greece by October 1944, but the infighting between the various partisan groups, the communists, ELAS and those on the right, EDES, who supported the King and wanted him to return. They were turning on each other."

"Gosh, that must have been so tough for you," said Laura, leaning over and touching Victoria's hand.

Victoria was drifting on a wave of nostalgia, almost talking to herself. "I always prayed for a miracle that he would come back, that he was just incommunicado whilst trying to get back to me. I thought I would wake up one day and there he would be, but as the Arabs say, *'Bukra!'*, which means a tomorrow that never arrived."

Victoria smiled and put her glass on the table. "I have had too much to drink; it's been a long day. Can we perhaps meet for lunch tomorrow? I need a good night's sleep."

"Of course," said Laura.

Victoria rose off her chair unsteadily and weaved her way towards the stairs and her room.

Laura had been bewitched hearing about Dennis Greaves but was starting to have some doubts. Something didn't ring true. Maybe he was not her grandfather, or even if he was, he moved on to another woman from her grandmother, and perhaps that is the real reason her Grandmother Martha didn't keep her child.

Laura lay awake in her room back at Arisaig House, her mind in overdrive.

*

Next day, Victoria and Laura met for lunch at the Crofters' Bar. It was relatively quiet, just two other ladies enjoying a lunch together. Victoria's opening gambit was:

"Your grandmother, I felt, was always a threat to Dennis and myself. He spoke fondly of Martha, always wondering what had happened to her. But Dennis always insisted she was just a friend and never admitted they had anything other than a platonic relationship. He just said they were pals, which is what I wanted to believe.

"There is an irony here, Laura, which occurred to me overnight, as it was a friend and fellow officer of my father, a fellow called Charles Podmore, who first introduced Martha to my family.

"Apparently, she was a refugee from Europe somewhere and had come up to Shropshire with the sisters of Charlie, all the way from Kent, to stay at Butler House in Harnage, Poddy's family home. The sisters, who seemed like spinsters to me, thought it safer than being in the firing line of the Germans in Kent.

"My mother and father called by one day, and my father was quite taken with Martha and suitably impressed by her language skills. So much so, the soirée where I met Dennis and his friend Harry was also attended by Charles Podmore, his wife, sisters and Martha, apparently at the invitation of my father.

"It was Harry who seemed to be transfixed by Martha and spent quite some time speaking to her. Then come midnight, everyone went their separate ways. The evening promised so much for me, but nothing to report, I am afraid.

"Once, when I was talking to Dennis about the first time we met, I asked Dennis innocently about his friend Harry and Martha that night at the house party we had at Ludford Grange. I commented they seemed to have been getting on well. He said he didn't recall but did admit to having once bumped into Martha in Shrewsbury whilst dropping in at a local café and apparently had directed her to the train station as she left." Victoria seemed to say it as if wanting to believe it herself.

"When Dennis didn't come back from his mission infiltration in Greece, I was distraught. I had to have some grief counselling out at Helwan and a little help. I had what you might call a nervous breakdown. Eventually, they shipped me home for the sake of my health."

Laura said softly, "I am so sorry to hear that but perhaps you are wrong and Dennis was just a friend of

Martha's. It is not certain that Dennis is my grandfather after all, just because…"

Victoria's face hardened; she put her hand up. "I am certain your mother is Dennis.'"

"But how could you know? I do not even know her surname."

Victoria fished for something in her large handbag and produced a black-and-white photograph, placing it on the table in front of Laura.

Laura picked it up and perused the black-and-white photo, which showed two people standing by what looked like a harbour wall with boats in the background. The man dressed in uniform, his arm around a very smart-looking lady, dressed in a pencil skirt with nipped-in jacket, heart-shaped face, both smiling at the camera and looking very happy.

"Look at the back," said Victoria, her face now like thunder.

Turning the picture around, the words, *Forever yours, love always, Martha XXX*

Laura did not know what to say. She was both emotional and so happy to at long last see a photograph of her grandmother with someone who was increasingly likely to be her grandfather but, a little concerned and confused, she refused to get too excited until she knew for absolute sure.

"This doesn't mean anything, even if she met Dennis socially, or indeed any relationship could have been just a wartime fling, for all we know."

Victoria then produced a letter.

Studying the beautiful writing addressed to Captain

Dennis Greaves, Laura delicately extracted the writing paper from the blue vellum envelope.

She immersed herself in the prose and how the writer spoke so gently in soliloquies, sharing her emotions, thoughts and feelings as if she was all alone. Laura was overcome by a raft of emotions.

Still holding the letter, she looked at Victoria through tear-filled eyes.

The address on the back, marked sender, was *Martha Swanson c/o Station Hotel, Morar.*

Laura was mesmerised. She repeated it in her mind: *Martha Swanson, Martha Swanson.*

"I found them when I was leaving Cairo. They had been locked in a small suitcase Dennis had left under his bed in Villa Tara, and they were given to me as next of kin amongst his few possessions when he did not return. Crazy as it may seem, I hadn't even bothered to open it until I had to leave Cairo. Don't ask me why I have never destroyed them, but perhaps I always thought one day Dennis would come back and I would confront him. Perhaps I wanted to find Martha and confront her. I do not know.

"But now, you see, I suspect he knew she was pregnant! Do you see the date on the letter? It was clear he had been in possession of the correspondence for a long time. He never shared this with me."

"Perhaps he never found out about the pregnancy," suggested Laura.

"No, we do not know," said Victoria, opening the palms of her hands and raising her eyebrows in a gesture to support her words.

"Laura, I feel happy for you that you have found your grandmother, well, at least her identity, and that possibly you now know who your grandfather is. I also feel strangely more at ease now that I have told you. I was becoming angry again, but somehow, I feel strangely ridden of a burden that has rested on my shoulders for many years. Can you understand?"

"Yes, I think I can!" said Laura, putting her hand on Victoria's.

"I know this is hard but what can you tell me about Dennis Greaves and his family, where he was from, and so on?"

Victoria's mind had wandered. "Do you know, sometimes I almost think my father liked Martha more than me."

"Why, what makes you say that?" said a puzzled Laura.

"The Atkinson family home is on the Shropshire/Herefordshire border at Ludford Grange, which has been in the family for generations. It is a large rambling old edifice and estate.

"I don't visit much. Dad occasionally mumbles her name even now. Last time I saw him, I opened the door of the snug and he said, looking up from his armchair, his tired grey eyes peeking out from under his bushy eyebrows, 'Martha, is that you?' and I said, 'No, it's me, Pops.' He grunted and returned to fiddling with the blanket over his knees, then he would occasionally look up at me and say 'Martha' again. I would just ignore it."

"Wow, he is still alive. That is amazing."

"Yes, he is ninety-nine years old, but I can't talk to

him about anything. He has Alzheimer's disease. He is away with the fairies most of the time. He still lives in the family home, which is far too big for him. He has outlived my sister, my mother and may well see me off! He has a very faithful housekeeper and some friends who look in on him.

"To answer your question, I didn't learn much about Dennis' family other than that his parents were dead and I think he had a younger sister. Susan, perhaps, or Sarah, I cannot remember. We didn't have a lot of time together to find much out about one another. We just enjoyed each other and the moment."

"I am sorry to hear about your father's ill health, it must be very difficult. Do you know where Dennis was from?"

Victoria shrugged then chuckled. "All I know is possibly South Herefordshire way, near the Welsh border. I guess we spoke more about the here and now, and the emotions we shared were heightened and explored because of the war. After all, it was very much *carpe diem*."

Laura picked up the photograph and letter and offered them back to Victoria.

"No! From today, they are yours. What good are they to me?"

"Thank you so much. I cannot thank you enough for all your help and for talking to me. I know it has been hard for you. I am sure Dennis loved you very much. It is just so sad he was taken from you so quickly."

"Well, that's life, let's have a glass of wine and order some lunch, shall we?" said Victoria.

Nine

Relative or not?

Laura spent that afternoon driving home to Comrie. She felt it better to share all this information with her mother, Elise, face to face.

Many thoughts went through her mind on the drive; so many, in fact, that she could barely remember the journey back, which became a blur. Turning the key in the lock, she shouted to her mother.

"I am home," said Laura, kicking off her comfortable low-heeled driving shoes.

Her mum came into the hall, wiping her hands on a tea cloth. As she did, her daughter gave her a huge lasting hug.

"My word, what's that all in aid of?" said her surprised mum.

"Mam, you are going to need to sit down. I do

believe I might have found out who your real mother and father are."

Laura regaled her mother with all the happenings since she had last seen her, not just the last couple of days with Victoria but all the stories preceding that meeting, Madge and then Alice Stanley. By 10pm, it was difficult to say who was more exhausted, Elise or Laura!

"Well, I do not know what to say," said Elise as she finally held a picture of her real mother and father.

"Of course, it is not one hundred per cent certain that Dennis is your father, Mam, but if I can find the sister of Dennis, we can do a DNA test – a new scientific way that I have established will check if we are all related – and maybe that will be the clincher."

"Oh! I don't know about bothering people who have accepted life for what it is. Perhaps let sleeping dogs lie, Laura," cautioned Elise.

"But, Mam, we need to know for sure."

"Do we, Laura, love? Sometimes, if you are happy with what you know, why go stirring things up?

"As far as I am concerned, Tam and Mary were my parents. They are the ones who brought me up. I never knew my mother or father, did I?"

Laura felt a little deflated. After all her efforts, she expected a little more joy and enthusiasm and also an accolade for what she had achieved and found out for her mum.

"Fine, Mam, I understand. I am off to bed. I am not going to drive back to Arisaig tonight, I am exhausted. I will make an early start tomorrow." She collected up the letters, notes and the photograph. Propping the photograph up against the mantelpiece clock, she said goodnight.

Laura tossed and turned; her restlessness was driving her crazy. She crept quietly into the kitchen, poured herself a glass of water and shuffled into the living room. Putting on the light, she picked up the picture she had been given of her potential grandparents. The more she looked at it, the more convinced she was that the lady in her dream had been her grandmother, Etive, and not herself.

Elise understood Laura's disappointment but let it go. Laura just didn't see her point of view nor understood how difficult the past had been for her and many others.

*

Over the next few weeks, Laura worked at trying to find out about her grandparents' war records and tracking down her grandfather's sister.

Letter after letter, phone call after phone call were met with disappointment.

A letter arrived from the National Records Office. It transpired that Martha's and Dennis' S.O.E. service records had been destroyed or mislaid and therefore did not exist, so there was no personal file information. Her grandmother's real name therefore could not be confirmed.

Finally, one day, a letter arrived from the Royal Engineers.

Dear Miss Dewar,

Thank you for your letter. We can confirm Captain Dennis Greaves did serve with the Royal Engineers 1940 to 1944, when we have him listed as missing in action in Greece. I am afraid that is all the record shows, as it seems to be incomplete.

We do have a home address from that time as follows:

Radnor House,
Church Street,
Hay-on-Wye,
Brecknockshire
We suggest you might want to try the Military Records, held in the National Archive.

Sorry we cannot be of more assistance.
Good luck with your search.
Yours sincerely,
Daphne Morris

Laura was pleased. For the first time in a few weeks, she smiled. *I have a starting place to look for the sister of Dennis.*

Tucking the letter back in the envelope, she reached into her office drawer for a road atlas. She discovered Hay-on-Wye was a border town nowadays, just inside Wales.

Laura made a call to the local tourist information office in Hay and established if Radnor House still existed, and it did indeed. In fact, it was a Bed and Breakfast run by a Juliet Harper, and the tourist office procured the telephone number for Laura.

That evening, Laura made a telephone call.

"Radnor House, how may I help you?" said the refined English voice of a lady.

"Hello, is that Mrs Harper?"

"It is indeed. How can I help you?"

"This might sound rather a strange request, but I wonder if you know much about the previous occupants of Radnor House. I am trying to track down the sister of a relative of mine. His name is Dennis Greaves."

There was a silence at the end of the phone.

"Hello, are you still there?" prompted Laura.

"Sorry, yes, what was your name again?"

"Apologies, I hadn't said. I am Laura Dewar."

"How might you be related to Dennis Greaves?" queried the now inquisitive yet terse tone in Hay.

"I believe he may be my grandfather."

"Oh no, dear! I think you may have the wrong Dennis Greaves, as my mother was Dennis' sister and we have never heard of a Laura in our family, let alone from… please excuse me for saying… from your accent, you sound Scottish."

"I am indeed. It's a long story, Mrs Harper. May I call you Juliet? Perhaps I could speak to your mother."

"I am sorry, that's not possible. My mother passed away a few years ago."

Laura hesitated then said, "I am so sorry to hear that sad news, but I do think we need to talk face to face. I believe I have a fascinating story to tell you."

Ten

Borderline

A month later, Laura headed south, driving to the little town of Hay-on-Wye. She crossed a quaint little toll bridge at Whitney-on-Wye and ten minutes later progressed up a steep bank into Hay, turned into Bridge Street and followed the car parking signs. A few minutes later, she was knocking at the door of Radnor House.

She admired the quaint white-painted lattice metal porch with roses rambling over it and up the wall of the imposing greystone three-storey building.

The door creaked open and before Laura stood a tall, slim lady. Laura's first impression was of an elegant mature woman, her hair tied back and wearing a string of pearls which rested on a lovat green silk blouse.

"You must be Mrs Harper, I am Laura," she said, proffering her handbag-free hand.

Mrs Harper cracked a rather forced smile and gestured for Laura to come in.

For such a large house, there was a very small reception room to the right, but Laura could see a larger room on the left and rightly assumed that was the breakfast room.

"Good journey?" asked Mrs Harper.

"Very good, thank you, mostly motorway then it was a little slower coming through Wales, but delightful countryside. Just down the road, I noticed some kayakers heading for the river," said Laura awkwardly.

"Yes, we have a few of those on the Wye. Tea?"

"Yes, please," said Laura, taking off her jacket and placing it on the coat stand as Mrs Harper disappeared from the room.

Warming herself by the fire, Laura took in the dark décor and wondered who the people in the framed photograph may be above the fireplace.

"My paternal grandparents," said the host, returning with a tray of tea and home baking and placing it on the coffee table, which divided the couch and settee set against the wall on either side of the room.

"I see," said Laura, acknowledging the answer to her unspoken question. "Thank you! The fruitcake looks delicious," praised Laura.

"*Bara brith* or speckled bread actually, whichever you wish to call it," corrected Mrs Harper.

"Ah yes! I should have spotted that. I had my first piece when I was in North Wales recently."

Coming straight to the point: "I am intrigued to know how we might be related," said Mrs Harper forcefully, almost as a challenge.

For what seemed the umpteenth time, Laura told her story, starting with her dream and then her subsequent curiosity, which had launched her on a mission to find out what happened to her grandparents.

Mrs Harper listened intently. Laura had expected her to be immediately dismissive.

Finishing her tale: "So that is why I am here. I also have a photograph of Dennis and Martha," added Laura, producing the black-and-white image that Victoria had kindly given her.

Mrs Harper studied it and held it to the light before producing a small pair of spectacles from her cardigan pocket and spending some time perusing the image before looking up at Laura.

"Excuse me a moment," said Mrs Harper as she left the room, returning a few minutes later with a photograph album, but this time sitting beside Laura on the couch by the front window.

Mrs Harper proceeded to talk Laura through the album, showing pictures of her mother and father and herself and siblings as children, before stopping at a page with a photograph of a man in army uniform. A much sharper image than the one Laura had. "This was Dennis Greaves, my uncle. Isn't he handsome?"

"Gosh, he is indeed, Mrs Harper, and an uncanny resemblance to the man in my picture here."

"Juliet, please call me Juliet."

A convivial conversation ensued and even a

chuckle or two as Juliet told stories of her uncle.

"I have fond memories of my Uncle Dennis. One day, I went down with him to Uncle Dilwyn's farm near Brecon, and Uncle Dennis decided he was going to shoot at a large crow on the chimney pots of the farmhouse but, as he was lining the shot up, Lucy the sheepdog shot past him, barking as she chased a rabbit. Well, it startled Uncle Dennis. He let off a shot and knocked the chimney pot right off. Uncle Dilwyn wasn't very happy!" Laughing out loud, they were soon in tears of joy as other stories flowed.

"When did you last see Dennis?" enquired Laura, sipping her now cold tea and grimacing slightly.

"I can make some more tea but, look, you will be staying, won't you? We can have some dinner and we can learn a little more about each other's families."

"Well, I had planned to possibly go back through Shropshire and stay the night in Shrewsbury. I have never been there."

"Oh! You must stay. Do you eat red meat or would you prefer chicken or fish?"

"That's very kind of you, anything would be fine."

"Do you have an overnight bag?"

"It's in my car. I parked in the large car park as you advised."

"Splendid. That is settled then."

*

"That was a superb dinner, Juliet. I am fit to burst."

"Thank you, let's have some coffee and a naughty

after-dinner mint or two," said Juliet, clearing away the plates.

As the evening flew by, Laura started to appreciate how much her grandfather was loved and cared for.

"My mother died of a heart attack in this very house," said Juliet. "She was a special lady. My mother did not suffer fools gladly but was very kind. This was her home actually. It was the family home and has been for generations. As I am the only child, my mother left Radnor House to me and my husband and we moved in. We had grand plans but it is such a huge house and somewhat of a money pit. We had to consider a form of income and I had always wanted to run a guesthouse. Thus, we opened Radnor House as a bed and breakfast, which has been very enjoyable. We have met lots of wonderful people, especially around the Hay Festival times in the summer, when the town is extremely busy.

"Sadly, my husband and I have separated. Our relationship did not endure, he left me five years ago. Unbeknown to me, he had another lady that he was seeing, so for the last five years I have been here alone. Initially, I was angry, then bitter, but now I am quite happy with my own company and catering for my guests. In fact, I prefer it."

"It must be really hard work."

"Yes, it is, Laura, but I enjoy it.

"I find it comforting to know my family still has this home and that Dennis once lived here many years ago. Do you know, I think he was a hero to my mother, Dorothy. She doted upon him. It broke her heart when he did not return from war."

"I wish I had been able to meet him," said Laura. "I thought his sister's name was Susan or Sarah?"

"Yes! There was a sister Susan, but she died rather young of consumption or TB as we know it today! Apparently, my mother said it broke Dennis' heart and it was after that he just could not settle, so he joined the army.

"Do you know, Laura, when I last saw Dennis, I was very young, maybe six or seven. He was in uniform. He looked so smart and important, so dashing. He swept me up and sat me on that very wall outside the house and gave me a big hug before departing, and I waved to him all down the road until he was out of sight. I never ever thought I would never see him again, and as you know, he was never seen again by any of his friends and family. He never came home."

"That is so sad. I hope you don't mind me asking, but on a serious note..." said Laura cautiously "...it seems more than certain Dennis is my grandfather, but in order to try and prove it beyond doubt, can you help me?"

"Well, how would we do that?" replied Juliet, intrigued.

"I have heard of these tests called 'paternity tests' that they do now, and by taking our blood or hair or something like that, they can see if they are matched or at least closely matched. If we both gave a sample, it might be the clinching factor!"

"Gosh, that is amazing. Well, of course we must do that. Let's have a brandy to celebrate!"

Both ladies wended their way up the steep stairs as Juliet showed Laura to her room for the night.

By the time they reached the third floor, even Laura was a little out of breath. She was shown into an attic room. It boasted a lovely big bathroom with walk-in shower. Its large double bed beckoned as she creaked across the creaking slope of the floorboards.

*

Laura slept well, showered and headed for the breakfast room. Juliet was already up. She had made breakfast for two other guests, who were just telling her what their plans were for the day.

"Well good morning!" said Juliet, who duly introduced them. "This is Mr and Mrs Craig from Gloucester. This is my cousin Laura from, and you might guess this, Scotland," she said before disappearing to the kitchen.

A polite conversation followed before the Craigs departed, and Laura sat at the small round table by the window, looking out across the small front garden to the fairly busy road beyond the wall where Juliet last saw Dennis.

Juliet returned with some toast, tea and local honey.

"So how did you sleep in your grandfather's room?"

Laura was dumbfounded. "My grandfather's room?" she gasped.

"Yes! That is the room Uncle Dennis was born in!"

"Wow, how special! Thank you!"

"So when can we do these new-fangled tests?" smiled Juliet.

Eleven

Kismet

The summer seemed to pass in a whirlwind of activity; Arisaig House was so busy with guests. Laura never ceased to be amazed at how many people were prepared to pay so much for staying at this characterful historic house, now a boutique hotel, but she only had to look out of the window from the Residents' Lounge across the terrace to see why visitors loved the exclusivity and seclusion of the property from which to explore the beautiful coast and hidden beaches of this photogenic area, and add to that the quality of food, service and accommodation, then she had her answer.

Every time Laura walked up the staircase, its handrail supported by an ornately carved pattern, she wondered what stories it could tell, and thought of her grandmother walking that very stair, holding on to the handrail.

From time to time, Arisaig House guests included someone who was more than familiar with the property in a wartime role, but these were becoming fewer and fewer as time marched on and former military men and women aged and shuffled off their mortal coil.

One day, a rather smart-looking couple driving a bottle-green Jaguar XJS pulled into the courtyard and entered the lobby, placing their small suitcases down with a sigh of relief.

"Hello, have you had a long journey?" beamed Laura, stepping from behind her desk, always keen to give a personal and friendly greeting, making guests immediately feel welcome.

"Good day, quite a trip, but we have overnighted on the way up the country, visiting friends in the Lake District," said the once tall but now slightly bent figure of a man who could still command one's attention just with his voice and intonation. Proffering his hand in acknowledgement, he smiled as he held Laura's hand within his mottled but firm grip.

"Welcome to Arisaig House."

"Thank you. Mr and Mrs Melton-Woodbridge, we have a reservation for three nights, I believe."

"Please come through to the lounge. We will take care of your luggage. May I get you a tea or coffee, or perhaps you would prefer something stronger?" said Laura, leading them the short distance to the lounge, before they settled on the large settee in front of the fireplace.

"Earl Grey tea, please, no milk or sugar."

Returning, Laura placed the silver tray with their requested beverage steaming away in a white ceramic teapot, with white china teacups and saucers accompanied by a plate of Scottish shortbread biscuits.

Mr Melton-Woodbridge had picked up a pamphlet from the coffee table and was studying *The History of Arisaig House*.

"There we are. I see you have found some information on our history. Is this your first visit to this neck of the woods, Mr Melton-Woodbridge?"

"David, please."

"I am Angeliki," added the strongly accented Mrs Melton-Woodbridge.

"I have been here before," said David. "Actually, I stayed here.

"I might add it was a long time ago, during World War Two, so not quite as relaxed and comfortable as we are now."

"Gosh! That is amazing," said Laura, her interest immediately heightened. "Excuse me for asking," said Laura, turning to Mrs Melton-Woodbridge, "where is your lovely accent from?"

"I am originally from Greece."

"How fascinating." Laura couldn't help adding, "My grandfather served in Greece in the war but sadly he didn't return."

"I am sorry to hear that," said Mr and Mrs Melton-Woodbridge simultaneously, before David added, "That is where Angeliki and myself met. Where did your grandfather serve?"

"I am afraid I do not know much about his service

as yet," replied Laura. "I have only recently found out he was my grandfather. I am sorry, it's a long story. I should let you relax and enjoy your tea."

"What unit was your grandfather with?" queried David, his interest piqued.

"As far as I know, he was with the Royal Engineers but then joined the S.O.E. – Special Operations Executive, that is – and was based in Cairo, but I do not know much more."

"That is astonishing. So was I," said David as Laura poured the tea.

Laura lost concentration and missed the cup as the tea splashed into the saucer.

"Oh! I am so sorry." Angeliki smiled and said, "Don't worry, no harm done."

"What was this fellow's name?"

"Captain Dennis Greaves."

"Well, well, well, I knew Den, fine chap." David's tone became more sombre. "I suppose you know he was reported missing in action."

"Yes! I have been told," said Laura softly but wide-eyed.

"So, Vicky is your grandmother then?" added David.

"Well, actually, no, it is rather complicated."

"Right, okay, well, a splendid chap. Sorry he didn't make it," said David awkwardly.

"I must let you relax and I will take you up to your room when you are ready." Laura smiled and turned to go, then hesitated. "You wouldn't happen to know where Dennis Greaves was last seen?"

"I am sorry, Laura, all missions were hush-hush, on a need-to-know basis, you see, and his service record, or should I say S.O.E. personal file, is probably still secret. However, a friend of mine, another former BLO, may well know the area he was parachuted into. Leave it with me."

Laura beamed. 'Thank you so much. That would be wonderful. How fortuitous meeting you. Just one question: what is a BLO?"

"A British liaison officer," smiled David, who was only too happy to help.

*

A fortnight later, Laura received a thank-you card for the wonderful time the Melton-Woodbridges had enjoyed and inside was a letter.

> Dear Laura,
>
> After our chat, I managed to contact an old colleague and fellow officer.
>
> Through him, I have established his amazing recollection that Captain Greaves disappeared on a mission into the southern mainland of Greece in late 1943, possibly early '44. It is believed he was only aged just twenty-nine. He was a British liaison officer sent in to help the ELAS forces, October 1943. He was with a fellow called O'Riordan, and his superior was a Major Reid.
>
> My old colleague also tells me he was pals

or at least worked with this O'Donnell fellow and remembers a conversation he had with O'Donnell about Greaves. He recalls O'Donnell telling him Dennis had been very perturbed about a massacre of Greek villagers which took place at Kalavryta, and the last time O'Donnell had seen him was Christmas 1943. Kalavryta is west of Athens, closer to the port of Patras in the Peloponnese. I am sorry to tell you this. Apparently, your grandfather disappeared. O'Donnell had initially feared he went AWOL, but the long and the short of it was, he was reported missing in action. Sadly, he was probably killed. By who? The Germans, Greek communists...? No one will ever know.

I did a little digging and was able to access a debrief report by this same chap, O' Donnell. Please find enclosed the salient part below.

Laura read and reread this report of a dreadful atrocity that took place on 13 December 1943. The entire town of Kalavryta was burned to the ground. The massacre was carried out by the German Army's 117th Jäger Division. The extermination of the male population of Kalavryta was in retaliation for the execution of sixty-eight German soldiers who had been captured by the Greek Resistance.

Early in the morning of 13 December, a convoy of new German army forces arrived in the mountain town, including many senior officers. The Germans rang the town's church bells and ordered all the people to gather in the elementary school, bringing with them a blanket and food for one day.

There, they separated the men from the women and children. The women and children were told to stay in the school, whilst all males over fourteen were led in groups to the nearby field called Kapi Rake. The field was on a slope and was the shape of an amphitheatre, offering a full view of the town. This also meant it was a difficult area to escape from. The Germans chose this site purposely.

The Germans proceeded to set the school on fire so that the men could see.

Women and children who were trapped in the elementary school were nearly consumed by the flames, but they escaped by breaking the windows and doors. Rumour has it that a Wehrmacht soldier – who was Austrian by birth – who the ladies had talked to whilst he was guarding them left one door open so they could get away.

That day in Kalavryta, 499 people were executed. Yet, astonishingly, twelve men managed to survive without the Germans knowing, whilst the total number of victims in the wider region of Kalavryta and the neighbouring villages was 677.

The thought made Laura feel sick. So, this must be what had perturbed her grandfather so much. Now she understood so much more.

Laura was awash with emotion and information and wanted to share it with her mother. It had been so busy and even though autumn had arrived, Arisaig House was still very full.

Laura had little time to pursue information and do more research on her likely grandfather, but one thing she had achieved, along with Juliet, was managing to send off their paternity tests. Tests completed, they were now awaiting the results.

Establishing that the Kalavryta Massacre had had a great effect on Dennis Greaves, as indicated by David Melton-Woodbridge, it played on her mind. She found out from guidebooks and library textbooks that this mountainous part of the Greek Peloponnese was located on the right bank of the Vouraikos River, 62km to the southeast of Patras, the region's capital. The guidebook she had found the information in described it as a typical mountain village nestled around a square, surrounded by plane trees and cafés, and a good base for winter sports.

It all sounded idyllic and at the same time alluring, for a different reason.

That evening, after her shift, Laura strolled through the meadows which led down from Arisaig House to the historic shingle beach of Borrodale with its dramatic views over Loch nan Uamh (loch of the caves) and the Ardnish Peninsula across to the hills of Moidart. As she gazed across this wonderful vista, something was changing, indeed, stirring in her soul. She was not quite sure what was happening, but she felt a change was coming.

Twelve

Farther and Father

Laura finally managed to get a day off. She found herself handing out the same old platitudes to the guests – *How are you? Have a nice day. How was your day?* – without really listening to the reply. Her sincerity was waning; she was facing burnout.

The trees were changing to their autumnal golds; it was a pretty time of year as she drove back home to Comrie, as the mountains turned more to hills as she entered Perthshire. She looked forward to seeing her mother and being home for a short while. She loved walking, and whilst Scotland sported plenty of pine trees, she loved getting back home and doing favourite walks like 'Lady Mary's Walk' at Crieff, just up the road from Comrie, and taking a leisurely stroll alongside the River Earn, lined with a plethora of oak, beech, lime and sweet chestnut trees, and at this time of year it was very special.

With trepidation, she opened the door of the family home. "Hi, Mam?" she called out.

Without reply, she realised her mum must be out. Settling in, she made herself a pot of tea and started to arrange all the information she had collected, including the cherished photograph of her likely grandparents, Dennis and Martha, on the large kitchen table. It was like a battle plan!

Before long, she heard the door, and into the kitchen breezed her mother.

"Oh! My word!" exclaimed Elise, a little startled. "I wasn't expecting you. Why didn't you call?"

"Sorry, Mam, we have been hell for leather and I just had an unexpected window to get a day off and wanted to come and see you."

"Well, it's good to see you," she said hesitatingly, kissing Laura on the top of her head as she placed a bag of groceries on the kitchen table. "Just as well I have been into Hansen's and picked up a lovely quiche that will serve us perfectly for lunch."

Laura felt relieved that her mum didn't seem to be upset. Laura had felt sad that she had left under a cloud last time she was home, and worse, she had been so busy at work that she had barely been in touch with her mum to share the continuing accrual of genealogical information and details of her Hay-on-Wye trip. But then the illusion was shattered.

"What's all this, Laura?" Elise frowned, gesturing towards the neatly arrayed table covering of documents and the special photograph.

"I have found out lots more about Dennis, Mam. I really think he is your father," she said enthusiastically.

"Oh, Laura! You are not still pursuing this nonsense, are you?" said Elise, taking her coat off. "I thought I said it was best to leave the past behind. No good ever comes of thinking about what might have been," she said dismissively, putting on her pinafore and flicking the kettle switch. "We should look forward, not to the past."

Laura said nothing. She had never seen or heard her mum so unsupportive. Something didn't seem right. She gathered up all the documents and other information she had collected, put it in her briefcase and went to her bedroom. That evening, they ate dinner in near silence and watched television with barely a word. Her hope that they may be able to go for a walk together and chat like mother and daughter should, was clearly not going to happen. Next morning, Laura drove back to Arisaig.

Laura was resolute and adamant that she was going to see this through, with or without her mother's help or approval. She decided to apply for her first passport. She was in a rut and needed to get away for a break, and Greece was the only place she wanted to go!

Picking up a passport form from the local post office, she filled it in and then realised she needed some photographs, one signed on the back by a teacher or doctor or some such luminary. Reading the notes with the form, Laura spotted she needed her birth certificate.

Darn, she mused to herself. *I should have thought about that,* as she knew her mother must have this.

Frustrated, she was going to have to contact her mum again but decided rather than tell her she was going to Greece and the motives for doing so, she would stay calm and disinterested and just say she was tired and in need of some relaxation; therefore, going for a holiday in the sun would not be unusual. She didn't even have to say where. *Why inflame things again?* she thought to herself.

That night, Laura rang home.

"Hi, Mam, how are you?"

"I am fine, how are you doing? Are you still tired?"

Laura was a little aggravated, knowing her mum had always thought that if she was being difficult, she was tired, hungry or both.

"Yes! Pretty full on here, Mam. I have decided work is getting on top of me, so I am going to take a break in the sun. That is why I am calling really. I have never had a passport and have found out I need a copy of my birth certificate. Could you send mine to me so I can sort this out, please?"

There was a silence on the other end of the phone.

"Mam, are you still there?"

"Yes, dear… why do you need to go abroad? There are plenty of lovely places to go in this country."

"A friend and I want to go and get a bit of Mediterranean sunshine," lied Laura.

"Which friend is that?"

"Oh, you don't know her, Mam. It's Beth from work. She has not been here a long time."

"I have never heard you talking about her."

"No, she has only been here a few months, Mam,

and as her employment is just seasonal, she wants to join me for a week or two."

"Well, I am not sure where your birth document is. I will have to have a look for it."

"No worries! Mam, if you cannot find it, I am sure I can send for a copy of it," said Laura, upping the pressure.

*

A few days later, Laura's certificate arrived with no covering letter, just her certificate sent recorded delivery in a brown manila envelope.

Laura was so pleased she could now put her plan into action. As she started filling the passport form in, she noticed a glaring exclusion on the form; it said *Father – Unknown*!

"What?" she said angrily out loud then looked around and saw one of the guests turn to look at her and frown before returning to his newspaper as he sat relaxing in the comfortable leather chair in reception.

Laura was both confused and angry. *Why is my father's name not on the certificate?* she asked herself. His name was Reginald Dewar; everyone knew that.

It was a long afternoon and she just couldn't wait. She went to the privacy of the back office and called her mother.

"Mam," she said, not waiting to listen for a reply. "Why is Dad's name not on my birth certificate?" Laura's mind somersaulted almost as violently as her mother's stomach.

There was no reply; the phone had gone dead. Laura tried again and again but just got a ringing-out tone from an unanswered phone.

Finally, in the early evening, Laura tried again.

This time, the phone was picked up.

"Mam," said Laura harshly, "why did you hang up? Why won't you speak to me?"

A weak and timid voice responded, trying to hold back the tears. Elise said, "I love you more than anything else in the world, and Reggie was a wonderful dad to you."

"I know, but—" said Laura.

Interrupting, Elise blurted out, "Reggie is not your biological father."

Laura was stunned. Finally, she regained her composure and said softly, "Well, who is my real father?"

After a few seconds' silence, Elise replied. "We need to talk about this, Laura. It's too difficult just to tell you over the telephone. Please come home when you can and we will deal with this then."

"What do you mean, difficult, Mam?"

"It's painful, *a bhobain*," she said, lapsing into Gaelic.

Laura told her employers that her mother was not well and asked for a short period of leave to take a day to go and see her. Laura could feel her mother's pain, and her own bemusement meant this would not wait!

Thirteen

A shocking discovery

Laura launched herself through the front door and straight into the kitchen. She stood rocking from one foot to the other, still absolutely seething, even after a three-hour drive.

"What do you mean, Reggie is not my father? Well, who the hell is then? Dad was always there for me. You said he used to hold me as a baby and sing Beatles songs to me, and you have pictures of Dad holding me in his arms and at the christening. What are you telling me, Mam?" said Laura angrily.

Elise hated confrontation with anyone, much less her beloved Laura. She had always feared that this day may come. She was sat passively at the kitchen table, her hands cupped around her coffee mug. She was trembling; with faltering voice, she spoke. "Look,

Laura, your father, Reggie that is. Well …" Elise wiped a tear from her eye. "We agreed we would bring you up as if he was your real father, and we vowed never to tell you. We felt it was for the best, even when Reggie passed away and you were only eleven years old. I had to keep that promise. I knew there was no alternative. Reggie loved you as if you were his own anyway."

"How could you, Mam? After you not knowing your parents, I would have thought you of all people would have wanted to share who my real father was."

Elise's tears flowed. Her mournful wail was more than Laura could bear, but instead of putting her arm around her mum, she stormed out into the garden.

Her frustration at breaking point, Laura stormed back in. "Who was he? Who was my father? What was so bad you couldn't tell me? I am thirty years of age and—"

"He was a German SS officer," screamed Elise all of a sudden, then there was a silence. Laura felt like her legs were not going to hold her. She reached for the table and lowered herself onto a chair, facing her mother.

Both of them were in shock; neither knew what to say. They looked at each other as if they were total strangers, but it was the realisation that the pain of the subterfuge was finally in the open, and it hurt them both equally.

After what seemed an age, the silence was broken by Laura as she regained her composure.

"H… h… how? H… h… how could you have met a German SS officer?" stuttered Laura as, with furrowed brow and totally bemused, she struggled to find the words she needed.

Elise twisted an embroidered linen handkerchief in her hands before dabbing her eyes and trying to breathe.

"I am so sorry I didn't tell you, Laura, but your biological father wasn't around when you were born. What was the point of you knowing of someone you were never going to meet?"

"But, Mam, it was 1965. How could you have met an SS officer twenty years after the war ended?"

"Make a pot of tea, love. I love you so much, I only did what I felt was best for you."

Laura automatically did as her mum asked and flicked the switch on the kettle, made a pot of tea and as it boiled, she looked at the ceiling then out of the kitchen window, searching for the logic to analyse this revelation. Taking a deep breath before she turned and knelt by her mother, putting her arm around her shoulders, she hugged Elise.

"I am sorry, Mam. I know you wouldn't want to hurt me. It is just such a shock to have never known that I was brought up by a step-dad, even though he was the most loving and caring man I have ever known."

"I know, I know, sweetheart. He worshipped you, Laura, he really did."

Laura brought over the pot of tea and a biscuit barrel.

"Can we start again, Mam? I am so sorry I was mad. I am tired and emotional. I am on my period. which doesn't help." They both smiled and then laughed as Laura poured the tea.

"Not long after coming to Comrie to work, I was doing a little waitressing at the Royal Hotel in Melville Square. It was a grand little hotel in those days and well respected, a bit rundown nowadays, but I have heard it has new owners and they plan to restore it to its former glory. I hope they do," Elise said, smiling.

"Anyway, one day, this very pleasant, rather tall and distinguished-looking gentleman came in for Sunday lunch. He was very friendly and over the coming weeks he came in regularly and I got to chat with him each time. He appeared to have travelled quite a lot and was very interesting. Then, out of the blue, he asked me if I did any other part-time jobs. Before I could answer, he said he was looking for a housekeeper at his house near Comrie, and as he lived on his own, he would really appreciate some help, as it was a rather large house.

"My immediate response was that I had no relevant experience. He smiled and said, 'I am sure you would do a good job, only a day or two a week. Please come and have a look and see what you think.' His clipped accent and kind yet rugged face beguiled me. I hesitated, but he was so charming, I thought what was there to lose? After all, I needed the money. I was trying to earn some money so that I might put myself through university. This was 1962.

"Somehow, life and ambition had a way of drifting on by. I never seemed to be able to get back to studying, as daft as it sounds. I was too busy working and, well, I suppose being a teenager, what was I thinking? I just thought university was going to be a passport out of little Comrie. That's why I was so happy when you went to university, Laura. I have lived my life vicariously through you."

Laura touched her mother's hand and said, "Thanks to you and Reggie, I have been blessed with a lovely childhood and a good education, leading to a happy life."

"Sometimes, Mr Lautenbach would ask me to stay for dinner, but I always declined, until one day in the summer of 1963. I remember it so well. It was a sunny day, the birds were singing and I stepped outside to shake a duster, and Mr Lautenbach, who was sitting reading on the terrace, asked if I would make a pot of tea and come and join him.

"It was a beautiful house with lovely views, so I did and we started talking. I asked him about his life and asked where he was from, and from this conversation, we started to do this more and more often. He was from near Munich and he waxed lyrical of the wonderfully scenic Bavarian Alps and told me about the beer festival every October and many other stories.

"One day, I was brave enough to ask him how he had come to live in Perthshire, and what he told me shocked me initially, but thinking about it, I became a little sad for him. It turned out he was a former prisoner of war at Cultybraggan, which was an internment camp near Comrie. Camp 21. It's still there, you know. When the war was over, he said he loved the area so much, he decided to settle here. He said he had nothing to return to Germany for. His family, all except for his mother and step-father, were dead. He lost two brothers and a sister in the war.

"In a later conversation, I could see he had something on his mind. What he told me really shocked me at first. He had been an SS officer and had commanded one of the concentration camps in Northern Germany until it was overrun by the allies. He had seen some terrible things but wanted me to understand he was only following orders. If he had not, he, himself, would have been shot."

Laura was astonished; there was so much to process. Her anger and perhaps fear returned as she struggled to take in the enormity of the unbelievable reality that she truly was the bastard daughter of a former S.S. officer, the 'Death Head' warriors so reviled and feared, whose like could have easily been responsible for her grandmother's demise and the reason she never returned to England safely and would never have the joy of seeing her daughter, Elise, or meeting her granddaughter, Laura. Then, she reflected, her grandmother thought Elise was dead anyway; therefore, would she ever have known? Perhaps she would have asked questions, such as where was her baby buried, and eventually found out the truth. Laura's mind was doing somersaults!

"Over time, I felt very relaxed in his company. Here was I, a slip of a young girl, barely twenty, and very impressionable he must have been, nearer fifty years old. Eventually, I accepted his invitation to dinner.

"He picked me up, and when we arrived at the house, he put on a long-playing record, LPs as we called them. He said it was Mozart. We drank gin and tonics whilst we chatted, it was beautiful. He cooked a very tasty dinner and he put another record on the gramophone. We went out onto the terrace. It was a windless, warm, long summer evening. He poured us a glass of port. I had never had one before. As he did so, a beautiful piano piece drifted on the air, caressing my senses. I closed my eyes and he said, 'Do you like this music?'

"'I do, I do,' I replied. He said it was Beethoven, and it was a lovely piece called *Für Elise*.

Laura, he was a gentleman, and from time to time we had dinner and eventually, within a year, we had an affair, even though he was about thirty years older than me. It didn't seem like that at all. He was kind, he was gentle.

"I became pregnant rather quickly, but it was clear I could not marry him. The whole town would have disowned me. I would have been in disgrace, shunned. It was such a small community and still is.

"He desperately wanted to marry me, but it just would not have worked. I have thought many times over the years, how did I get myself into that predicament? I have also thought it was wonderful, and for a young girl, an impressionable one at that, it was exhilarating. Every time I look at you, I don't feel pain and dishonour. I feel proud and lucky and do not regret my love affair for one moment. A time of discovery, it was the first time I had really been made to feel special.

"I could not even consider an abortion back then, so I ran away and with no real plan took the first train I could. I ended up in Glasgow, and that is where I met

Reggie. He was a lamp man on the railway and the night I arrived in Glasgow without a plan, he saw me crying over a cup of tea in the station buffet and asked what the matter was, and as daft as it sounds, I just blurted it all out. He lived with his mother and, despite my initial protests, he took me home. If he hadn't, who knows what would have happened to me and to you, Laura? Until this fortuitous meeting and his kindness, I had nowhere to go. I was a lost soul! I could have ended up in one of those dreaded mother and baby homes, and you would have been taken from me and adopted somewhere. I couldn't bear that thought.

"Before long, I gave birth at Glasgow General and took you home to his house, and the rest is history. He wanted to make an honest girl of me, and it was an answer to my dilemma. I wasn't in love with him, we hadn't even kissed, but we grew together and he was wonderful! Reggie was truly heaven-sent."

"What happened to Mr Lautenbach and what was his first name?"

"Hans Lautenbach. I went back to Comrie a few years later with Reggie, for old times' sake, to show him where I worked at the Royal, and I found out Hans had sold his house. Reggie and I drove by the house and we spoke to the lady in the little post office close by, and I was told he had gone back to live in Germany with his widowed mother. Other than Reggie, no one ever knew the identity of your father, until now."

It was so much for Laura to take in, but Laura had no option but to accept what she had been told.

Seeing her mother's relief that finally she had been

able to divest her conscience of this secret after all these years, Laura took the opportunity to tell her mum what she had found out about Dennis. Laura could see Elise seemed relaxed and genuinely interested now, like her old self again. It was as if a cloud had passed over and a weight had been lifted from her mother's shoulders.

*

Next morning, over an early breakfast of Scott's porridge oats, toast and honey, the world for Laura and Elise was back to normal.

"So, Mam, the truth is I really want to go to Greece and see where Dennis Greaves was last seen and where he died, just to pay my respects. Would you like to come with me?"

Elise held her daughter's hand and looked her in the eyes. "I have done enough worrying and searching in my life, Laura. I never knew my real father, much like you never knew Hans. Go with my blessing and at the very least enjoy some sunshine."

"Thanks, Mam. I hated falling out with you, I love you so much." With that, they hugged one another once more, best of pals. The relief was palpable. Both hated confrontation.

Fourteen

Discovery at Ludford Grange

Holiday booked; it was not going to be Greece at its warmest, being late October, but Laura told herself that flying into Athens and getting a car would be an adventure. She was excited. Then the phone rang. Before Laura could say hello, Victoria blurted down the telephone, "Laura, is that you? My father has died."

A torrid, heart-rending thirty-minute conversation ensued. Condolences from Laura were followed by the revelation that Victoria had found her father's diaries and specifically his wartime diaries, which she was amazed still existed.

"It must be wonderful to learn about his thoughts and experiences in a younger life, Vicky."

Vicky hesitated before adding, "I have found

something relating to your grandmother and what happened to her."

"Really?" Laura hesitated, struggling to breathe. Her mind drifted momentarily, but before she could say more, Vicky cautioned her.

"I don't want to tell you anything over the phone, Laura. You really need to read it yourself."

Laura didn't know whether it was the emotion of her genealogical journey or all the travelling she had done this year that was starting to take its toll – she suspected a combination of both – but it was like a drug. She couldn't walk away; she needed to find answers.

Once more, she asked her understanding and compassionate employers for some leave. Taking the train down to Shrewsbury, she found the journey quite pleasant, albeit fraught with haphazard train connections. It enabled her to get her thoughts in order and prepare herself. Laura was also intrigued as to just where Vicky Greaves lived.

Vicky had kindly arranged to meet Laura at the amazing gothic architecture building that was Shrewsbury Station. Descending the metal-studded stairs from the platform, she headed for the exit and was greeted by a small car park set on a slight incline. She studied the various vehicles for sight of Vicky. As she did so, she admired the attractive Victorian edifice, towered over by Shrewsbury's Norman castle.

A horn sounded and Victoria waved from a cherry-red Range Rover.

The journey took about an hour and on the way,

they caught up, both saying what they had been up to. Vicky, of course, had a lot to arrange and organise after the passing of her father, and Laura explained loosely what had been keeping her busy. She decided not to tell Vicky about her real father, as she was still trying to evaluate the bombshell which her mother had dropped upon her and it continued to trouble her.

The beautiful town of Ludlow appealed to Laura. "Gosh, look at that delightful black-and-white building. Oh, it's an inn."

"Yes, the Feathers Inn, it has some fabulous ornate touches inside as well as terrific woodwork and Jacobean furnishings, which I think you would appreciate, Laura."

They drove to the top of the busy broad thoroughfare before descending and crossing the very quaint Ludford Bridge, traversing Britain's longest river, the River Severn.

More narrow roads followed before they were turning through a high ornamental gate set between solid sandstone walls and a gatehouse, and riding up a wide drive within extensive grounds either side of the single-track drive.

Before very long, they were crunching to a stop on the chipping-laid frontage of a most imposing 17th-century redbrick manor house that sported an equally impressive pillared porch and entrance.

That was not where the grand impression of Vicky's home ended. Inside, it had wonderful dark wood-panelled walls, leading into an attractive drawing room. In fact, all of the rooms had stone fireplaces, superbly decorative ceiling roses with fruits and flowers abounding around each light and plasterwork extending over the whole ceiling. Laura was just open-mouthed.

Seeing Laura agog, Vicky said, "I know it looks fabulous, but the upkeep is daunting."

"I bet it is, but wow, it's positively regal, Vicky."

Entering the large Aga-warmed kitchen, Vicky digressed whilst making a pot of tea. "We could never get it out of Dad, but it is rumoured that Ludford Grange was used by the S.O.E. in World War Two."

"I would not be shocked. It is certainly large and secluded enough to fit the bill."

"Would you like a cup of tea?" asked Vicky as she prepared and carried a tray of baked refreshments out of the kitchen and along the corridor, followed by Laura, before settling into a good-sized yet comfortable lived-in room. This space was dominated by the large portrait of a rather handsome moustached man in military uniform which sat above an exquisite fireplace, its open grate boasting a log fire, adequately protected by a large metal fireguard.

Half a dozen shelves of dust-covered books over to the left side of the room, which Victoria described as a 'snug', caught her eye. Laura couldn't help but compare and think of her bijou home; this was larger than her mother's lounge. Laura sank down with a thud onto a less-than-responsive old settee, which had seen better days.

"No servants nowadays, Laura, I am afraid," she said, putting another log on the fire. "Those staff went long ago, well, all except of course Dad's faithful housekeeper, Mrs Boucher. She even came in and laid the fire ready for our return and prepared some scones for us," she said with a resigned look as she poured the tea. "Alas, even Mrs Boucher is no longer employed here, but it feels like she is part of the family after all these years. A little like a mother hen, or the grandmother I never knew."

"Is the portrait your father?" asked Laura.

"Yes indeed, a handsome chap, don't you think?"

Nodding, Laura could not help but feel the man in the portrait was following her every move with his eyes.

Evening was soon upon them. Vicky elected to take Laura out for dinner in Ludlow, as there was rather a good selection of restaurants for a small rural market town.

On their return, they settled into the kitchen with its large farmhouse-style central island. Vicky poured them both a glass of red wine.

"It's so warm and cosy in here," said Laura.

"It's the warmest room in the house, thanks to the Aga, especially at this time of year. The rest of the house is just too expensive to heat. I have put the electric blanket on in your room. You will be glad I did. Cheers," said Vicky with a knowing smirk as they chinked glasses.

"I bet it's been strange being back here and on your own without your father," commented Laura.

"Yes indeed! Still, we must get on with things. I have a meeting with the solicitors again next week.

We may have to sell this place. It really is a drain on resources when it comes to maintenance."

"I suspect you are sad about that, given it has been your family home for a number of generations."

"Yes! It will be a wrench but it's no use being sentimental, though. It is too big to be rattling around in, especially with all the memories and no dad here now. Frankly, it's an easy decision to make, as the finances do not work out otherwise," lamented Vicky. "Anyway, I am bushed."

Going to the side of the Aga stove, she returned with a grey mottled box folder. "I have some bedtime reading here for you, Laura. There are a few letters and other newspaper articles, but most important to you, my father's diaries from the war. It felt strange looking through them, especially when he mentioned us children, which was not too often, but it's clear he loved his career.

"Let me show you to your room," said Vicky, picking up her glass and the half-empty wine bottle. Leaving the warm kitchen oasis, the cool air embraced them as they ascended the tired but once impressive staircase which divided to the right and left before the final creaking step announced their arrival at the first-floor landing.

The large guest room with its lofty ceiling allocated to Laura sported a dauntingly high, flower-quilted wrought-iron bed. An old-fashioned washstand complete with large ceramic jug and matching bowl and a very large period wardrobe dominated the one wall. Bedside tables and an ornate dressing table completed the furnishings, which all sat on bare wooden floorboards, except for one small patch in front of the dressing table where a very worn, once colourful Persian carpet lay. There was a distinct smell of mothballs.

The dressing table sported a small mirror. Upon it, alongside, were a set of ancient hairbrushes as part of a grooming set. Above the ubiquitous fireplace rested a large old mirror, discoloured by age. It seemed appropriate, as it reflected a room of faded grandeur.

As they said their goodnights, Laura took the box file from under her arm and lay it on the bed. The large functionally obsolete bathroom with matching green bath and sink dating from around the sixties was cold. Nevertheless, this tough Scottish lassie was used to Scottish winters. She quickly showered, put on her warm winceyette pyjamas, which felt soft and warm against her skin, and scaled the elevated bed before settling herself under the duvet, so thankful for the electric blanket. She could see her breath in the room. Bedside light on, she opened the box file with trepidation.

Wartime articles about El-Alamein and the fall of Singapore stared out from yellowed newspaper cuttings. The diaries, eight in all, seemed to date from 1939 to 1946.

As she opened the first diary, an envelope fell out before tumbling onto the floor. The patina of age and postmark dated 1946; the month was a little blurred but told Laura this may be important. She retrieved the envelope and liberated the multi-paged, beautifully handwritten letter.

Dear Bernard,

I am well, thank you, and back teaching as a language master again nowadays.

How are you, the delightful Victoria and the rest of the family? Bad do about Dennis. Please pass on my sympathies to Victoria.

Yes! I agree the horrors of war cannot be forgotten just because an armistice has been signed. We lost many friends and colleagues to this awful and unnecessary conflict, thanks to that despot Hitler and his cronies, and do not get me started on the Japanese.

I am so sorry for what you have endured, added to by the mental anguish and guilt you feel on discovering Martha had been so cruelly taken from us.

It is clear from your letter that you had great affection for Martha and feel responsible for her demise. This must make life unbearable, but rest assured she wanted to be part of this and of what she could do to make the Nazis pay for the hardship and pain caused to her family. I know she was like a daughter to you, but I am also aware she cared and appreciated your kindness, support and your belief in her. You were like a second father to her.

To answer your question on how she ended up in Waldbrücke, nothing is certain, but this is what I have discovered from my Baker Street contacts and some subsequent enquiries I have made with de Gaulle's boys.

Martha's code name was 'Etive', operational name, 'Butlers'. After a small hiatus due to a health issue in Scotland, she continued her training and was highly thought of for her willpower, dedication, determination, language and excellent firearm skills.

Initially, because of her knowledge of Austria and language skills in German and the 'hoch Deutsch' of the region, she linked up with the Office of Strategic Services, the Americans. It was planned to drop her into the Southern Tyrol to work with Hans Egerter, code name 'Barbarossa', and the mission to support his 'Patria' group, the Austrian monarchist movement. It soon became clear there just was not enough support to make a difference in Austria, and the occasional sabotage attempts on the German infrastructure and the eventual Vienna resistance leaders all being captured and executed underlined the unlikely chance of success.

S.O.E. resources were concentrated into France. It was decided to use the French language skills she had developed through studies, holidays and time working in France; thus, Etive was apparently back with the S.O.E. and dropped into France with disastrous consequences.

Initially, she was scheduled to go in with former S.O.E. agent, now OSS agent, Virginia Hall, by motor launch to Brittany, but the S.O.E., in a rare liaison with RF, came calling and she left England on a hastily arranged mission to replace agents that had been captured. This was in early to mid-March 1944. It was planned to infiltrate her into France during January but the weather had been too inclement, so they waited for the February/ March new moon periods.

Just before Etive flew out, Madeleine Damerment, a very experienced agent, parachuted in as a courier for the 'Bricklayer' circuit, along with France Antelme and Lionel Lee. Courtesy of 161 Squadron and a specially adapted Halifax bomber, they used a drop zone in fields near Chartres on the night of 28/29 February 1944. The Gestapo were waiting for them, thanks to intelligence from previously captured agents who had been interrogated. We think German radio operators using the captured agents' codes had used the wireless sets and codes to lure them in. Damerment was transported to Gestapo headquarters on the Avenue Foch in Paris, where she was interrogated.

Apparently, the same fate would have awaited Martha. Why Buckmaster or others had not worked this out, who knows? It was clear there was a traitor in their midst. Martha would have been tasked with trying to connect with the 'Cinema-Phono' circuit then to head west and see what happened to the 'Parson' circuit. Alas, her destination would have been Paris and Avenue Foch, Gestapo HQ, but this plan was aborted late on too. As fate would have it, Martha had injured her ankle on one of the training runs, so she needed a little recuperation time. By then, another operative had been sent in her place and duly disappeared.

This is where it gets hazy, as I believe she was sent further south to the Hautes-Pyrénées area.

Either way, Martha, it appears, was captured somewhere in France then possibly after time in Paris was likely shipped to Karlsruhe and then sent to Neuengamme on the banks of the Dove and Elbe Rivers in a suburb of Hamburg in northern Germany and then eventually to Waldbrücke, situated on an isolated sand hill amidst the heather. The area of the camp occupied about 86 acres and consisted, as many camps did, primarily of wooden barracks, which sadly you know only too well from personal experience.

I would say the agent I spoke to – 'Collette', real name Anne-Marie Walters – had met Etive briefly. Collette talked about someone from the French resistance called Cathy Arvieux – code name 'Edith'– who survived Ravensbrück. After the war, she had found and contacted Anne-Marie in her personal search for Etive, who she had become friends with and was clearly fond of, only for Madame Arvieux to learn Etive had never made it home.

Anne-Marie knew another agent, Jean Legarde, who had flown over with Martha (Etive). Jean remembered spending time with her at Gaynes Hall, where they billeted the night before they flew from Tempsford to near Toulouse. They actually had a bonus night there and took the opportunity for some leisure time by going for a drink at the Thornton Arms in Everton near Tempsford after there was a twenty-four-hour weather delay to their departure. He had described her as a good-hearted, intelligent, bubbly, confident character. She went as a 'pianist', a radio operator, that is.

After their last meal, they were transferred the short distance to the pre-flight briefing in Gibraltar Farm Barn, close to the runway, which, as was procedure, was where they were checked for likely incriminating British possessions. Should they be caught, she had a small photograph with the name 'Dennis' on the back. I don't know if that means anything.

Anyway, it was taken from her because the photo could be identified as from Britain. Then they were given French identity and ration cards, plus some clothing coupons, some French francs and a small suitcase containing some temporary rations of cigarettes and chocolate. More worryingly, an 'L' pill – L for lethal – containing cyanide for use in case of capture. Apparently, Buckmaster saw them off and gave them a gift of a gold powder compact and they were told you can always barter or sell it if you get into a tight spot. Vera Atkins may have been there, but possibly a conducting officer who had been responsible for their pastoral care or maybe

Noreen Riols or someone from de Gaulles' RF chaps.

After the briefing, they put on their jumpsuits, sometimes referred to as 'striptease' suits. Jean remembers he was quiet, almost morose, fearing what was ahead, but Etive said hello to the crew and commented on the beautiful sunset as they boarded the 'Tempsford Taxi'! The despatcher offered them both a hot drink and they took off. It seemed a long bumpy ride but before long, they were hooking their silk lines to a link on the side of the converted Halifax bomber interior so that the cord of their parachute opened the chute when they exited the aircraft.

Jean watched as, fearlessly and without emotion, Etive sat on the side of the 'joe' hole, specially cut out of the base of the aircraft and before long, he saw the red light come on, then the green light, and almost like magic, Etive disappeared into the night sky of the propeller-driven aircraft. After what seemed an age, he was making the same descent as the slipstream first of all took them towards the back of the aircraft at speed, then the stillness of the night took over as both agents descended silently through what Jean estimated was about 400 feet above the land. He seemed to drift away from the drop zone and unfortunately landed in a tree, breaking his leg. His mission was going to be cut short.

He recalls Etive was wearing a black coat. Underneath, she had a black skirt and white silk blouse and, somewhat bizarrely, black heeled shoes, so that once the jumpsuit was off and the parachute buried, she would look like any other French woman. He also noted her ankles were heavily bandaged, presumably to help give her support on landing.

What happened to her neither Jean nor Anne-Marie knew for sure. Jean was cared for by a local doctor and extracted by a Lysander a week or two later, after his disastrous landing.

Anne-Marie understood, or perhaps presumed, that Etive had been captured by the Germans following a possible betrayal by one of the resistance, but that is speculation and all I can find out for now.

I am so sorry, old chap, she was a lovely girl! Anything else I can do, please let me know. Best wishes, Harry

Laura could barely see through her misty eyes. The place name 'Waldbrücke' resounded in her head like a pinball bouncing around a gaming machine. So, was this where she met her destiny?

Turning back to the diaries, Laura skimmed over some pages before reaching a bookmark, where Vicky had kindly pointed out she might want to start.

Charlie Podmore came tonight with Martha, a splendid young lady, very bright, pretty too. Apparently, a refugee from Europe. Austria, I think. I introduced her to Harry Ree. I felt his boys may be able to gain some information from Martha, as she had not so long ago been living in Europe. Plus, her linguistic skills are excellent. Fluent in German/English and I believe French. Harry seemed quite taken with her and spent a lot of time with her this evening.

A few pages later and a Post-it note, left by Vicky:

Looks like I was right! I spoke to Harry Ree on the telephone today. He says Jepson has invited Martha for an interview.

Late summer '43: *Much redacted letter from Vicky in Cairo. It appears she had gone and got married to some chap called Dennis Greaves, who I have met, but I cannot really remember much about the fellow. As long as she is happy! Her mother is not very pleased, though. I suspect she always wanted a traditional wedding for our Vick!*

Early 1944 entry: *It appears Victoria's husband is missing in action, poor old girl. War is an abominable sap on lives and emotions.*

In spring 1944, another entry said: *Received a call from a friend of Harry Ree today. It appears Martha has done very well and is most suited to her new role.*

January 1945: *Christmas has come and gone and it's New Year, will be glad when this awful war is over. Witnessing some dreadful sights, lost a good friend today, Sergeant Major Taff Phillips. RIP, old chap. Still seems strange to be part of an armoured squadron now.*

April 1945: *This war in Europe cannot be far from over. Germans are in disarray and the race is on to beat the Russians to Berlin. We are coming across many labour camps, 'Konzentration Lager'. Light but sometimes stubborn resistance. Lucky to get through these last few days. My 'Honey' reconnaissance tank took a hit. Fortunately, I escaped with just a few abrasions: a knot on my head and one almighty headache. Back is pretty sore too. Must have been an anti-tank mine. Tank is a write-off, blew a track off too and sent us hurtling down an embankment. One dead, one seriously wounded. I had only known Bixby a week, poor fellow.*

Today, myself and Sergeant Philpott filled two vacancies in Bravo Patrol tank. We are on our way to a small place called 'Waldbrücke'. Advance recon tells us there is another concentration camp near there.

Reached Waldbrücke, situated about 43km northeast of Bremen. No 3 Squadron and a company were halted by fierce resistance.

Close to camp now, but it's dark so decided to take it on at 0500hrs. It is across a narrow river, all bridges destroyed. Platoon left to observe. We have a few boats to bring up if they arrive, we will be on the move.

Ordered three platoons to lead. Lt Jock Laurie in charge to draw fire. We crossed a little further up. Three prisoners taken. SS are apparently controlling Waldbrücke Camp.

Not enough of us to proceed, must wait for rest of the Grenadier group to come up before we stage an assault.

3pm. First wave of Grenadier Guards went in with supporting fire from two tanks, with shells and machine guns. Very strangely, we had little resistance.

Before we knew it, we were at the gates, and myself and Philpott pushed the gate open with the tank.

A flanking force from the north had received some resistance in a short but bloody exchange. Fortunately, only a few wounded, no dead on our side.

As we entered the camp, the sight before us was heartbreaking. Scantily clad skeletal figures were emerging from huts; it was like a miniature Belsen. A medical team arrived behind us in a Jeep. A platoon of the guards stealthily entered with us. A phalanx of German uniformed men was on the parade ground, their weapons stacked in front of them. "Hände hoch," I blurted out. Doing as they were told, the infantry advanced and secured their weapons. I told the guys to corral the Germans. There, they were told to sit and put their hands on their heads. Philpott covered them with the tank weaponry.

Other soldiers arrived and started searching the camp and trying to assist the poor wretches, who were now emerging from huts and congregating. I had passed orders to the men that we were not to give them food, not even a sweet or toffee, as it would make them unwell, indeed, positively sick. Besides, the camp was rife with typhus. We needed to treat them.

I took the senior officer and his apparent deputy to the main office. With two of my men, I demanded to see the camp register and asked if there were any British prisoners. Shaking his head, he took off his cap and dropped his gloves into it and sat opposite me. He was courteous and handed over the register. It was a model of accuracy and well kept, right up to yesterday's date, as you would expect.

As I briefly glanced down the list, my blood ran cold. I saw a name I knew.

"Where is this woman?" I bellowed.

The German SS officer took a look as his face reddened.

"I am afraid to inform you she died yesterday, along with three of her associates."

"Where is her body?" I shouted, losing my temper.

"We have typhus in the camp. It has been disposed of," said the SS officer coldly.

The Kommandant's number two stepped forward. "Excuse me, sir, but she is still in her cell, where she unfortunately died this morning." The Kommandant's face was like thunder.

"Take me to her now," I said, drawing my pistol.

We escorted them both, forcing them to walk ahead of us. They walked as if approaching the gallows. We approached a nearby block. The smell as we entered the building was awful. I took my handkerchief and covered my nose. We proceeded to the end cell on the left of the block, The door was open and there was nobody, just an empty cell.

I grabbed the Kommandant's adjutant by the throat and put my pistol to his head. "Where is she?" I bellowed in his face, my spittle speckling his face and uniform.

"She must have already been taken," came his wide-eyed and frightened response.

"Where?"

The Kommandant, momentarily perturbed, regained his composure and calmly yet maliciously said, as he lit a cigarette and blew a smoke ring in the air, "To be disposed of. I told you, there is typhus." I was hit by the realisation that the smoke I had seen before entering the camp was likely Martha.

We marched them to the crematorium. As the door opened, the hot air hit us. Two men stood back with a start, putting their hands up at the sight of my gun. They were dressed in striped pyjama-like clothing, four stretchers on the ground. Three were empty. On the fourth lay a corpse covered by a sheet. The three ovens were operational.

I knelt by the stretcher and pulled back the covering. The face was contorted, a young lady who had suffered before her death, but it wasn't Martha.

I exploded, I am not proud to say. I was less than measured and even less an officer with my reaction. I stood, drew my pistol and looked the Kommandant in the eye, brandishing my gun and calling him all sorts of obscenities. He was impassive, barely a flicker of reaction. It made me so mad, I was burning up inside.

I demanded to know where Martha was, but the Kommandant remained resolute. However, his number two said, 'Follow me,' as we returned towards the original prison block. Just before, there was a smaller building, which contained four cells. The German officer, much to the disdain of the Kommandant, entered and as we came to the end of the cell block, the German officer pushed the door slightly and the door creaked open.

At first, I didn't believe it was her. She was so emaciated. Her once lustrous hair was tufted with grey, which made her look older than her years. Martha lay to one side as if she had been sitting, but slumped sideways. Her lips were bloodied and swollen, her thin cotton dress torn at the front. A striped uniform lay on the floor. As I picked it up, I noticed there was a number stencilled on the left side of what I presumed was her prison clothing. Martha had become a number – 51311 – alongside which was a red triangle and an upside-down yellow triangle, intimating she was a political and Jewish prisoner.

No doubt Martha had become a victim of the 'night and fog' decree of the Nazis as they endeavoured to extinguish all trace of people like Martha as secret agents, but how and why they classed her as a political prisoner and a Jew, we will likely never know. It hurt to think that Martha, this vibrant human being before her death, had been reduced to this awful state. She had no number tattooed on her arm, just this. But looking at the torn yellow dress who knows what had befallen her before her death.

Her feet were bloodied; she was still wearing one wooden clog. I knelt by her and gathered her broken body into my arms. As I held Martha, I realised she had been shot in the back of the neck. Those Nazi bastards had executed her. This once attractive, intelligent, kind, principled and determined lady was gone. My tears of pain and guilt turned to anger, I saw red.

We hustled the two Germans back outside to the parade ground, back to their men. The Kommandant started to say something to his men and laughed. My blood just boiled over. I spun him around and I shot him in the stomach from close range. I later figured I would report I had told him to stand with his men and have them line up and that he refused to do so and drew a luger on me, so I shot him in the stomach at close range.

He squealed like a pig. I ordered the corporal to my right to bayonet the man and put him out of his misery, which without hesitation the soldier duly obliged me. I just saw red. All the Germans lined up, their eyes wide with fear. I sent the other troops to help clear the various huts. I turned to Sergeant Philpott in the tank and said to him, "Use the cannon." For a minute or two, Philpott stood up in the turret and looked at me. "God damn it, man, that is an order."

I am ashamed of this, but Philpott, on my orders, machine-gunned the Germans with 50mm cannon shells, making an awful mess of them. We scattered their weapons amongst them and took a photograph, and the official report said they were all resisting arrest.

Other men came rushing over. I told the men to build a bonfire, which they did, with rubbish, debris and tyres, and put the bodies on them, including the head SS officer.

I returned with the medical team to the cell and we collected the body of this brave and once very alluring lady.

I was beside myself. I felt so guilty; it is my

fault she was here. My fault she had met such an awful death.

17th May 1945: *Today, Martha's body was flown back to England by the Red Cross. I saw the coffin onto the Dakota myself and asked for it on arrival in England to be taken to Ludford Grange for burial in the grounds of my family chapel.*

I will live with my actions for ever, I feel dead inside!

The whole camp brought you to tears, as corpses were sprawled in piles, some in the barracks, some just where they seemed to have died. They looked like human bonfire pyres. Of the estimated 9,500 camp prisoners who arrived during April 1945, by 29th April, only 6,800 were still alive, and many more would die as the result of disease, hunger and exposure over the coming months, I am sure. We decided, as per orders, to burn most of the barracks to the ground to stop the spread of typhus.

Over the next few days, we interviewed prisoners and various guards and 'Kapos'. These were prisoners who were selected by the Nazis to take charge of prisoner work gangs, called 'Kommando'. It was their job to ensure fellow prisoners, sometimes with brutal treatment, did forced labour, whether they were injured, sick or starving. But no one told me anything of value. What I did learn was a little of what life had been like here.

They all said life in the camps was brutal. Stripped of identity and self-worth, they laboured every day until they died or by the grace of God were liberated as they were now. Here are one man's words: "When we arrived at the camp, we were registered and given a prisoner number."

I contemplated poor Martha. From this time on, she would likely only have been referred to by her allocated number rather than her name. Routinely Martha would have probably been assigned a barrack and work details at this stage.

This prisoner told me: "After registration, the prisoners were told to undress. They were then forced to have their heads shaved, and forced to shower, usually in front of hundreds of other people and the leering SS guards.

"Their clothing was taken away and replaced by a striped uniform.

"This humiliating process was designed to remove any remnants of human dignity.

"Life was repetitive and only punctuated with tortures and beatings.

"Every dawn felt like a deep wound was reopening, such was the hell of waking up and realising this was not just a bad dream. You could be woken at 4am and 4.30am, a little later for winter prisoners. Prisoners spent about thirty minutes using the ablutions, dressing and cleaning the barracks as well as having breakfast.

Thousands sharing dirty water with no soap or toilet paper, anyone not arriving in time for 'Appel' would be punished.

"Appel (morning roll call) was often in freezing conditions in the winter, and their clothing did nothing to keep them warm on the Appel Platz (the square where the roll call took place). It was drawn out, sometimes for hours, as all prisoners would be counted twice, and any miscounts meant that they were recounted. Weak prisoners were often held up by fellow inmates, because if they collapsed, or worse, didn't make roll call, they faced beatings, torture or execution.

"Then, exhausted, they were marched to work. Sometimes, there was a noon roll call, when they stopped for lunch.

"At the end of each day, those that had survived the day were marched back to camp for another roll call.

"At 9pm, lights were out.

"Women wore a dress or skirt with a jacket, headscarf and clogs.

"Food was not enough – just thin gruel and bread for the most part."

God! Please bring this war to an end! We must never forget these horrors and never let anything like this happen again!

Laura was in tears. She felt for the major but she was distraught to know how her grandmother had died, and for what? Her eyes slowly closed as she ran a kaleidoscope of images through her mind before she fell into a fitful sleep.

Fifteen

Grave developments

Next morning, Laura, still tired from staying up until the wee hours, put the heels of her hands into her eyes and massaged them as if trying to bring them to life. She swung her legs to the side of the bed. Dropping to the floor off her high perch, she grabbed her dressing gown, wrapped it around her and shuffled towards the steamed-up windows, wiped the condensation from the thin glass and realised she was looking out to the front of the house. In the distance across the oval lawn, which acted as a turning circle, she spied in the neighbouring meadows a herd of black-and-white Herefordshire cows ruminating nonchalantly; a quintessentially British scene.

Laura couldn't face another shower in the cold

bathroom, so washed her face, cleaned her teeth and dressed.

As she descended the splendid staircase into the main hall, all was quiet. She sought out the kitchen which, through the labyrinth of corridors, she found surprisingly easily but there was no one about. Returning to the capacious cold hallway, she collected her coat, pulled a woollen tartan scarf from the pocket and stepped out into the brisk morning air.

Feet crunching on the drive, she went over to the spring-loaded kissing gate set in the three-tier rusting metal perimeter fence and followed a wood-chipped path, which was in need of freshening up. The pleasant walk took the path into a copse of oak and sycamore trees before breaking out into a wonderfully secluded and quiet oasis of calm. Here stood the family chapel, resplendent in red sandstone. Laura stood for a short while and took in the yew tree-shaded burial grounds; it gave her goosebumps. She listened to the birdsong. The soft sweet song of a blackbird was competing with the raucous laughter of a magpie and the soothing coo of a wood pigeon. She went forward in the stillness, reaching the chapel and the solid metal-studded entrance door. She turned the circular iron handle and the latch clicked, and with shoulder-nudged assistance the door creaked open.

Shutting the door behind her, Laura stepped through the porch entrance way and into the nave of the small chapel. Assimilating the solitude, the serenity was palpable. She wondered if her grandmother had ever been inside this church; she rather felt she had.

It was a small yet attractive chapel, which made it even more special. The nave and sanctuary were divided by a beautifully carved timber screen which had an arched central entrance. Wooden hatchments adorned the rear west walls, commemorating the death of family members of Ludford Grange – names like de Gracey – unfamiliar to Laura, who figured these dated back to well before the Atkinsons were living at this historic pile.

Laura nodded her respect before proceeding towards the cross set atop the altar and perfectly framed by the screen entrance. At that very moment, as she progressed up the aisle, the morning sunshine burst brightly through the east window, bathing her in light, as if beckoning her onwards. She knelt at the oak altar rail, looking up at the splendid stained glass window depicting the crucifixion. She prayed for her grandmother and grandfather and their deliverance from the evil they had endured, and beseeched the Almighty that they may rest in peace!

Stepping out into the bright sunlight, Laura circumnavigated the church, stopping to examine the few gravestones on which she could make out the inscriptions. Much of the periphery of the graveyard was overgrown; a few headstones were leaning against an old brick wall as if holding it up.

A small walkway led away from the main path to an overgrown patch of land; it had not been tended for a long time. Laura's attention was drawn to the idyllic view from this vantage point as the field beyond descended sharply towards a pond in the dip and a panoramic view of the hills in the distance. She wished she had her camera. As she turned, a robin flew past her before landing on the old heavily rusted metal boundary fence, before hopping down onto something in the long grass. She returned towards the fence and parted a swathe of grass, weeds and thistles. Treading down the undergrowth, she pushed her way forward to reveal a gravestone. She rubbed some of the accumulated moss and lichen off the memorial inscription.

As she examined the marble stone more closely, she could gradually make out the inscription.

Marta Sansom
You did not die in vain
Your foe is vanquished now
Releasing you from pain
May God your soul endow
SHALOM

Died 28 April 1945

Laura knelt, putting her fingers on her grandmother's real birth name as she wept.

*

Vicky finally stirred and was pleased to see Laura had made herself at home and made some toast and tea.

"Good morning," said Vicky drowsily. "I need some caffeine! Did you sleep well?"

Laura gave a somewhat melancholy facial expression and a tilt of the head.

"Not good then," jested Vicky as she made herself a cafetiere of the strongest coffee she could find.

"Vicky, thank you so much for sharing your father's diary with me. Needless to say, I have read the salient entries you so kindly highlighted, as well as a good deal more. Your father must have been incredibly brave, and he must also have been tortured by the things he endured and witnessed."

"I think we both understand a little more about your grandmother and my father now," lamented Vicky. "I had no idea whatsoever. I feel dreadful for some of the selfish thoughts I had and the hard time I gave Dennis, but how was I to know she was going to meet such a tragic end?"

"You didn't, Vicky, and your emotions and jealousy were perfectly natural.

"I believe the ladies and men of the S.O.E. were unbelievably valiant and very brave and selfless to give up their lives for the benefit of all those that survived, and indeed for us to thrive today and have the freedom to do what we care to!"

"I am sure they were full of fear, but maybe that is what drove them on to achieve what they did," theorised Vicky. "Strangely, Dennis seemed to me to be enjoying it. Perhaps that was all a front."

"I feel that I need to go to Waldbrücke one day. I need to see where my grandmother died. There may be nothing of the camp left, who knows, but I want to go to where she was murdered and pay my respects."

"Indeed," nodded Vicky. "It was only after reading the diary I realised why my father was not the same after returning from the war. I just heard Mama say war is a difficult time and that was that when I was younger, yet I hadn't experienced real hardship or experience of the tough lives the servicemen had had in Cairo, well, not to the extent poor old Papa witnessed it. Now I do understand it was also personal.

"Hold on to the diaries and letters, Laura. They may be helpful to you in your search."

"Thank you, Vicky. Did you know before you read your father's diary that Martha was buried in your chapel grounds?"

"No! I didn't. That has come as quite a surprise to me."

"I found the grave this morning."

Laura went on to explain how the robin, like a guiding spirit, had guided her towards her grandmother's final resting place in such a tranquil and beautiful spot.

Vicky tilted her head, her eyes filled with tears, as she listened to Laura.

Laura looked up at her and saw her sadness.

"There is no need to be sad, Vicky. At least your father made sure my grandmother was brought home to a beautiful place of rest."

Vicky shook her head, unable to speak as the

emotion welled up in her. She stood, walked to the window then turned.

Her arms crossed, her eyes brimming with tears, she said, "My father had not been out of the house for months then early one morning he somehow made it across to the churchyard. That is where they found him, lying on his back, his eyes open, staring at the sky. He was close to the location you describe. He had suffered a massive seizure."

*

All the way back to Scotland, Laura ran the various scenarios of how her grandmother had come to be at Waldbrücke. She must have been taken there after interrogation by the Gestapo in Paris, which seemed to be the fate of many captured agents she had learned about. Laura wanted to know more; somebody must know. If she could find Michelle Arvieux perhaps, just perhaps, she could learn more.

For now, she felt she could not share this information with her mother. It seemed so horrible to even contemplate the nature of her final days and hours. What had she endured? Who might have been at the camp to tell her more? She vowed to find out.

Returning to Arisaig House for her final ten days of shifts before heading to Greece, she made a list of who to contact to find out more about Waldbrücke. Vera Atkins was top of the list.

"Hello, Liz, how are you?" she greeted one of the domestic staff who was just leaving for the day.

"All good, looking forward to putting my feet up."

Derek McInnes, one of the older members of staff, who had been standing in for her, came out of the office.

"Great to have you back, lassie, we have missed you. A couple of pieces of mail arrived for you," he said, handing them over.

"Thanks, Derek," she said. "How has it been?"

"Nae problem, just busy as ever. Mrs Branfoot had a little tumble in her room, probably a little too much of her usual medicine, but she is okay," he said, chuckling.

Laura laughed and tapped Derek on the arm.

"You are bad, Derek. I need a shower, see you later," said Laura as she retired to her room.

Showered, she made herself a cup of tea and sat on the edge of the bed, picking up the two envelopes. The first one was a car insurance reminder, which she set aside; the second looked official.

Laura used her letter opener to slowly reveal its contents as she carefully read and reread the letter and its attachment.

Heading down to the office, she rang the number she had first called a couple of months back.

"Hi, Juliet, it's Laura."

"Laura! It's great to hear from you. Did you get a copy of the DNA results?"

Laura beamed to herself as she replied, "I did indeed. I hope you are not too disappointed that the tests show beyond doubt that we are both related to Dennis Greaves, cousin Juliet!"

Sixteen

Etive's assignment

Vera was incredibly helpful, as she put Laura in touch with Harry Ree's son, Jonathan, who was surprised and delighted in equal measure to hear from Laura. He promised to survey his father's notes and diaries. He confessed he had kept them with an interest and desire to one day be writing his father's biography. He was sad that Laura could not have met his father, who had died four or so years before.

A couple of days later, Laura received a phone call from Jonathan. He had found gold, giving Laura a phone number and an address in France where Michelle Catherine Arvieux resided, or at least she had until a year or so before his father's passing, but so far there were no notes relating to Martha or Etive.

An hour later, in Laura's lunch break, she was

listening to a telephone ringing out as she stood surveying the wild trees blowing in the wind, which had picked up as a precursor to a storm brewing in the Lochaber region. She was just about to put the phone down when the phone clicked and a voice softly said, "*Bonjour, allo.*"

"Hello," said Laura. "Is that Madame Arvieux?"

"*Non!* But it is Mademoiselle Arvieux. Who is calling?"

"I am so sorry, my apologies for my presumption. Mademoiselle, you will not know me but I believe you knew my grandmother, Martha, or you may have known her by her code name, Etive."

There was a long pause. "*Oui, d'accord*, I did know Etive," said the voice, tinged with melancholy. "But I lost touch with her. Did she come home eventually? I did try and find her."

A frisson of excitement and sadness went through Laura's whole being. She felt she was somehow on the brink of discovering something very important about her grandmother, but her mixed emotions thinking about her grandmother's demise tempered her joy.

Laura shared the story of her search for her grandmother and the discovery of her involvement with the S.O.E. and clandestine operations. She stopped short of recounting the circumstances of her death as she was found in Waldbrücke, just saying she had died there.

There was no response from Mademoiselle Arvieux when she had finished her tale.

"Hello," repeated Laura, thinking she had lost the connection.

"*Oui*, I am here. I am just a little… how do you say? Surprised to hear her name after all these years and I am so sorry. *Je suis navrée*," her voice breaking.

"Did you know her well?" prompted Laura.

"Of course, please excuse my English. It has been a while since I have spoken your language. Etive and I worked together in France. She was a very brave and resourceful lady. You can be proud of her. I can still see her bright blue eyes and her kind face, but they hid a… how do you say? A steely resolve, Laura!"

"When did you first meet her?" said Laura, trying to contain her excitement, her stomach churning full of butterflies.

"That would be middle to late March 1944 when she parachuted into an airfield near Toulouse. Myself and a few men of the 'Françoise' circuit were at the drop zone. We collected her and another agent and buried their parachutes before relocating them to a nearby farm to hide out in a barn loft, until we could arrange for them to be taken to more suitable accommodation. A fellow agent I now know as Yvonne Baseden had landed a couple of weeks before Etive.

"Your grandmother was keen to make contact with Le Patron, 'Hilaire', head of the Wheelwright circuit. It appears she was briefed and trained as a wireless operator and with the farmer's assistance, they hid her radio set just in case of the Gestapo making a surprise visit to the farm. It transpired that a male agent who flew in with her and broke his ankle or leg was repatriated, and Etive took on his courier and other roles too.

"This meant she would be liaising with networks, finding suitable landing sites and helping organise and escort evaders and escapees as well as meetings with Le Patron to pass and receive information for transmission to and from Londres. She was an amazing lady, I am proud to have known her. I even called my child Etive after her, God rest her soul. Etive Catherine only lived a short while, and soon after, her father was captured and murdered by the Milice as he tried to escape. It felt like my life was over, I was distraught, but life is strange in how it affects you, as very quickly my attitude hardened and my will strengthened my desire to make the Germans pay! We didn't have chance to marry and bring up our child and I felt the Nazis had taken this from me."

"I am so sorry to hear that, Mademoiselle."

"Such was war," lamented Mademoiselle Arvieux.

"My grandmother's real name was Martha," said Laura.

"Ah yes, I did know this later, but Etive seemed so French and different. I loved it.

"A day or two later, Madame Dissard – Françoise – ordered me to take Etive south by train to the Haute-Pyrénées to meet Hilaire so she could report back to Londres. At this time, many airmen and indeed Jewish refugees and escapers were trying to get back to England, and escape routes over the Pyrénées were critical to this goal.

"The meeting was set in the small Haute-Pyrénées

town of Saint-Girons at a local café. We were met not by the boss but by a young boy who escorted us out of the town and up a small track to a hut. I then waited outside and kept watch whilst Etive met with Hilaire. Twenty minutes later, we retraced our steps and caught the train north to Toulouse.

"Thinking back, I recall noticing that Etive would head off to meet Le Patron – the boss – with increasing regularity, sometimes accompanied by me or escorted by one of Madame Dissard's trusted right-hand men, like Jacques Latigue, but as time went on she went alone. Then she would return and keep moving premises so she would not be discovered when transmitting the radio messages to London. Invariably then we would all wait for the 6pm or 9pm BBC news broadcast to hear a coded message, giving us instructions, be it to meet a new agent, wireless operator or courier, or more and more arms drops, especially before D-Day. In April and May 1944, the intensity and frequency built up, so we knew something was in the wind. Hilaire trusted Etive implicitly and she clearly admired him.

"Occasionally, Hilaire would arrange to meet us. I remember him coming to a little farm near Condom about 8 kilometres away from the town. Another agent, Colette, had been living there on a farm called Nasoulens. It had a red tiled roof with brown shutters. I even remember its red-and-white check curtains and the lovely flowerbeds at the front. We of course were cautious and checked our escape routes and noticed the bamboo bushes at the back of the house gave us some cover. Before long, we heard the small *vélo moteur* –

motorcycle – its little three-quarter horsepower engine putt-putting away as it approached, and Le Patron getting off, and he always wore a 'Canadienne', a short heavy waterproof jacket.

"He seemed to chain-smoke, as his nicotine fingers betrayed, but perhaps he needed that to steady his nerves. He smoked French cigarettes, notably the brand 'Balto'. He always lit up straightaway whenever we saw him.

"Colette, I seem to recall, was there sometimes. She was a pretty girl, quite young, maybe twenty or twenty-one years old, a bit of a flirt. She liked the men for sure, I would say, whereas your grandmother was far different, more serious and considered, but we all did our jobs, whatever it took.

"Our hosts were the lovely Cerensac family, old Farmer Henri, his dark shining eyes peeking out from under his beret.

"I remember Le Patron telling your grandmother to wear her hair higher at the front in the local style to avoid standing out, and to buy some *sabots* – local clothing – to make her fit in more.

Madame Cerensac… who brought a fabulous *pastis* to the table. She had baked this local Gascon pastry filled with Armagnac and sodden apples and no doubt cooked it in the traditional way under wood ashes. Henri Cerensac, her husband, opened a bottle of Armagnac and we made some toasts, not least of which to Victory.

"Instructions and information were exchanged. We often stayed the night, had a breakfast of pâté, alongside a metre-long loaf we shared and a bottle of red wine, then we would all go our separate ways to implement the plans we had been given.

"We would watch Le Patron depart. He barely made eye contact before mounting his *vélo moteur*, and he would disappear into the distance and out of sight.

"Hilaire was a fascinating and beguiling man. He was of small build, maybe in his forties, but his grey eyes seemed to hypnotise you with their intensity. He was almost bald and sported a small moustache. I had great respect for him, as we all did.

"He seemed nervous at times, but I suspect he needed to be on edge to survive and keep moving. He was a dedicated resistant, very keen everyone did their duty and take responsibility for their actions. He never asked me or indeed anyone to do anything he couldn't do. Perhaps the wireless set was an exception to that. That is why Etive and other 'pianists' were so important to the resistance movement.

"Occasionally, we would meet in Condom under the arches of the 13th–century monastery, which bordered the square with cobbled streets going off from there with high houses hemming in these conduits of activity, especially on Saturday morning, market day, but this became more and more dangerous.

"It was safer to travel by bicycle and Etive often cycled up to 50 kilometres to meet and deliver messages to Le Patron. She would sometimes come and help retrieve some of the supplies dropped to us, often in long cigar-like containers which were very heavy and needed as much manpower as we could muster, perhaps up to 400 pounds in weight. Not just that, we had no horses so had to transport the delivery hidden under hay or piles of vegetables on a cart pulled by cows and, believe me, the progress was painfully slow, and the more time it took, the more chance there was of discovery by the Germans.

"Sometimes, Etive took the train if the message was very urgent, but she would often be stopped and her identity card checked. Sometimes, it would be queried and then you would be put under intense pressure of being found out by questions like why is your identity card so new, where are you going and why, what is in your bag or case? Yet Etive always seemed so calm.

"Etive's fellow British agent Yvonne gave me a tip which I passed to your grandmother, Etive. It was to wear large hooped earrings, which were fashionable, whenever in Toulouse and this made her fit in more.

"Etive was well versed in what to do and what not to do, like never order *café au lait,* as coffee was only available without milk. The coffee was awful, usually made from acorns and referred to as 'Ersatz coffee' or sarcastically as 'Pétain's coffee' – a nod to the puppet government in Vichy of the former First World War hero for France, General Pétain. He was old, weak, and likely had no choice.

"Our rations were awfully meagre. We also had a ration card and a clothing coupon book, which in the earlier days allowed us 10 ounces of bread a day, 2 ounces of cheese a month, 25 ounces of fats, 20 ounces of sugar, 10 ounces of meat, 6 ounces of that foul-tasting coffee, all a month not a week.

"Men had a cigarette ration, two packs a week, but no such ration for women, so that was another red flag and warning that women could not smoke in public, as they would be questioned where the cigarettes came from.

"Many of the men had been taken away under an order called '*Service du Travail Obligatoire*', which was enforced labour, primarily to rebuild damaged roads and buildings. Frenchmen hated this so many disappeared but in reality joined the Maquisards to resist the Germans.

"Of course, Laval's Milice would endeavour to hunt them down and was a big reason why the Milice were hated by their own countrymen.

"Etive travelled under the cover of being a district nurse, and later a cosmetics saleswoman. Her identity card name and profession would change as suited certain situations. It was a lot to remember, especially when stopped or, worse, interrogated.

"The Milice, the French police, were like a French Gestapo, their blue uniform a sign we should be wary.

"As soon as de Gaulle returned to France after D-Day, he was witnessed entering liberated towns and cities, one after another. It is said that the S.O.E. were told they must leave the country, which I felt was despicable after all they had given up and for those that died fighting to free our country.

"In fact, a close colleague from those times told me de Gaulle referred to George Starr and his like as mercenaries. It was ironic; it was because of people like George and the leaders and people in each circuit that de Gaulle could return in triumphal pomp. Apparently, I heard George's reaction to de Gaulle was '*Mon general, je vous emmerde*.' Vive Le Patron!

"I remember reading in an English newspaper, years later, maybe as much as twenty years later, that de Gaulle was planning to pull out of NATO, and he is alleged to have commented to the American secretary of state Dean Rusk that he wanted every American soldier out of France. To his credit, Rusk replied calmly yet sharp as a whip, asking de Gaulle whether that included the dead Americans in the military cemeteries of France.

"De Gaulle felt that somehow he had been maligned, even ignored, and sidelined by the British, Americans and other allies during the war, especially not being included in key decisions.

"De Gaulle was arrogant and had his own agenda and was very much full of his own importance. His vision was to return to France to promote the myth of him as a victor leading a victorious people who had risen up as one to overthrow a hated conqueror in the Germans, thus establishing this myth of heroic France the Invincible. No heed was paid to the fact that so many allies died achieving liberation and a free France.

"I think he succeeded as far as the French people were concerned. However, I will never forget all the brave men and women from many countries as well as many French people, be they communists or Gaullists, who endured, suffered and gave the ultimate sacrifice so he could return from exile and make such claims and enjoy such adulation. Still, the past is the past. We must look to the future.

"Take your grandmother and all she did for France and its people and helping airmen and others to escape to fight another day, and her ultimate sacrifice.

"Sorry, I am rambling.

"A few days after Etive's first meeting with Le Patron, we had a meeting with Françoise, an unlikely resistant figure but a prime operator in the efforts to help people escape the clutches of the Gestapo. She had taken over from Pat O' Leary, better known as Albert Guerisse, who had been betrayed in early March 1943 by the traitor Roger Leneveh at the Café Super in Toulouse! Françoise headed to Bergerac to lay low whilst the hullabaloo and fallout settled down. She was back in Toulouse by July 1943.

"Françoise was so committed and brave and frankly didn't seem to see fear. She was very creative. Apparently, she had been a teacher and a secretary and had run a haute couture dress shop on the Rue de la Pampe in Toulouse. She dressed somewhat theatrically in large straw hats decorated with flowers or feathers and even fruit. She was somewhat eccentric and always favoured large handbags made in satin or velvet. Yet she walked on a cane, stooped over with pain, probably rheumatism.

"She was a wily old girl, though in her sixties, I suspect, at that time. She once pretended to be drunk at a German checkpoint, almost making out with the German soldier, flirting and then being hurried through and on her way, as they all thought she was drunk and crazy. She was strange but we adored and respected her, and I know Etive felt the same. Little did the Germans and the Milice know she was achieving a huge success rate in smuggling out airmen and all escapers and evaders to safety, over 250 by the end of the war, I was told. She had a large black cat called 'Milouf', which she adored.

"This unlikely heroine had two prominent front top teeth, somewhat affected by the nicotine from her chain-smoking, which she did rather elegantly, using a bamboo cigarette holder, almost like playing a part in a play at the local theatre. She had an amusing knack of drinking at the same time as keeping the cigarette holder between her lips. Her grey hair was wound in two plaits over her head.

"I first chatted properly and at length with Etive at Madame Dissard's apartment. It was the first time we had been together for any period of time, and later we worked a lot together, getting groups of airmen together and escorting them to the *passeurs*, who would guide them over the Pyrénées to safety in Spain and back to Great Britain. It was not just about resistance-loyal people trying to defeat the Germans and the secrecy and trust needed to protect each other in the resistance, but money was the motivation for some. I was told the *passeurs* wanted about $200 for every escapee. After all, they risked their lives with escorting them over the difficult terrain of the central Pyrénées, avoiding German patrols and potential capture, torture, imprisonment or indeed death.

"We only tended to know a few close people who

in turn knew perhaps one or two. The idea being that if anyone was caught, they could not destroy the whole network, but the German intelligence and unfortunately traitors combined to destroy many a network over the course of the war, sometimes for money but usually out of fear and threats to them and the lives of their families.

"If you were caught, we all knew our fate was unlikely to be a good one, and we were all instructed to hold out for forty-eight hours or as long as possible to allow other members of the resistance we knew and had worked with to escape and hide."

"What did you think of my grandmother, Etive when you first met her?" enquired Laura.

"She was quiet but I sensed she was taking everything in and… how do you say? Weighing things up! She was a pretty lady but I always felt she was thinking of something or remembering someone back home, perhaps a lover or relative. Or maybe she was just planning her moves, like a chess player.

"Sometimes, we would be working together, cycling somewhere or walking. Then she would just start humming the same old tune. I asked her what the song was and she told me it was *We'll Meet Again*. I raised my eyebrows and said who is the lucky man? She just smiled and sang a few words. I remember the words even now. It made me think of my daughter's father, Jean Claude."

There was a silence then Cathy started to sing.

"'*We'll meet again, don't know where, don't know when But I know we'll meet again some sunny day*

Keep smiling through, just like you always do
Till the blue skies chase those dark clouds far away
And I will just say hello to the folks that you know
Tell them you won't be long
They'll be happy to know that as I saw you go
You were singing this song
We'll meet again, don't know where, don't know when
But I know we'll meet again some sunny day."'

"That was beautiful, thank you so much for sharing that song, in perfect English too. You have a wonderful voice."

Laura could almost hear Cathy blushing, then her mind contemplated the words and she wondered if her grandmother had been singing about Dennis, her grandfather.

"Thank you," said Cathy. "Apparently, it was sung by Vera Lynn. I believe she was known in England as the 'Forces' Sweetheart'. I have it on a record somewhere. I used to play it a lot to remind me of your grandmother."

"I am sure I have heard my mother singing this song, I will ask her," Laura replied.

"Etive soon proved a very forthright and confident individual who did not suffer fools gladly. She was a tour de force at times. One time, we were escorting a large group of evaders, mostly American and Canadian airmen, at dusk with an experienced courier, Paule Viatel, when a truck came around the corner of the road, catching us by surprise. We jumped in the ditch and the truck passed us a little way, braking hard, then a number of German soldiers and plain-clothes Gestapo got out. We were like rabbits in the headlights. What bad luck, caught red-handed. We were just outside Saint-Girons, having overnighted at a pension in Seix run by Paul Broue's parents. Paul was a boy who often acted as an *agent de passeur*, tasked with getting escapees to the *passeurs* at great risk. Paul is still alive, of course. Paul had himself escaped over the Pyrénées in 1943 and joined the French Army and returned to help liberate France.

"We realised quickly that one of the men in the group of our assailants was a man called 'Mareval' and for some reason he had become a traitor and he pointed us out to the Germans, having recognised me and Paule, as it was Mareval and Paule – code name 'Claire' – who had set up the network. It transpired they had been on their way to arrest other members of the network when they bumped into us.

"Initially, I was disgusted with the traitor, but I could see the signs of interrogation on Mareval and began to understand. We were all dragged roughly by gunpoint out of the ditch and taken to a nearby farmhouse where, along with Mareval, we were locked in a large room with some of the Germans staying to guard us, albeit they went to the kitchen and got the farmer's wife to make them pancakes.

"Somehow, with an implement Etive had hidden in her shoe, she picked the lock and slid out but locked the door after her so the Germans would be unaware of her escape. She had more chance alone.

"Paule knew what would be coming, with torture and interrogation on the horizon, and knew we had to escape. The Gestapo had gone off to locate and question another local inhabitant in Saint-Girons. We heard later he had been shot. On capture, Paule and myself had been hit with rifle butts and had bled from our noses, lips and other cuts, so we asked the soldiers if we could go to the bathroom and clean up. To our surprise, they allowed this.

"Fortunately, we were able to get out of the window and we ran frantically through the woods, half expecting to be shot. As we ran, every twig and stick seemed to crack loudly beneath our feet. Suddenly, as we scrambled up a steep undulation in the forest, we heard a different sort of click and above us we saw a Wehrmacht soldier with his rifle trained on us, out of breath and perspiring. We stopped in our tracks, then, out of nowhere, Etive appeared behind the soldier and like a cat crept behind him and within seconds his throat had been cut. We sighed with relief and all three of us ran for our lives.

"Taking circuitous routes and without trusting anyone, we pilfered eggs, drank water from streams and three days later we came across a safe house known to Paule and fortunately as yet uncompromised. The owner was a retired architect. He put us in touch with the Françoise network and we were spirited back to Toulouse. A few months earlier, we would have headed for Villa Pamplemousse, a villa Madame Dissard rented for the network, but it had been compromised after an operative codenamed 'Sherry' had been picked up, and in a notebook he foolishly had with him, the Germans found details of Villa Pamplemousse and

Madame Dissard who, although she was in Brive at the time, on hearing the news of the capture of Sherry, as a precaution hurried back to evacuate the airmen before leaving again to wait out the fallout in Toulouse, I believe, but she soon came back to operate successfully.

"Sadly, myself and Etive ran out of luck when one day we boarded a train from Toulouse Matabiau Station to head south towards Saint-Girons, but the Gestapo were waiting for us as they boarded at a small station en route to Mazères-sur-Salat. We were not a long way from Saint-Girons, maybe our guard was down. We had likely been betrayed. I felt we were done for as we were escorted back towards Toulouse on the train.

"After a little while, Etive asked to use the toilet and a guard followed her and stood outside the door. As she came out, she lit a cigarette and asked the soldier if he would like one, which he did. She stood with her back towards the carriage door and apparently distracted him as the train came across a bridge above a river, and as the train exited the bridge, she opened the door and jumped out. It seems like she rolled down the embankment.

"A few hundred metres up the track, maybe more, the train screeched to a halt after the emergency cord on the train had been pulled. A number of Gestapo and soldiers disembarked and ran back towards the bridge, but Etive had disappeared. When they reached the next station, one of the Gestapo got off and no doubt arranged for a full-scale search, but she was never found, well, not then."

Cathy went on to say, "I thought Etive had escaped and recall the sad moment when Etive arrived at Fresnes Prison in Paris just a few weeks after my own incarceration there, having been caught trying to escape via Saint-Girons over the Pyrénées, after making her way to Saint-Girons at the confluence of the Lez and Salat Rivers with the help of Hilaire, the leader of the Wheelwright circuit, and his fellow resisters."

In the course of time, Cathy learned that here, Etive had met a group of airmen in Saint-Girons who had arrived from Montsaunès by bus and that night they started off into the mountains, trudging through hip-high snow, reaching a hut where they sought rest and refuge, but not long after arrival, they were aware that a German patrol was approaching the hut. The escorting *passeur* stealthily exited the rear of the hut and headed up the mountain with four of the men as another snowstorm started. The less mobile in the group were escorted by Etive down the mountain but, alas, the German patrol decided to follow their footsteps in the snow, which tracked down the mountain, and they were all arrested. The men were shot and Etive was taken to Toulouse, interrogated by Klaus Barbie and his henchmen, and then she was taken under heavy guard to Paris. She even tried to escape at Paris Austerlitz Station on arrival, asking to use the bathroom, but she was followed and closely monitored. There was no escape this time.

Cathy heard after the war that the *passeur* and the other men in the group Etive had been with from

Saint-Girons on that fateful night had escaped using the high mountain pass over the Pyrénées and, whilst exhausted and some with frostbite, they managed to drop down to freedom in Spain. "Anyway, when Etive was captured, fortunately, Hilaire, who I now know was George Starr, was not there.

"Let me tell you, on capture, your grandmother was resolute and very brave, accepting her fate may never be to return home, but she was stoic throughout interrogation at the Rue des Saussaies headquarters of the Sicherheitsdienst and imprisonment at Fresnes Prison in Paris, where the conditions were deplorable.

"The noises in Fresnes Prison echoed through the night like torture itself. Some paced the 10 by 7-foot cells if they could still walk. Others sobbed and cried out. A number, defiant to the last, sang patriotic songs, as did Etive before one day she was taken away by a truck and this was the last her fellow agent saw of her.

"But every day, one or more of us were taken to Avenue Foch and tortured. We feared the dreaded *baignoire* more than the beatings often meted out by a name I will never forget: Josef, Josef Stork. He would force our heads under the water of a bath. We were close to drowning and the water was full of previous victims' bodily waste.

"One day, Etive came back, hobbling, walking on the side of her feet. Her toenails had been ripped off with pliers, and they had started on her hands. Her back had burns on it, yet she never gave her captors any useful information. I am so sorry to share these horrors with you, but people must know what we endured."

Laura's eyes had filled with tears; she could barely speak. "Thank you for sharing this, Mademoiselle. It is hard to hear but I am proud of her for sure and indeed of you."

"Please call me Cathy."

"So, what happened then?" Laura tentatively asked, fearing the reply.

"I was sent to Ravensbrück, but I do not know what happened to Etive."

"That must have been awful, to be sent to a concentration camp," said Laura.

A silence ensued then a stuttered reply: "I... I... it was hell."

"I am so sorry."

"From the time we arrived, we were stripped of our clothes and belongings and they tried to destroy our self-confidence and dignity, and we were persona non grata, for sure, but I decided I must keep my mind healthy to survive, whatever they did to me. *I must survive*, I told myself every day!" Her voice cracked and Laura could feel the pain and indeed fear.

"It was easy to become depressed and to give up. We witnessed awful things and depraved actions, and of course we endured pain and other horrors. We all looked like we were dying on our feet, some like wounded animals. It was easy to give up and hope for a quick death. We slept on a concrete floor in a reception building the first night. I was put into a solitary cell for complaining and being outspoken. There was no window, just a brick or two with holes in to let in air. Nearby were the punishment cells, and all through the day and night, I could hear screaming and the agony being inflicted on human beings.

"Eventually, I was in a barracks close to the crematorium, which we realised was the final walk to the so-called showers, for delousing. You could smell the bodies burning and see cinders floating off into the sky. I always thought of it as the souls of these poor people ascending to a more peaceful place.

"One day, as I left the hut we slept in, I saw a teenage girl, her head newly shaved, her slender emaciated body shrouded in the striped uniform of imprisonment. She was shuffling in front of a German officer. He shouted to her to stop. She turned, her eyes met mine, and then he shot her in the head before nonchalantly turning and walking away. Her body crumpled to the ground, taking her last snapshot of life with her, but as her motionless body lay on its side, her eyes, wide open, were staring directly at me. She left me with an image that has haunted me all my life. Within seconds, fellow prisoners appeared, stealing her shoes and anything of use to them, just to survive.

"I just hope your grandmother did not suffer. I hope this has helped and not made you too sad. Barely a day has passed since the war when I have not thought of Etive. God rest her soul.

"Etive had a poem she used to recite. I still remember it.

"'Beside the waters
Clear and cold
Unbridled love
made us bold

The sky above
as blue as ice
Reflected love in paradise
The dusk revealed
the lover's lair
I often dream
that I am there."'

Laura's voice croaked a reply. "That is so beautiful, Cathy, thank you so much for sharing that with me. That is such a wonderful gift!"

"*Mon plaisir*, Laura! It is you who have given me such a pleasant surprise today. Just to talk to you, her granddaughter, about Etive has been very special to me."

"Maybe we can meet one day, Cathy!"

"I would like that. Come to Toulouse. This wonderful city was liberated in August 1944. It is not perfect but it is known for its pink buildings and stunning array of violets, you will like it. I would also like to meet the granddaughter of Etive, sweet Martha. I must rest now, à *bientôt*."

"À *bient*ôt and thank you," said Laura as she held the phone to her chest, wiping the tears from her cheeks. She needed air.

She made her way out to the terrace at Arisaig House. Fortunately, it was deserted, allowing her solace to assimilate all she had heard from Cathy Arvieux. Laura surveyed Prince's Beach in the distance across the meadows, took a deep breath of freedom and allowed her tears to flow unhindered down her cheeks once more.

Seagulls passed overhead; the mournful call of one lone bird was almost like a squeaky wheel repeatedly sighing as it laboured towards its destination.

Laura was indeed very proud of her grandmother and all the brave souls who resisted the Germans so that she could live so freely today! At that moment, Laura felt a presence. She looked above her and saw the majestic sight of a rare sea eagle with its large wingspan and distinctive white tail; it circled on the thermals and then dipped its wing and headed out over the loch. Watching this magnificent bird disappear into the distance, she whispered, "Thank you, Etive!"

Seventeen

Greek Odyssey

A fortnight later, Laura was staring out of the aircraft window as she descended to Athens Airport. It was a rather spectacular approach during perfect weather for late October, with beautiful views of the city of Athens. Laura could make out the Acropolis, and a large island which the Greek lady in the seat beside Laura informed her was Evia Island. The port of Piraeus seemed busy with a flow of ships and boats of all sizes coming in and out, before the Boeing 737 straightened its course and descended, landing almost imperceptibly, as if it had floated like a feather onto the runway. As the door opened, the dry still air was like a warm blanket, so different to the cool morning at Glasgow Airport she had left four hours before.

After the usual melee of passport and customs

control, she was in the arrivals hall. A sign showing her name was in evidence as a swarthy, stocky middle-aged man seemed to pick her out before she did him, even without knowing her. Taking her bag, he smiled and gestured for her to head towards the exit. She followed him to his vehicle and they set off. Laura had abandoned the idea of a car hire and driving herself. Before long, she realised she had made the right decision, as the hooting of car horns and drivers gesticulating to one another in deprecatory ways underlined why she would have been a little daunted by the traffic and even more so by driving on the right-hand side of the road. She sat back, relaxed and looked forward to her journey as they headed west towards the Peloponnese.

Stavros was a pleasant enough chap, even though he was not very talkative; his English was not the best. It started to head towards dusk as over two hours later they arrived on the Gulf of Corinth coast, at the small beach resort of Akrata, which the travel agent in Fort William had recommended, as according to her resort guide description, it was well known for its beaches. Apparently, the River Krathis flows from the Aroania Mountains to the sea right through Akrata.

Laura's accommodation for the next ten days was the Georgiou Guesthouse on Porovitsa Beach, and the guesthouse was indeed situated right on the beach. The brochure said, '*Its views are majestic and one can sit for hours taking in the coastal views*'. Rooms were clean but basic and service came with a smile. A great place to recharge the batteries, relax and explore the area from, and a number of restaurants on your doorstep. It wasn't as if Laura had much of a choice, as most of the resort's accommodation had closed for the season at the end of September.

It turned out that the guesthouse was a little out of the main town of Akrata, perhaps a couple of kilometres. From the road, the large three-storied frontage looked uninspiring, but it was getting dark and there appeared to be balconies above her. As Laura stepped through the recessed door into a cosy lamp-lit reception area, it was like going into someone's house. This looked like their lounge, and maybe once it was.

"*Kalispera*," greeted the rather short, plump, grey-haired lady, her hair swept back into a ponytail, as she popped up seemingly from nowhere. "You must be our British friend, Dewar."

"Laura, Laura Dewar," she replied, holding her hand out in greeting.

"Ah! *Yiasou*, Laura. My name is Eleni. Welcome to Georgiou's, which is your home for your stay. Spiros Georgiou is my husband," she said proudly. "He is out at the moment. You must be tired. Let me show you your room; we can deal with the formalities in the morning. Have you eaten?"

"No! I am a little hungry. Perhaps I can get a snack somewhere close by?"

As they entered an open terrace, the evening was getting cooler. Some tables and chairs were scattered around.

"This is where we have breakfast, 7.30am until

10am, but it is too cool to eat here this evening. I will bring up a plate of fruit and cheese if that is okay."

"Perfect, just perfect," replied Laura, thankfully.

Climbing the outside staircase, they reached a walkway and came around the corner past a rather weathered wooden table and chairs, the table sporting a bowl of oranges and what looked like the remains of a geranium in a flowerpot.

Laura became aware of the sound of the lapping waves. She stopped, leaned on the railing and took in the sea breeze as it played with her hair. Eleni turned and smiled.

"You will be able to see the sea in the morning from your balcony."

That night, Laura slept like a log. She awoke as the morning light pierced the window's shutters, which she had left slightly open, creating a ladder of morning sun across her bed. She could hear the sea and make out the surf as it lapped the shoreline. For the first time in months, Laura felt relaxed and contented. Walking across her small but adequate room, she peered out of the window. The cool night air had started to disperse as the bright morning sun warmed her face. She closed her eyes and felt as if her batteries were starting to recharge. It was 9am as she sat at the terrace table and very soon a young girl appeared.

"*Kalimera*, Madam, may I get you a tea or a coffee?"

"Coffee, please! Your English is very good," complimented Laura.

"Thank you. I learned at school and my family helped too."

A few minutes later, she reappeared with a silver coffee pot and some rather flowery bone china, very similar to some her mother had at home in Comrie.

"My word, that is splendid. What is your name?"

"Melina."

"That is a very pretty name."

"It is her grandmother's name too," said Eleni, arriving with some toast, honey and a bowl of fruit.

"Wonderful, so are you related?"

"She is my niece." Melina smiled and disappeared.

"Did you sleep well, Miss Laura?"

"I did indeed. The bed was very comfortable and clean," said Laura, before she could stop herself.

Eleni chuckled. "I am glad you found things clean."

"I didn't mean to offend," said Laura, thinking she may have upset Eleni.

"No offence taken, *agape mou*," replied Eleni in a familiar tone.

"Can I cook you something, no?"

"This is just fine for me. I want to get out and explore."

"Are you here on holiday?"

"Yes and no."

Eleni leaned her head to one side, waiting for Laura to explain.

"I am here to pay homage really to my grandfather, well, not so much homage but to try to find out where he died and pay my respects, because I never knew him."

"Your grandfather was Greek?" beamed Eleni, enthusiastically.

"Well, no, he was British but he died here during the war, or at least we think he did. He went missing, you see."

"Many died in the war, and the civil war after the Germans were dealt with," said Eleni, her tone hardening a little then sounding a little doleful. She added, "It was a terrible time. I was a mere child but our older generations suffered badly. You should talk to Spiros; he might be able to help you, or at least tell you who can."

"Thank you, I will."

With that, Laura sat and listened to the birds in the vegetation surrounding the terrace and looked down the path towards the whitewashed gateway pillars and through the gate held open with a large stone. It provided a tantalising glimpse of the greeny blue sea beyond. It was mesmerising; as the sun played on the surface, every now and again, the sea changed colour as the sun peeked from behind the clouds then disappeared again. She seemed to be the only guest, and her mind moved to thinking about Dennis Greaves.

Laura considered her options, before realising in all her efforts she didn't have a lot to go on. Her only lead was Kalavryta, and she accepted that was a long shot.

Donning her sunglasses, she headed past the gnarled old olive tree, which the terrace seemed to have been built around, and down to the crazy paved walkway, which gave way to a deserted white stone and pebbled beach. Laura looked at the panorama of surprisingly green hills that put an arm around the bay to her right, then raised her face to the sun and closed her eyes as she assimilated the welcome autumnal sunshine to top up with some vitamin D.

"*Yiasou*," came a deep voice behind her. Laura turned, hand across her chest.

"Wow, you move stealthily. How I didn't hear you on this pebbled beach, I am not sure."

The once dark-haired man, his hair now peppered with grey, smiled.

Heavily accented, he introduced himself. "Sorry I startled you, Miss Do-wah, I am Spiros Georgiou. Sorry I was not here to greet you, I always seem to be busy running around. Your breakfast was good, yes?"

"Excellent, just right for me," proffering her handshake. "Please call me Laura."

"Lowra, a pretty name," came the heavily accented reply.

Spiros didn't immediately let go of her hand. Instead, looking into her eyes, he said, "Your grandfather was here in the war."

"Yes," hesitated Laura. "Well, yes, at least I think he was, but I am not sure exactly where. He was a British liaison officer who parachuted in to help organise local partisans to fight the Germans."

"We did pretty well ourselves," said Spiros, dismissively.

"I am sure. Your wife said you might know someone who can help me with some local knowledge of those days, fifty years and more ago."

"There are not many left who can help with first-hand experience of the war now. The fighting in the civil conflict saw to that, and many do not want to be reminded. What makes you think he may have been in Akrata?"

"Oh! I am not sure he was here. All I have to go on really are some reports from other British officers that stated he was in this vicinity at some stage because they refer to the fact that he was very shaken by a massacre that happened at Kalavryta. Sorry, did I pronounce that right?"

Spiros recoiled. "Bad, very bad." He barked, "The Germans were murderers, less than human. The British didn't help much. We needed more arms, more support. They seemed to disappear when they were needed, even siding with EDES over ELAS, it is said. Germans were butchers, butchers, I tell you, killing women and children, burning homes and doing unspeakable things in some parts of the country," said Spiros, shaking his head, his face like thunder. "They left us starving."

"I am so sorry," said Laura, surprised at how strongly this pain was still carried by the people of this area.

"Old Antonis!"

Laura hesitated before repeating the name. "Was Old Antonis a relative or family friend that was killed?"

"No! Antonis spoke to surviving witnesses. He knows a lot more than me. I was too young. I just remember my parents being angry, horrified and frightened when we heard of the massacre, and it was not the only one... many more, like at Distomo, and so on.

"Where was your grandfather killed?" queried Spiros.

"I have no idea. He just never came back from his mission, but men who were in this area and knew him did."

"So, you know very little?"

Laura shook her head forlornly, as she could not disagree.

"Not much that can be done then. Enjoy your day, Miss Lowra," he said, turning.

"Excuse me," said Laura, chasing him and grabbing his sleeve.

Unhanding him, she said, "I would like to visit Kalavryta and perhaps, if possible, meet Antonis, wherever he lives. Could you help me?"

Spiros looked at Laura. He inclined his head, opened his hands in a gesture, as if to say *why?*

Laura looked at him, her eyes melancholy. "If nothing else, I would like to pay my respects and learn a little more about life on Kalavryta then and now."

Spiros looked at Laura as if trying to see inside her mind. He nodded and walked off.

Not knowing quite what to make of Spiros, Laura watched him depart and turned towards the sea before strolling along the beach and stopping at a small taverna; its only other occupants, two wizened old men with characterful faces, weathered by time, as if they had always sat on those seats and been assaulted by the elements. She said hello as she passed by and took a table close by as the men nodded and continued talking.

"*Kalimera,*" came the breezy greeting from the young man who bounded towards her table. He wiped it with a cloth and, pleased to see he actually had a tourist customer, said in perfect English, "It is a fine day today, no?"

"Lovely day. A cup of tea, please."

"Sure," and he disappeared through a curtain of rainbow-coloured horizontal plastic strips, which no doubt tried to keep the insects and flies from the kitchen within.

Later that day, after a relaxing afternoon reading a book, the first one she had read in earnest for a long while and which had sent her off into a restful doze, she was startled by a rap on the door. Not realising where she was for a moment, she straightened herself up and checked herself in the wall-hung mirror as she passed it before answering the door. Surprised to see Spiros, before she could say anything, he said:

"Tomorrow, I take you, 9am. Wear something warm," and with that he walked off.

Laura was perplexed; she was happy Spiros was helping her but puzzled by his evident anger and abrupt manner, as if directed towards her. She could understand the memories of war and the underlying bitterness in his tone; perhaps something else was bothering him.

Eighteen

Kalavryta

Next morning after breakfast, sure enough, Spiros met her in reception. His thickset build seemed to fill the door; two brown eyes like laser beams in his weathered dark-skinned face seemed to pierce Laura's exterior. She wondered what was going through his mind.

"*Kalimera*," he said, not waiting for a reply before turning on his heels, and Laura rose and followed in his wake.

The sun was intermittent, regularly disappearing behind clouds as they took the narrow coastal road alongside the Gulf of Corinth. The land was beginning to get higher inland. Laura decided not to make conversation until Spiros instigated it. He looked like he had had a rough night; his shirt collar was up on one side and he had stubble, unshaved from the day before.

Before long, they came to a blue signpost with place names in Greek upon it. One said *Kalavryta 32kms.*

"We go up into the mountains now," said Spiros, his tone a little softer.

"We are heading for Kalavryta, 32 kilometres?" said Laura, a question in her voice.

He nodded.

"How long will it take us to get there?"

"It is a reasonable road but it is steep and the road bends at times. Our journey is maybe ninety minutes, maybe less. It is beautiful but cold in the mountains as we approach November. They ski up here in the winter."

"Really? That's amazing. I didn't know you could ski in Greece. I have always thought of Greece as a land of sun and Zorba the Greek."

Spiros raised his eyebrows and for the first time that day grinned.

Before long, they entered Kalavryta, which is surrounded by mountains. Arriving just before 11am, they pulled into the main square of Kalavryta by a church.

"What a lovely church," commented Laura. "Kalavryta is bigger and more modern than I thought it would be. I envisaged a small village."

"It is a good size population, maybe over 2,000, but that is only a quarter of the municipality population. I love this church too. It is called the 'Assumption of Theotokos Church.'"

"Gosh, that is impressive, do they have a memorial here?"

Spiros turned off the engine and got out of the car, followed by Laura.

"Yes, Lowra, they have a monument on Kapi Hill called 'The Place of Sacrifice!' Please follow me first; I have a surprise."

Intrigued, Laura tried to keep pace with the long strides of Spiros, before he stopped outside a whitewashed two-storey café with terracotta roof tiles, set just off the main street. An old man wearing a cap and glasses reading a newspaper sat at one table in front of the *kafenion*, and a couple of other customers sat at the other outside table.

Georgiou stopped and stood by the table with the old gentleman. "Good morning, old man. I have the lady I spoke to you about," he taunted in jest.

Lowering the newspaper, the man stood. He was surprisingly tall and erect; he sported a large unkempt moustache and inspected Laura with his penetrative piercing brown eyes set like stones beneath large tufted eyebrows. He shook the hand of Spiros, who turned to Laura.

"This is Antonis. He will help you learn about Kalavryta and the time your grandfather was here."

Nodding towards Laura, "Please," said Antonis, holding both his hands out towards the empty chairs around the small table, indicating for them both to join them.

A waitress quickly joined them and coffee was ordered.

"You are Laura," said the old man, whose calm voice delivered cultured English with barely a hint of a Greek accent.

"Yes! It is, thank you so much for seeing me."

"My pleasure. What do you need to know?" he said, his eyes intent and focused on her with a high intensity of concentration.

Laura explained about her grandfather's involvement in Greece and how he never returned but how the terrible events at Kalavryta had obviously shaken him.

"I can understand that," said Antonis. "It was a terrible time. I was just a child, but I remember it as if it was yesterday."

"Do you mind talking about it?"

"The world must never forget," he replied.

"It was a holocaust. Yes, the town of Kalavryta suffered a holocaust, awful atrocities committed. Some say it was the guerrillas' fault, others the British, the allies. But for me it is the Germans and no one else to blame. Sure, it was revenge for a guerrilla attack in October 1943 when the guerrillas attacked Germans near Kerpini village and eighty German soldiers were captured. The Nazi forces demanded the prisoners be freed and threatened terrible reprisals. However, the guerrillas refused to free the Germans, in spite of the attempted intervention of the Church."

He paused and listened to the church clock strike 11am, almost on cue. It was as if this reminder of time heralded an epic tale.

"Then on the 8th of December, the German troops

destroyed the villages Kerpini and Pogi and killed their male population. After this, the Greek forces in retaliation executed and mutilated the German prisoners. Only one of them managed to escape.

"On the 10th of December, a Friday, the Germans entered Kalavryta, looking for the Greek resistance soldiers, the partisans. I remember they were on one balcony searching houses and saw a shepherd in the meadow through binoculars, and the German soldier raised his rifle and shot him, laughing as he did so. We knew things were going to get worse at this stage. The Germans were angry beyond measure and out for blood. It was clear no mercy would be shown.

"Before long, they had identified some houses used by members of the resistance, like Major Gikas of ELAS, and burnt them to the ground. Hotel Helmos was burned and some men and boys taken to Hotel Dalianis for interrogation. Each day, the tension grew. We were all living in fear as houses were requisitioned.

"Sunday the 12th of December was St Spiridon's Day, the patron saint of potters, a feast day, but no one felt like worshipping and food was not in great supply, as the Germans were starting to drain the village of anything we had. We were fearful, frightened.

"The Germans could see there were no resistance people, be they guerrillas or anyone else. We had even given them a splendid meal.

"Daybreak arrived on that fateful day, Monday, the 13th of December, 1943. It was a foggy morning as the cold day started. A tall German with pistol drawn and wearing a helmet motioned to us all to get out of the house and gather outside. We were told to take food and a blanket for one day. There were my parents and six children. The man next door was slow coming to join his family. I later learned he had hidden some kitchen utensils under the cabbages, as he feared the houses would be burned. It is strange what we do in times of duress," said Antonis, wistfully.

Laura nodded, absolutely transfixed by the story she was hearing.

"My mother had made some porridge so she brought that with her in a bowl. Then hauntingly, and I can hear them now, the church bells tolled, but it was a different sort of toll to the normal feast day and Sunday service celebrations. It was almost mournful, as if warning of some apocalyptic event about to happen.

"My father turned and said goodbye to my mother. He said, 'I might not see you again.' My mother was so overcome with emotion. Can you imagine how this would feel?"

Laura just shook her head.

"Everyone was collected and herded to the elementary school. As we entered, the women and children were ushered to the right, the men and boys over twelve to the left. One or two boys lied about their age and stayed with their mothers and younger siblings.

"I had seen one lady, Mrs Vaya, she had blood running down her legs. I pointed this out to my mother and she assisted her. She was barefoot. I heard my mother saying, 'This is terrible, you only gave birth yesterday. You should have been allowed to stay in bed.' Her daughter was holding the baby, barely in this world for a day!

"The women and children were crammed into the classrooms. We were in the one under the courthouse. There were so many of us in there. It was really stuffy and claustrophobic. People opened windows for us to breathe.

"Then we could smell smoke, and an old man pulled himself up so he could see through the windows properly, and he told us houses were burning and then proceeded to tell us which houses as the fires took hold. The smoke started to filter in and we feared we were going to be burned alive. A panic ensued and people rushed out of the classrooms and by now the men and boys had been taken somewhere. The ladies forced the back door and spilled into the street. A soldier left on guard looked bewildered. He did nothing, he just watched us, but there were so many, over 2,000 of us. Other soldiers saw us and pushed us downhill as we turned back, hearing the breaking of glass and crackling of the burning buildings. The school was now on fire. It was truly awful!"

All the time, Spiros sat, said nothing, sometimes looking to the distance, other times focused on Antonis.

Antonis took a sip of coffee and then some water. He greeted an old gentleman, who took the now vacant table across from them.

"After the Nazis had locked up the women and us children in the school, they took all the men and boys to Kapi Hill, just outside the town.

"The men stood and some sat on their blankets as the Germans told them to stop where they were on the hill. Some Germans at that location dropped into a gully there. They insisted they were taking the men elsewhere and said on their honour they would not hurt them. Then it began, from three different positions, machine guns opened up firing, strafing the helpless men and boys, cutting them down like dogs.

"Can you imagine the carnage, Laura?"

Laura's eyes filled up as she shook her head and put her hand on Antonis' hand.

"For ten, maybe twenty, seconds at a time, the bullets flew into defenceless bodies. Boys murdered before they could have a life. Then silence, men came forward and pulled the bodies that had fallen on one another apart, checking for signs of life, and if there was any... well, it was ended."

"Cowardly bastards," came the voice from the next table.

Laura turned to see the old man who had just arrived joining in.

"I know because I was there," carried on the rasp of the old man's voice.

"How did you survive?" said Laura, before thinking how difficult it must be for this man to speak.

"I am here thanks to the grace of God. It was not my time." He stood and tottered over. Parting his thinning hair, he showed two indents in his skull. "They shot me twice in the head and once in the leg, but I survived somehow. Here, feel." He took Laura's hand and pressed her fingers into the indent in his skull.

Laura stood and gave the man a hug. "I am so pleased you did live."

The man's eyes welled up. He moved his head from side to side and looked her in the eye.

"But my father and four cousins and uncle did not. I can never forgive the Germans for what they did."

At that, the old man shuffled away, not being able to talk about things anymore. Laura could see just how painful it was for him.

Sitting back down, Laura saw Antonis glance at Spiros.

"Maybe that is enough," said Spiros. "Now you know."

Laura nodded. "What was that man's name, Antonis?"

"Aghiri. He was one of thirteen survivors."

"I am amazed that thirteen survived. How did the wives, sisters and grandmothers of those murdered deal with this, when they realised what had happened?"

"It was a nightmare, everyone was frightened. The women lit fires, we had nothing to eat. The Germans had taken everything, all our animals. The next day, when it was thought the Germans had now all gone, we tentatively made our way up towards Kapi Hill and everyone looked to find their loved ones. Women were crying and wailing and some just couldn't even do that. They were shocked by the slaughter. At least we found some still alive, but almost 700 were dead.

"The women and older children set about burying the dead as they were untangled from one another and lifted on blankets to be taken to the cemetery. We had no tools. People used their bare hands, but the ground was hard. We could barely make shallow 5 centimetre-deep graves. We tried not to look at their faces. Some ladies covered their loved ones' faces with handkerchiefs before shovelling dirt on them.

"The ground was red with blood. It glistened in the sunshine as we collected the bodies and we stood in their blood. It was dreadful, no one should ever have to endure this. It took us until dark to bury them all.

"Next day, one lady went and found the metal hoop off a burned-out wine barrel and used that to dig. We covered the bodies with the loose soil from the sides of the cemetery where possible, as the rest of the ground was frozen hard. It was winter after all.

"People collected stones to try and protect their loved ones' graves and mark them.

"Vultures and ravens circled above and dogs would come and dig at the graves, so we lit fires and banged tins to keep them away. Some slept with the deceased, but sadly some bodies and graves were desecrated.

"The following days were awful. The women had buried their beloved family members, but they were bereft. They were homeless and had nothing to eat because the Germans had burned the whole village and nearby fields of crops and had taken all available food with them. All I can remember is the misery and hunger and in most cases, we were so poorly clothed that the cold got to our bones. It was snowing and minus 4 or 5 degrees.

"One thing that sticks in my mind growing up is something my sister remarked upon. For years after, people in general, not just the women, would wear black, and Maria said the right wing of the church on Sundays would be almost empty, as there were no men, whilst the left wing was full of women in black."

"I do not have the words to express my sorrow and sadness, Antonis. I am so sorry for your losses," said Laura, as compassionately as she could muster.

"It was and still is dreadful. We had no shelter, just the odd hut or some structure that had not been fully burned, no roof but some wall maybe, so most people tried to survive in the open.

"Slowly but surely, we became stronger. Teachers started teaching the children again. We were destroyed morally, emotionally and in many ways physically. But we survived. I think the problem is, like Aghiri, we feel guilty we survived. All families had losses; the Katsaros, Tsarouchis, Kalderos , Lotsos, Vaya families, and so on, everyone."

Laura stood and went and hugged Antonis as he dabbed his eyes with his handkerchief.

"The Germans continued. After us, they destroyed villages nearby and the monasteries of Agia Lavra and Mega Spilaio. They killed monks there too, as the Germans believed them to be collaborators with the partisans."

Spiros had been very quiet and finally spoke. "There is a memorial dedicated to the people of this town who perished. It is on the top of Kapi Hill. It is where the men were killed. Let us take a drive up there."

All three alighted in the small car park below the hill. Laura looked up at the large white cross that dominated the skyline. Then she followed Antonis and Spiros as they looked, probably for the thousandth time, at the stones inscribed with the names of these men.

They entered a small chapel, and Laura soon realised there was a nameplate with the name and the age of each man and boy; in front, hundreds of candles, burning for them. She noticed both men lit candles and joined them in doing so to pay her respects, and as she did so, she made a wish. Both men put their fingers on some of the names displayed.

Antonis sat in the sun whilst Laura and Spiros followed the steps and path up to the fine white cross beside a flagpole on which the familiar blue-and-white stripes of the Greek flag fluttered, then looked back over the town of Kalavryta. It was an emotional moment for them both. How could this awful carnage have happened in the quiet meadow below them? On the bank of land just under the cross, 13 12 1943 was spelt out in white stones.

After a few moments of stillness and reflection under the azure blue of the autumnal cloud-pocked sky, with the breeze and cool wind tugging at them, they descended swiftly to Antonis and drove back into town. As they pulled into the town square, Antonis pointed out that the impressive cathedral of the town, which Laura had admired on arrival, was rebuilt after the massacre but the left tower clock remained stopped at the time when the crime, as Antonis described it, began, at 2.34pm on that fateful day.

"Remember the school where the women and

children were locked up? Well, we now one day hope to have the Kalavryta Holocaust Museum there. We just need the money to make it happen. We want to leave some floors of the school remaining, showing the burned and scorched areas. It will be mostly for tourists. Our memories are always in our hearts."

Laura got out of the car as Antonis bid them goodbye. She hugged him.

Tears in her eyes, clearly moved, she said softly, "Thank you! One question, do you remember any British soldiers coming to the village?"

"No, I am sorry, I was only young. Maybe there were some. I heard my parents talking of British, but I do not remember anything they said."

As Spiros went to get in the car, Antonis gave him a slip of paper and a friendly pat on the back.

Very soon, they were leaving the town. Laura felt emotionally wrecked; she was exhausted and couldn't begin to imagine how Antonis felt. As they drove down the winding road to the coast, they chatted generally, Spiros asking Laura about what she did back home and was she married, and so on. On the coastal road once more, Laura turned to Spiros and said, "I hope you do not mind me asking, but you seemed to know some of the names on the memorial stone at Kapi Hill."

Spiros swallowed and she could see he was struggling to speak.

"It's okay, I understand," said Laura.

"It was my father and older brother and uncle." Now Laura understood the pain Spiros felt.

Laura didn't know what to say.

A few minutes passed before she could speak herself. "So, were you born in Kalavryta too?"

He nodded. Regaining his composure, he said, "I was a babe in arms. I never knew them. My mother never recovered, she was a shell of a woman. It was very hard for her bringing up myself and my older sister."

"It must have been dreadful for your mother and sister," said Laura softly.

A few moments later, they pulled up in front of the Georgiou Guesthouse.

"Thank you," said Laura. "I now understand how hard that was for you to arrange and deal with again." She leaned over and kissed him on the cheek.

He turned and looked at her forlornly. "Life must go on. Now I have my own children and grandchildren. Of course, we will never forget."

Both stepped out of the car and walked slowly to the door.

"I am going now. I need to see someone. One other thing," he said, bringing the folded piece of paper out of his pocket. "Antonis has found a woman who may know something about your grandfather, or at least people he served with." He gave Laura the note and turned, saying as he went, "Enjoy your evening."

Dusk was settling. Laura smiled, a little shell-shocked, and thanked Spiros once again as he departed. He raised his hand as he walked off into the village.

Laura turned and entered the dimly lit reception area. Clutching her note, she made her way to her room, put on the light and sat on the edge of the bed beneath the bedside lamp. She opened the note with trepidation. It bore the telephone number of a lady, one Marietta Papadopoulos!

Nineteen

Kapetanios Greaves

Next morning, Laura awoke early and decided to go for a quick dip in the sea. She had been in Akrata a couple of days but it seemed a lot longer. She needed a swim. The morning was overcast as she tiptoed gently over the pebbles and soon immersed herself in the therapeutic salt water of the Gulf of Corinth. It felt a little cool at first but nothing like as chilling as the wild swimming she had done in Loch Morar.

Laura felt alive; she felt so good and happy she had made this journey. Even though she was pursuing information about her grandfather, and despite the intense nature of yesterday's chilling storytelling by Antonis, she felt she was getting her life back. She had been on a treadmill of work all year and loved the change of pace.

Picking up her towel off the beach, she pulled her long blonde hair to one side and dried it before dabbing herself down and putting on her sundress and returning to the terrace for breakfast.

"*Kalimera*," greeted Eleni, who was sweeping the path.

"*Kalimera*," replied Laura. "It's a gorgeous morning."

"What can I get you for breakfast?"

"The usual, please," as she was now a regular.

Coffee soon arrived.

"Eleni, I wonder if you could please help me make a telephone call"

"No problem, when you are ready."

Forty-five minutes later, Eleni was listening to the telephone number ring out.

After what seemed an age, a scratchy voice answered. Laura could not understand a word of what was being said by Eleni, nor gauge the replies from her expressions. After about five minutes, Eleni hung up the phone then sat down, exasperated.

"Are you okay?" enquired Laura, concerned.

A little red-faced, Eleni laughed. "Marietta is a little hard of hearing. I had to keep repeating myself."

"Would she be prepared to see me?" said Laura, raising her eyebrows in hope.

"She says her English is not good and she is not sure how much she can remember, but she confirms she can remember some British soldiers who were in Kalavryta in the winter of 1943/1944. She has asked me to ring her back in thirty minutes, as she is asking if her niece, who lives in Plantanos, maybe twenty minutes away, can come over and interpret for her."

"That would be wonderful."

Laura showered, bemoaning the water pressure, which seemed to be good one minute and a trickle the next.

As she dressed, a knock at the door proved to be Eleni.

"Mrs Papadopoulos would like you to join her niece and herself for lunch. I have the address. I have taken the liberty of booking you a taxi for midday."

"Eleni, you are wonderful. I cannot thank you and Spiros enough for all your help."

"No problem, we are so happy we can help."

The sun was bright but the cool breeze had picked up off the sea as the taxi drove into the small village of Plantanos Beach. Marietta Papadopoulos lived in a small maisonette set a few blocks from the sea on the ground floor. Laura pressed the buzzer to the apartment and shortly an intercom voice cracked forth. Soon Laura walked through to an attractive, dark-haired young lady, a little younger than Laura, she estimated mid-twenties.

"Welcome, my name is Euthymia. It is hard to say, no? It means something like serenity or cheerful in English."

Laura said, "That's a pretty name, thank you so much for coming to interpret for me."

"My pleasure," she said as they entered the bijou lounge. Laura could see a lady sitting on her terrace, wrapped warmly in a blanket.

"Hello, I'm Laura," she said as she came in front of a sharp-featured, silver-haired lady; her dark eyes were tinged with red.

Nodding and smiling, she held out her hand as Euthymia put her hand on her great-aunt's shoulder.

"My great-aunt and I have made some traditional Greek food. Is this okay for you?"

"Absolutely, it is so kind. Please express my thanks to your great-aunt for inviting me and for helping me with my search for my grandfather."

The terrace was sheltered from the wind and the warmth of the sun was on them, making the temperature comfortable.

Euthymia brought out a small flagon of red wine and some glasses. Laura poured them all a small offering.

"I will go and get our lunch now."

"Please may I help?" asked Laura.

"Sure," thanked Euthymia, whilst Marietta Papadopoulos just nodded and smiled.

A lovely meal of moussaka packed with aubergines, potatoes, minced lamb and delicious herbs, and no doubt a little red wine, really made Laura's digestive juices flow.

"That was scrumptious, really tasty," said Laura, sporting a clean plate in front of her.

"My great-aunt is a fabulous cook," said Euthymia.

"A toast," said Laura. "To you, Marietta, you look fabulous and you are a wonderful cook. Thank you once again for inviting me."

Marietta raised her glass "*Yamas*, Laura."

"She is toasting our health," confirmed Euthymia as she repeated Laura's message to Marietta.

A sumptuous *baklava* later and Laura was almost ready for a siesta. They had chatted small talk over lunch. Laura had learned that Euthymia was single and had been to university in Athens, studying politics, but now helped her mother and father run a restaurant in Akrata.

Table cleared, they sat with a coffee then Marietta, who had been looking at Laura closely for the entire time she had been there, spoke.

"Kapetanios Greaves and Kapetanios O'Donnell."

Laura was a little surprised to hear her grandfather's name spoken by a Greek.

Marietta was playing with some worry beads, looking down at them then back at Laura.

She continued in Greek, Euthymia translating. "I knew of these men. I have been thinking of them since you called."

"You did," said Laura excitedly, remembering that the diary entry she had received from Melton-Woodbridge, whom she met at Arisaig House, mentioned an O'Donnell. "What can you tell me about them?"

Once again, for the second day in a row, Laura listened intently. Marietta paused for a sip of coffee then water every now and again, but all the time she caressed and moved her worry beads, known as *komboloi* in Greek. Laura noticed she would start at one end of the thread and pull the thread forward with her thumb and index finger until one of the turquoise beads was reached. Then the cord was tipped so that the bead fell and hit the shield. This was repeated until all the beads had been tipped and then it was repeated.

"They had been with the ELAS guerillas a week or two before, but I was told they were not involved with the guerrilla ambush of the Germans that led to the massacre." The bitterness felt palpable.

"Then a week or so, maybe sooner, after the massacre at Kalavryta, they arrived. They were unbelieving of the devastation and were visibly emotional. They did not have much they could help us with. One or two of the survivors of the massacre, the injured, they helped construct makeshift shelters for them and notified the Red Cross. We told them the Germans had taken everything – chickens, mules, pigs, even clothing and money, and anything they didn't take they burned. They did come back and gave us some gold sovereigns to buy food with and a few sparse provisions they had collected, but then they were gone.

"I remember Kapetanios Greaves promising they would return, but we never saw them again.

"Maybe he was killed, who knows. The communists didn't really care for the British. They didn't trust them."

Laura nodded and put her hand on Marietta's shoulder. "I spoke to Antonis in Kalavryta. He told me the full story of the massacre. I cannot express how shocked and sorry I am to hear of this evil act."

Marietta's eyes were tired and full of tears.

"Some of us had to move away; we couldn't bear it. I was young but it still hurts. I lost my uncle, my father and two brothers. My mother died not long afterwards, maybe a year or so. I was orphaned. I was brought to Patras by one of the rich sheep farmer landowners and worked for them, then I met someone and the rest is history."

"Did you have children?" asked Laura.

Marietta hesitated. "No, sadly not. I think my body and mind have never recovered, and in some ways, I wouldn't want them to ever go through what we had to go through!"

"I understand," said Laura, putting her arm around her.

Euthymia was quiet this entire time.

"Did anyone else work with the British who might still be alive?" quizzed Laura.

"The communists did, of course. There were stories I heard of the partisans from ELAS turning on the British. One of the British officers being shot; I am not sure what happened to the other allies. They were not all British. Some were Australian or from New Zealand.

"There was a sweet girl called Daisy who had joined ELAS. I remember talking to her when she came to the house to ask for a food contribution for her and her comrades. She wasn't pushy; it didn't seem like she had her heart in it. But then when she began speaking, after I had asked where she was from, she said she was from near Athens. She was Jewish.

"Her father's shop had been closed down by the Germans and they feared being taken away. Daisy went to search for some food. When she returned, her family were traumatised, the door open and damaged.

The Gestapo had paid a visit and taken a number of Jews away from the area that day. I feel upset thinking about it. She kissed her family good night and then during darkness left, leaving a note saying she was going to try and fight back against these invaders.

"I felt she was too kind and good-looking to be a partisan. She came with the ELAS guerrillas and I am sure helped turn the heads of a couple of young villagers who left our community with the ELAS fighters, in fact, because they were betrayed by neighbours fearing for their own safety. Maria Savlakis and her brother Dionysis had their family's house targeted and burned by the Germans. Their family were on the street. Most partisans eventually seemed to disappear, some crossing the border into neighbouring countries like Albania. Later, they were in Russia. Some were captured in Greece and sent for reprogramming in one of the prisons or on those dreadful island camps like Makronissos. There was no escape from there or Trikeri. From 1947, Trikeri was used as a concentration camp for female anti-fascist political prisoners during the Greek Civil War. Maria and Daisy could have ended up there, unless they were killed. The women and children here were relatives of members of the EAM-ELAS, the resistance forces that had fought against fascist occupation during World War Two."

"I think you are getting tired now," said Euthymia to her great-aunt.

Marietta nodded and said, "Time for my siesta. Thank you for coming to see me."

Euthymia added, "She said she is sorry she knows

little more and says you might want to speak to my brother. He is helping someone write a book on the history of Kalavryta."

Marietta continued to ramble. "I wonder whatever happened to Maria and her brother, I liked them a lot. Their mother was devastated. She lost her fifteen-year-old son and her husband when the Germans murdered them and lost her other two children to the guerrillas. She had no home; she was a broken woman with nothing to live for."

Laura thanked them both and kissed Marietta's hand before starting to leave with Euthymia.

"I can run you back to Akrata in a short while if that would be helpful. Just let me settle my great-aunt."

"That would be great. I need to take a walk, get some air, back in twenty minutes. Is that long enough?"

"Perfect," thanked Euthymia.

Just as they were leaving, Marietta shouted to them and they returned to see her standing in the lounge, her hand steadying her by the armchair. "Maria and Dionysis had an aunty who lived in Kerpini, not far from Kalavryta, but I am not sure if she is still alive. It is only a small mountain village, over 1,000 metres above sea level. Perhaps she knows more." Once again, Laura thanked Marietta.

Laura strolled down to the small unspectacular beach of pebbles and sat on an upturned boat that was likely used for fishing.

Looking out over the idyllic gulf, she wondered how this beautiful land could have been so blighted by so much horror and pain!

Twenty

War and civil war

Laura had not learned much, other than experiencing the joy of hearing her grandfather's name. Nevertheless, she felt it was a piece of the jigsaw she had found, which she now placed into the large hole in the middle, just needing the connecting pieces to form the full picture; aware she may never have the entire picture, only the faded memory box to store it away in.

Euthymia had kindly brought her back to her accommodation and the next day invited her to the family taverna for a drink and a chat with her brother, who, as it was Saturday, was home for the weekend.

At 11am the next day, Laura strolled into the town. Eventually crossing the river, she dropped down to the narrow road that skirted the beach and ambled in the autumn sunshine, which bathed her in warmth and relaxed her as she reflected on the journey she was on. *Who would have guessed?* she thought to herself. *Here I am searching for the grave of a grandfather a year ago I never knew existed.* The gentle lapping of the sea was soothing as she soon arrived at Nikos' taverna, idyllically set and straddling the small access road that ran the length of the beach of Akrata. One side the vine-covered pillars of the main building and outside terrace, on the beach an extension of the business, all with blue and white striped seat covers in a nod to beach life and the Greek flag.

"Laura, we are over here," came the now familiar voice of Euthymia.

"*Kalimera*," greeted Laura.

"Good morning," nodded Euthymia. "This is my brother, Aris, and my father, Nikos."

"It is so good to meet you all, and thank you for seeing me to hopefully help with my quest in the search for my grandfather," said Laura, seating herself at the table.

"Our pleasure," said Aris, in perfectly good English.

Introductions complete, Nikos departed to get them some drinks and Aris opened a satchel, placing a ring-binder file onto the table, clearing the cutlery and glasses to one side.

"I hear you are helping someone write a book about the terrible wartime atrocities at Kalavryta," said Laura, keen to get started.

Aris nodded and added, "Actually, I have written a thesis on the terrible massacres that took place in Greece during World War Two and also during the civil war, which was sometimes even more harrowing. The story also follows those imprisoned by the government and who were interned for years after the conflict was officially over. It is this information I am helping another local man with, as he wants to write a book as a personal story of his family, who were affected by the Kalavryta massacre."

Laura listened, fascinated once more. She was on a daily history lesson and improving her knowledge and understanding no end.

Laura commented, "I had no idea Greeks were imprisoned by other Greeks. I have a lot to learn."

"Sadly, that was the case. Terrible atrocities and bad treatment took place, especially against the communist women in captivity. I could tell you some dreadful stories. But for now, let's concentrate on what you would like to know."

"Thank you," said Laura, doe-eyed for the handsome chestnut-haired Aris, his open white cotton shirt sporting a firm chest and his brown eyes so soft and beguiling.

Before they went further, Nikos arrived with a jug of white wine, a dish of salad and a plate of sardines topped with sea salt.

"Wow, they look fabulous. Were the camps near here?" said Laura, referring back to the civil war incarcerations.

"There were a number of prisons used throughout Greece and also on other islands, but the worst was surely Makronisos in the Aegean Sea, as it was an island and prison from 1940 to as late as the 1970s.

Makronisos was used as a military prison island and concentration camp during the Greek Civil War, until the so-called 'Regime of the Colonels' was over in 1974. It has been kept as a memorial of the civil war. The island and the buildings on it are protected by law. People were sent to Makronisos for 'reprogramming'."

"Makes them sound like robots. Have you been there, Aris?" queried Laura.

"I have, Laura. I took my father, as his grandfather had friends imprisoned there. It was strange. There were only around five people on the whole island, just taking care of the buildings."

Laura's mind started whirring. Was Nikos' father an old communist? Was he with ELAS perhaps, or EAM? All these acronyms were becoming confusing for her; it was difficult to figure out who supported who.

Nikos returned with a tray of fried calamari rings, mussels, marinated anchovies, mullet, shrimps and Greek salad with feta. The three of them all tucked in, chatting generally about life and places they would like to travel to. Aris and Euthymia both said they would love to visit the UK.

Laura was more than full. Still, Nikos returned with yet another tray, this time dessert of *baklava*, coffee and a small flagon of a regional brandy, called *tsipouro*.

Nikos sat down with them this time.

"Thank you so much, Nikos. This food is fabulous," said a rather bloated Laura. "I have not eaten so much good food in a long time," and gesturing towards the sea with her left arm, she said, "and what a view too. Perfect!"

"You are welcome," said Nikos as he poured a small tumbler of *tsipouro* for them all.

"*Yamas*," he toasted, and they all joined in.

Laura started to splutter and cough a little as she imbibed; they all laughed.

"Are you okay, Laura? You took a big gulp. I should have said. *Tsipouro* has about forty-five per cent alcohol, so pretty strong," said Nikos, smirking.

Regaining her composure and sipping on a glass of water, Laura said, "Now you tell me! Nikos, we are talking about the Greek Civil War and before, around the time that my grandfather was here and went missing. I suppose you were very young then."

"Indeed, I was. I cannot remember much. Was Marietta able to help you?"

"Amazingly, she did remember my grandfather being in Kalavryta but not much more. She said he seemed to disappear. She did recall the Savlakis children, Maria and Dionysis, joining ELAS, and also a young Jewish girl called Daisy."

"Perhaps Maria may be able to help you. She was still alive the last I heard," Nikos commented, smiling nonchalantly.

Laura looked at him. "Could she still be alive?"

Nikos nodded. "I hear she couldn't face coming back to Kalavryta for a number of reasons, not least the memory of her family, all of which were now dead. Can I get anyone anything else? Now I have to go and see a friend. Nice meeting you, Laura." With that, he made a rapid departure.

"Euthymia, do you remember Marietta mentioned

yesterday that Maria and Dionysis had an aunty in Kerpini?"

"Yes! I do."

"I wonder if Maria and her brother are still alive and living in Kerpini with their aunty possibly. Perhaps she recalls my grandfather and might know something."

Aris looked at Laura and said, "I could take you with me tomorrow if that helps. I planned to go and drop some information to the author I am helping. He still lives in Kalavryta. We could start early and go to Kerpini just to put your mind at rest, and I can deliver my notes on the way back."

Twenty-One

The mountains hold secrets

The next morning was like déjà vu, as Aris picked Laura up at 8am and they soon ascended the winding roads to over 1,000 metres into the mountains.

The air was clear and cold; Laura could make out some snow on a distant mountaintop. Before long, they were passing through Kalavryta and she gave a thought to Antonio and Aghiri and then to the many lost souls from the massacre she had learned about. They arrived into Kerpini very shortly afterwards.

Kerpini was a small village nestled on the mountainside about 5 kilometres above Kalavryta, mostly red-roofed houses but some properties seemed to be unoccupied. *Perhaps holiday properties*, thought Laura. A dwindling population of around 170 people, it was a sleepy settlement where nothing much happened.

Pulling into the small square, they parked up and Laura followed Aris to a small taverna-cum-*kafenion*, dappled under the shade of plane trees in the bright but weak morning sunshine. The tonic of the normally heat-producing sunrays, whilst pleasant, barely warmed the body, and it felt so much cooler here at the altitude of 1,080m they had reached in the mountains. Laura thought of how cool and overcast it could be on the 1,000m plus Munros back in Scotland and felt blessed and thankful for the Greek morning light brightening her day.

A few old men sat drinking their coffee and chatting away in Greek, of course. Clothed in jackets and trousers with warm sweaters on, they took a cursory glance at the incomers and then went back to their conversation. As they sat down at a table bordering the square, an older woman came out to serve them. "Two coffees, please," said Aris.

"This is so kind of you, Aris. I find this part of the world so wonderful and the people so friendly. I really did not know what to expect. But it is also clear to me there is still a lot of sadness from the past."

"Once they get used to you, people are welcoming, more so here than in the cities and even towns like Akrata. Perhaps it is the same in Britain," suggested Aris. Laura nodded.

The coffees arrived. "*Efharisto*," thanked Laura, practising her limited Greek language repertoire.

Her host nodded and smiled.

"Do you know if Maria Savlakis or her aunty still lives here in Kerpini?" said Aris, questioning the lady who it appeared was the patron.

Collecting some used coffee cups and plates from a neighbouring table, she replied, "Since I can remember, Maria has lived here. They sometimes come down to the café in the evenings."

"Can you tell me whereabouts the house is?"

Laura was so pleased to hear the news as Aris translated. "So, she said they are just up the road out of the village."

"She said they. Is she married, do you think, or is it her brother, Dionysis, or her aunty?" speculated Laura.

"Perhaps her brother survived the war and is still living with her, maybe her aunty, but she would be quite old," said Aris with a shrug.

Finishing their coffees, they took a stroll up a couple of narrow streets to the edge of the village, before reaching their destination. A traditional stone house, built in the 19th century, Aris guessed, as they opened a side gate into a large yard with a covered oven, and beyond, a vegetable garden came into view; nearby an old threshing floor and stone hut. Laura was stunned by the panoramic views of the surrounding olive tree-dotted hills.

"*Boró na se voithíso*? Can I help you?" came an indignant voice from the rear of the characterful old house.

Slightly startled and a little embarrassed, both turned towards an older lady, perhaps in her mid to late sixties. It appeared they had interrupted her efforts to brush up some fallen leaves, as she stood before them holding a traditional Greek broom. As they came closer, her stunning dark ebony eyes fixed on them.

"Hello, I am Aris, and this is a friend of mine from Scotland, the United Kingdom, that is. Do we have the right house? We are looking for Maria Savlakis."

Cautiously, the lady set aside her broom, wiping her hands on a pinafore. She approached them. "What do you want with Maria?"

"I am doing some research regarding World War Two, and Laura is on, shall we say, a pilgrimage," said Aris, looking at Laura then back at Maria. "Laura has come to see where her grandfather was during World War Two, and whilst she may never find his resting place, she is just seeking as much information as possible to fill in the blanks."

Lapsing into very good English, she said, "Welcome, Laura. Welcome, Aris. Perhaps you should come in."

"Your English is very good," said Laura.

Maria smiled.

"It's a long story but a Marietta Papadopoulos mentioned your aunt used to live in Kerpini."

"Then my father said he had heard you were still alive and that you lived in Kerpini," interjected Aris.

"I see. I did not know I was so famous," said Maria sarcastically whilst raising her eyebrows, her mouth developing a slight grin.

Crossing over the threshold of the well-kept but basic traditional home, they followed Maria, stepping down into a surprisingly sparse and stark interior which presented an open room with a kitchen space just off to the left, various drying herbs and garlic bulbs hanging from the ceiling. A small doorway then led further into the interior of the house.

Maria closed the door. "I will make some coffee." She nodded towards the seating and disappeared back into the kitchen. Whitewashed stucco walls gave way to low dark wood-beamed ceilings. The colour, with bright blue shutters and doors, seemed at odds with the rest of the décor. A goatskin rug softened a waxed hardwood floor. An armchair that had seen better days and a very comfortable but old settee were set around a hearth, which bore large pots and pans hanging over the fireplace.

Maria returned with the coffee and some local pastries.

"Oh! Those look delicious. Did you make them?" said Laura. Maria smiled and nodded in acknowledgement.

As they settled themselves on the settee, Maria perched upon a wooden stool from which she proceeded to organise pouring the coffee.

Wondering how to approach it, Laura bucked up the courage to ask.

"Is your brother here with you?"

Forlornly, Maria kept pouring without looking up. "Sadly, he passed away a long time ago."

"Oh! I am sorry to hear that, Maria. It's just the lady in the taverna said you came down to the taverna occasionally to eat, and I was under the impression there were two of you. I thought it might be your brother."

"No! That will be me," said a voice from the small doorway, now completely blocked with the figure of an elderly man, stooping slightly, his grey hair thinning;

a small moustache, well-groomed on his tanned and weathered face.

Their guests looked suitably shocked as he joined them.

"I believe I detect a hint of a Scottish accent," he said.

"W... w... well, yes," said Laura, stuttering slightly. "Have you ever been there?" she asked, her mind somersaulting with perplexity.

"Yes, many years ago. I suspect it has changed."

"I am Laura and this is Aris, a friend from Akrata I have recently met."

"Very good to meet you both. It is so lovely to meet someone from the old country. We do not get many tourists in Kerpini. They sometimes come as far as Kalavryta for the skiing, or just visiting."

Taken aback, Laura looked at the rather good-looking gentleman; a quizzical frown gave her whirring mind away.

"You said the old country?" said Laura, inviting a response.

"Indeed! I have not been back in many years. Sorry, I didn't introduce myself. I am Dennis, as in the Greek god of wine. Pleased to meet you!" Laura's hand quivered in his and she became pale.

"My word! You look as if you have seen a ghost!" said Dennis.

"Let me get you some water," said Maria, somewhat perturbed herself.

"Are you okay now, dear?" said Dennis, crouching towards Laura, who was sipping the water.

"Yes! Yes, it is just, well, I know it might be…" Trembling, she couldn't finish her sentence.

She blurted out, "My grandfather's name, I believe, was Dennis Greaves."

"That is astonishing," said Dennis, settling himself in the armchair opposite Laura. "That happens to be my name, but I must have a doppelgänger when it comes to names because I have no children."

For over an hour, Laura proceeded to tell her story. Dennis sat open-mouthed. When she had finished, he stood wearily and put his hand on her shoulder. She looked up at him, her tear-filled eyes mirroring his. He pulled her up gently and hugged her, then kissed her on top of the head.

Then he left the room, returning a few minutes later with a rather creased and well-worn black-and-white photograph of a couple in which it appeared they were having a picnic. Laura recognised her grandmother kneeling behind Dennis, who was lying in front of her, his head resting on one arm. Both in uniform, looking very happy, they smiled at the camera as if they did not have a care in the world.

He looked at Laura, his heart breaking, his eyes full of compassion. "I never knew any of this. This was the last time we had a photograph together. I have treasured it all these years.

"I did meet Martha once more by chance in Fort William, at a cinema, would you believe? I could not believe my eyes. She was with a small group of military personnel, a couple of Frenchmen and two other F.A.N.Y.'s, but that is a story for another time."

Laura nodded and knelt by his chair and held his hand. A teardrop tracked down his cheek as he continued to look at the moment captured on film. Maria and Aris looked at one another, both realising the significance of the moment.

Maria said nothing; Aris was just as transfixed.

"You must stay and have dinner with us this evening," Maria finally interjected.

Over a wonderful lamb dinner and with red wine flowing freely, they shared their memories, aspirations and thanks for this day to have come!

As the evening progressed, Laura asked, "It might be a silly question, but why did you not come back to the UK, or even tell the authorities you were alive?"

Dennis looked at the wine glass in his right hand. He twisted it around and around then looking up, he said, "Laura, I cannot explain what a brutal time it was. I had been attached to the Royal Engineers when I met Martha and until now I had no idea she was in the S.O.E. or attached to any of those secret organisations like the OSS or RF, such was the secrecy in war. As fate had it, I too was selected for S.O.E. Balkans operations and did training for that very purpose, in my case to enter Greece. When I was in Cairo, I was sent to Mount Carmel and then did parachute training at a place called Kabrit.

"In October 1943, I was parachuted into occupied Greece as a British liaison officer – BLO – with S.O.E. Middle East, known as Force 133. My mission was to make contact with the local *andartes*, the partisans, and arrange to receive arms supplies for the Greek resistance in the Peloponnese, with a view to helping them stage sabotage and harass the Germans as often as we could.

"It was during this time that myself and my fellow officers and other ranks were caught up in a big German operation which led to the massacre of hundreds of men and boys in the Greek village of Kalavryta on the 13th of December 1943, just down the road from here; as you know all about now.

"It all came about because communist ELAS partisans captured eighty-one German soldiers from the 117th Jaeger Division near Kalavryta. The Germans were ambushed near to this village, Kerpini, and Rogoi. A small number of Germans were killed. Three were taken to hospital at Kalavryta but were later attacked and bludgeoned to death by the partisans, *andartes,* call them what you will. The other Germans who had surrendered were kept as prisoners of war until a fateful decision to kill them. Many were shot and some thrown over a cliff, they say from the impact of the shots. But one or two survived and got back to German lines.

"The Germans reacted as they always did. By the 8th of December, they were in full revenge mode. Our informants told us an operation was underway and we in turn warned people we had got to know, Greek friends that is, to leave Kalavryta and take to the hills, the caves, anywhere, as we knew and most knew that there would be reprisals.

"On the fateful day, the 13th of December 1943, we were miles away, having been pursued by the Krauts ourselves. We were hungry, thirsty and surrounded. We could have done nothing even if we knew. We could actually hear the shooting echoing across the mountainside and witnessed bombers attacking other villages. The Germans were naturally incensed and determined to teach people a lesson. The trouble was, they were all innocent.

"You have already heard of the carnage and devastation they left.

"When we could, we made our way back through Kalavryta and I was one of the first British officers on the scene. We tried to do what we could but we had little to help them with. They needed shelter and food but so did we – we were constantly on the move. We did get a message to the Red Cross. We radioed for relief supplies of tents and food to be dropped as soon as possible and of course reported the dreadful massacre. Drops took priority over continued arms supplies. It was winter and bitterly cold. Remember, it was snowing on the higher ground.

"The first thing I remember as we stealthily approached the small town to make sure no Germans were still lingering was the wailing of the women. The sound was awful, the pain almost audible, the loss and fear still palpable.

"I have rarely been back to Kalavryta, not even to Mass on the 13th of December each year. Maria has, of course. After all, her family are on the memorial on Kapi Hill."

"More wine?" said Maria, emptying one bottle and starting another.

"Where were you at this time?" said Aris to Maria.

Maria sat and looked at the wall beyond. "I was young myself, as was my brother, Dionysis. We were always moving to avoid the Germans. Occasionally, I was sent into villages, as I was young and female and not as likely to arouse suspicion. My job was to find information and collect any food I could. I dressed as a villager might, of course. I was heartbroken by the deaths in my family and of friends. I truly questioned what I was doing and feared, like many have since blamed us, that it was our fault this retribution took place, but if it hadn't been us, it would have been other *andarte* bands. We loathed the Germans and this was war."

Laura could see the pain in Maria's eyes. She wondered how such a young lady coped with this way of life, when all she had to concern herself with in her teens was what she was going to wear and when she would go out with her friends.

"So how did you both end up together here?" said Laura.

Dennis looked at Maria with such fondness and love.

"Maria saved my life.

"A month or so later, maybe longer, myself and a small group of other allied soldiers who had been infiltrated recently, a couple of Kiwis amongst them actually, were once more trying to evade a pursuing German unit and we bumped into a rather rough band of Greek communist guerrillas and, much to our surprise, we were duly arrested by them. We constantly seemed to be at loggerheads with partisan groups, even though we were helping them. We were abused occasionally before being released; they figured, and rightly so it proved, we would eventually side with a Nationalist government. ELAS were happy to take British arms supplies, but their ideological guidance pointed towards Soviet Russia. Churchill felt ELAS planned to survive the German occupation then take over power in Greece and make it a communist state.

"On this occasion, we were approaching a mountain village. We had a couple of mules carrying our supplies. The communists' excuse was they didn't think we were who we said we were. They accused us of being spies instead of British officers. We were relieved of our weapons and kept in a village house, but fed and not badly treated, then one day, Bill Mackillop, one of the Kiwis, went out to remonstrate with them. He had just about reached his limit of tolerance. He was joined by his pal Jim Balfour. We just laughed at first, as we knew Bill had a bit of a temper, then we heard gunshots. We all raced outside and Bill and Jim were dead. We tried to talk to them but I got hit round the head by a rifle butt and that was all I remembered until I awoke in a locked room a while later on my own.

"Each day, a young attractive *andartes* girl came in and put a tray of food by my bed. She would bathe my head wound and re-bandage it. Then after about four or five days, she left a message under the bowl containing the small meal. It said after she had collected the empty bowl and cup that evening, I was to listen out for the sound of a bird call, like a pigeon or dove. I was to lower myself out of the shuttered window but to be careful, as I was on the second floor, and to be as quiet as possible. She would be waiting for me.

"I mulled this over all day. I wondered if it was a test, a trap, but I had built a rapport with this girl and she seemed sympathetic to my plight. I decided to gamble. I did not know her motives. I was feeling a little stronger and feared the alternative might be execution.

"Sure enough, after what seemed an age, I heard the distinct sound of a bird cooing.

"I doused the small lamp in the room and opened the shutter. I could barely see a thing. It was a perfect night, very cloudy, and a cold icy wind was getting up. I straddled the windowsill and lowered myself by my fingertips before taking the risk to drop into the unknown. I landed with a jolt and fell backwards, but I was still intact. As I looked around, the small frame of my saviour came towards me. Pulling my arm, she said, 'Follow me.'

"Quietly, we moved slowly towards the back of the village and up the mountainside. I took the knapsack off her back and followed her as fast as I could. She was fleet of foot and obviously knew the mountains well. We walked for hours, following the stony ground, then rested in the lea of a large stone. We could see some light and the odd campfire in the village way below. It was bitterly cold.

"I looked at her and said, 'Thank you so much for helping me escape. I am sorry, I do not even know your name.'

"'Maria, Maria Savlakis.'

"'Well, thank you, Maria Savlakis. So, what now?' I said I had no way of contacting anyone for assistance, of course. Our radio and everything had been confiscated by the guerrillas.

"'We keep walking,' said Maria. 'We have a long journey and we need to be as far away as possible from these people before they realise you have gone. They will soon work out I have gone too.'

"We slept in caves. We ate the meagre rations of bread and smoked meat and were soon melting snow on the high ground to have water to drink. In the caves, we huddled together to keep warm. It seemed to take forever, but we eventually reached Kerpini, and this house. This was at the time the home of sympathisers to the nationalist cause.

"We stayed here, hidden for months, then when the Germans left in due course, Athens was liberated. The Germans had hightailed it out of Greece for fear of being cut off by the Russians. We were at last able to wander out.

"But the real threat was still the communists and with ELAS we naturally feared terrible reprisals. Maria went down into Kalavryta, to see if it was perhaps better for us to be in a bigger town than a small village, but it was clear wherever we were the communist influence was taking full hold and civil war was on the horizon. She made contact with her aunt."

Aris, who like Laura had been listening patiently and intrigued, commented, "What were you to do? Did you ever think you and Maria could contact the British and be spirited away from here?"

"Indeed, Aris, a very astute observation, but I also feared I might be treated as having gone absent without leave and court-martialled. However, by now, I had fallen in love with Maria, so what was I to do?"

Laura pondered her next comment. Hesitating, she felt compelled to continue and she had to ask. "But you were still married to Victoria?"

"Yes! I was and I suppose I still am, but somehow it didn't seem right to go back to a world I felt I had left behind a year or more before, which frankly felt like decades, another life entirely. I truly wanted to help rebuild the communities here and with Maria I really was in love.

"Don't get me wrong. I feel a bounder as far as Vicky is concerned but, I don't know, I just feel it was all so quick and, well, if I am honest, Vicky and I were not so much in love as living in the moment. The marriage proposal was impulsive. Who knew if tomorrow would ever come? I know it's not good enough as an excuse, but Maria and myself felt a bond, a chemistry, and indeed it's still very real today, a true love." He looked at Maria.

Maria stood and put her arm around the still-seated Dennis.

Maria added, "We had to be careful here. Dennis took on the name Dionysis, my brother's name, which ironically is Greek for Dennis, so fate conspired, and he, to all intents and purposes, was my distant cousin who had come to see my family, having lost his own in the war, as far as others were concerned. His Greek had become more local and he could just about get away with it, especially if he didn't talk too much." She laughed. "My most abiding fear was that the ELAS guerrilla band who abducted Dennis would turn up and seek retribution against us both. You could never really trust anyone. Rumours spread quickly."

Dennis smiled. "Very true, my Greek was rather classical Greek to start with, as I had studied Greek at school in Shrewsbury and at university."

"In one of the purges by ELAS, they ransacked homes and stole provisions, as they were being pressed more and more by Nationalist forces, backed first by the British and then the Americans. The Kavalides family were hounded out of here, their animals taken, and the house became overgrown and ramshackle.

"Dennis and myself had moved to Athens. We decided we were best hiding in plain sight, and Dennis was able to somehow get us through by using his British know-how and an assumed name. As soon as we could, we returned to Kerpini to find the house abandoned, so we set up home here. I contacted my aunt, who was now on her own, and she came to live with us, which was perfect cover. We kept a low profile as guests and to all intents and purposes, it was her home now."

"I take it your aunt has passed away," said Aris.

"Yes, she never really recovered from the trauma of the massacre and she died in the sixties, leaving us to live our lives alone here."

It had become late. "You must stay the night with us. I will make up a bed for you, Laura, and perhaps, Aris, would you mind sleeping on the settee?"

Aris nodded. Saying their good nights, they all retired, all with so much going around their heads.

Twenty-Two

A few home truths

Laura had barely slept when she saw the first light of dawn creeping through the window. She stood, walked to the window and saw Dennis sitting on the terrace, smoking a cigarette and sipping a coffee.

"May I join you?"

"Good morning, Laura! So good to see you bright and early, I trust you slept well."

Laura smiled.

"Did you love my grandmother?" said Laura straight out.

"More than anything in the world," said Dennis without hesitation. "From the first moment I met her. Did you know I had met her before Vicky's party at Ludford Grange?"

"No!" said Laura, rather surprised.

"It was a chance encounter, but she stole my heart instantly. It was just fortuitous we met at Major Atkinson's soirée. I guess in some ways it was always going to be difficult to follow Maria, and Vicky never really stood a chance. I do regret the way I have treated Vicky, Laura. I am so sorry; I am coming over as a cad. How is Vicky? We never really got to talk about her."

"She is fine, on her own now."

"Did she remarry?"

"Do you know, I haven't a clue. We spoke about you most of the time. I felt she had remarried and perhaps been divorced or widowed, but I really don't know, so you are off the hook, I guess, if she did."

Dennis felt the barb.

"She does drink a lot, and it seems as though she never found what she was looking for after you never returned." Laura regretted her comment almost immediately.

Dennis nodded, a little melancholy and guilty in equal measure as he surveyed the hills, which sported a slight sugar coating of snow from the previous night. Winter was approaching.

Laura had become extremely protective of Martha and questioned with vigour. "Tell me about when you first met Martha."

Dennis took a deep suck on his cigarette and exhaled, putting the cigarette out in the ashtray, and took a sip of his coffee. The morning sun, as cool as it was, seemed to illuminate him like an aura.

"That morning in Shrewsbury, I remember vividly feeling the chill of the cold lodgings I was in as I washed and shaved. The dampness on the inside of the latticed windows gave me advance warning what the light frost on the ground confirmed, as I went out pulling up my greatcoat collar against the cold autumnal November morning that greeted me. I remember distinctly pulling the heavy door closed and, small brown leather case in hand, surveying the bright blue sky above which was tinged with red. 'Red sky in the morning, shepherd's warning,'" quipped Dennis.

"I had headed down Swan Hill towards the market square. I had enjoyed catching up with an old friend and some of my old masters at Shrewsbury School. I tightened the muffler around my neck to protect against the chill morning breeze and quickened my pace. Skipping up the steps into Sidoli's, opposite the west end of the old market hall, I was relieved to get into Sidoli's café, my eyes watering as the warmth and cacophony of sound of people chatting over morning coffee greeted me. I recall one or two looked up, more disconcerted by the blast of cold morning air as the door opened and closed, before returning to their conversations. Funny what you remember, isn't it?"

Without waiting for a reply, Dennis continued. "I placed my coat, scarf and homburg hat on the coat stand and looked forward to one of the frothy Italian coffees which were a rarity in provincial rural Britain. The steamed-up windows of the café were somewhat comforting now I was on the right side of them.

"The Italian chap – or at least I presumed he was Italian – asked me to repeat my order three times at the counter, as the first efforts had been drowned by the hum of conversation from the very busy café behind me.

"I then recollect putting down my small brown suitcase as I fished in the pocket of my tweed jacket for some change to pay. Something comforting about the smell of coffee and the steaming sound of the coffee machine, don't you think? Anyway, I turned to locate a seat in the busy café. All tables seemed to be taken, then I spied a lady wearing a wide-brimmed blue felt hat who appeared not to notice me as I approached the table. She was totally absorbed by the book she was reading.

"'Excuse me, may I join you?'

"Slowly raising her head, she inclined it and shrugged her shoulders simultaneously, smiling in the affirmative.

"I have to say, I was immediately smitten by the attractive auburn-haired lady who had returned to concentrating on her reading material by now.

"I could not help but stare at the elegant long neck and narrow shoulders, whilst trying to pretend to look beyond her. She looked up at me and frowned. I suspect she sensed my attention.

"She said, 'Yes, can I help you?'

"But all I could say was, 'It's a fine cold morning.'

"She smiled, took a sip of her coffee without losing eye contact and gently returned the cup to the saucer. Her generous lips and blue eyes just like yours. Beguiled, I felt hypnotised.

"I was grasping for any line of conversation, Laura. I had noted she was reading *The Power and the Glory* by Graham Greene. I lamely said, 'Is it a good book?'

"'Yes!' was the rather curt and simple reply.

"'Excuse me for saying, but do I sense a slight accent? Is it Italian?'

"She said, raising her eyebrows, 'No, but close geographically. I thought I was losing my accent but obviously not. It is Austrian actually.'

"'You speak very good English. Where did you learn it?' I countered, trying to make her more at ease and pay a compliment.

"'Thank you, I learned at the Schwarzwald'sche school, a school in Vienna where Maria Montessori's methods and other new education helped me greatly, and since I have been developing my skills within my work and local community,' came the reply.

"'What do you do?' said I, blunt as ever.

The young lady frowned. 'I get the feeling I am being interrogated,' she said with a smirk.

"'I am so sorry, how rude I was, just curious, you know, making polite conversation.'

"'Do you live in Shrewsbury?' she asked me, putting her book down now.

I was intrigued by her accented pronunciation.

"'Ah no, I am just visiting an old friend and some masters from my old school, Shrewsbury School,' which the young lady noted conflicted with her pronunciation of the county town. I added, 'I used to go to school here. I was born in the neighbouring county of Herefordshire but spent most of my youth in Kent in the south of England.'

"'Really, Kent? I visited there once, as the school I work at was originally sited there before being transferred to Shropshire because of the war requisition of the building called 'Bunce Court'.

"'What a coincidence. I know it, it's not far from my grandparents' home. It is an old 16th-century manor if I am not mistaken. I am so sorry I have not introduced myself. Dennis, Dennis Greaves,' I said, leaning over, proffering my hand.

"Taking my hand, she replied in a teasing manner, 'Martha Swanson. I take it that is just one Dennis, not two.'

"'Well, very pleased to meet you, Miss Swanson,' liking her sense of humour.

"She looked at her watch and abruptly closed her book, tucked it into her handbag and stood.

"'Good morning, very pleased to meet you too. I am sorry I must leave. I have a train to catch or I will be in trouble.' She turned a few male and female heads as she elegantly weaved her tall, slender figure between the tables and made for the coat stand.

"Following her, I just made it to her to assist her putting on her close-fitted coat before she fastened the buttons over the chartreuse green cinched waist dress which accentuated her modest bust. She nodded to thank me, donned her black gloves over her delicate porcelain hands and draped a silk scarf around her neck before pulling at the wide lapels to settle her coat on her slight frame. I could not help but notice her shiny patent Mary Jane shoes and thought she seemed far too elegant for Shrewsbury, a small market town in the backwaters of rural England.

"I remember wiping the condensation from the

window and watching as she stepped down into the square, the weak but bright autumn sun making me squint as I watched her progress towards the Penfold post box. She stopped momentarily at the top of Gullet Passage, looked back at the café and smiled before disappearing from sight.

"The waiter was bemused as he stood at the empty table with my coffee in hand and watched as I returned for my suitcase before hastily grabbing my coat, hat and scarf and braving the morning chill in pursuit of the mysterious lady. My Martha.

"That was the first and I thought the last time I might see her, although I had learned where she was working temporarily.

"Next time I saw her was Ludford Grange. There, a good friend of mine, Harry Ree, monopolised her and I was distracted by Major Atkinson and his wife, a few others and of course Vicky, who, if I am honest, I didn't really register too much, as she was a little younger than me."

"Like me," said Maria, appearing behind Dennis, basket in arm.

"Yes, dear, like you but not as beautiful as you, of course," he said, patting her on the hip.

Maria sneered in fun and walked down the steps to go and feed the pigs, chickens and goats.

"I know I do not deserve it, but I have been blessed with the ladies in my life," said Dennis.

"So, when did you see Martha again?"

"Ludford Grange, at the party, of course, but Harry Ree rather dominated her attention and Victoria mine, although I could not help but keep glancing at her from the corner of my eye.

"Well, knowing what I know now, I should have worked it out, as I next saw her in London. Purely by chance we met at Lyons Corner Café at Marble Arch. Reacquainted, we were amazed at the coincidence and I asked her out for a date. We had a wonderful couple of weeks together and then it was she that had gone. I am presuming now she was undergoing training with the S.O.E. She had a splendid uniform on, the First Aid Nursing Yeomanry, like a barathea material with maroon buttons, much smarter than the old WAAF and ATS rough cloth uniforms. It suited her and I figured she was a driver for an officer or something. I don't think I ever asked; we were too consumed by one another. Time was too short to wonder really.

"The rest is history, Laura."

Aris shuffled out onto the terrace, a little bleary-eyed, running his hands through his curly black hair and stretching, before lighting himself a cigarette. He offered one to Dennis, who declined.

"Was the settee a little hard?" laughed Laura.

Aris chuckled. "More a little short," he said, bending his knees and stretching his almost 6 feet-tall frame.

Maria returned to the terrace, smiling at the state of Aris. "Perhaps the red wine and *retsina* had something to do with it," raising her eyebrows to accentuate the probability.

Laura said, "No one go anywhere. I will be back in a minute."

Returning with her handbag, she extracted a small

instamatic camera and said, "We really must have a photograph. I want to show proof to my mam – your daughter, Granddad," nodding at him.

She took a couple of snaps as Dennis, still seated, put his arm around Maria's waist and pulled her towards him, cigarette in his left hand. He smiled the smile of a contented man. She clicked off a couple of shots of Aris too, not looking his best, but his smile lit up her morning.

"You must be in these pictures," said Aris.

Dennis put out his cigarette, stood and pulled Laura close to his other hip, and the generations were connected; Maria one side and Laura the other.

"I now have another pretty lady in my life," he said, teasing Laura, and smiled at that moment Laura accepted him.

Laura was elated and sad all in one; so happy she had found her grandfather, amazed he was still alive, but also so sad for him too, that he never had the opportunity to know he had a daughter and to get to know her.

*

Maria stood in front of Dennis, who stood erect, straightening his tired aging frame, placing his hands upon Maria's shoulders. Laura wound her window down and looked at them, their peace now being restored after forty-eight hours of revelation and incredulity. She wondered if she would ever see her grandfather again.

Dennis' eyes watered. Laura felt something very deep and painful in that moment. Why didn't she get out and give him a hug? But she didn't.

Both waved goodbye as Aris and Laura headed down the hillside towards Kalavryta for a quick drop of the notes Aris had promised the author, then back to Akrata.

In the short time Laura had left, no plan had been made to see her grandfather again. *Perhaps that is just as well*, thought Laura.

As they drove into Akrata, Aris said, "You have been very quiet all the way home."

"I have had a lot to think about, Aris."

"An amazing couple of days, for sure. Do you think you might return to see your grandfather?"

"We will certainly keep in touch. I think it depends on how my mother feels as to whether I return."

Aris nodded his understanding.

Dropping Laura off, he said, "When do you travel home?"

"In a couple of days. Time for a little sunbathing yet, ha ha!"

Aris smiled, understanding the sarcasm aimed at the cooler Greek weather which was impending.

"Perhaps I could take you for dinner tomorrow night on your last night, a sort of farewell."

"That would be lovely," said Laura without hesitation.

Laura entered her room. She lay on her bed, tired from the last few days' exertions and the emotional upheaval of discovery. It was stuffy in the room, so she put the ceiling fan on. As it whirred away, so did her mind. She began to re-evaluate her grandfather, grandmother, Vicky Greaves and indeed all those she had been privileged to meet. Wartime had been a torrid time where no one knew from one day to the next if they would survive. It was into this context that she realised relationships like Dennis with Martha, Vicky and Maria all had their place and were all with merit.

It was clear to her that Dennis really did have affection for all three ladies but felt more than anything that her grandmother was his real love. Why else would he keep the photograph all those years? His recollection of his first meeting felt like Laura was a fly on the wall; such was his recall of detail. Vicky, he asked about almost in passing, whereas Maria was the reason he had life and had survived.

Laura wondered what she might have done in all those circumstances, as she weighed up the complex web of relationships, all with one common denominator: her grandfather. She remembered his eyes and the feeling he exuded for Martha when telling of that first encounter. She smiled and drifted off into a whirlpool of dreamy bliss!

*

Her last evening came quickly. Aris collected her and they drove back to Akrata, but instead of a little taverna, he stopped in front of a block of apartments which overlooked the coast road and Akrata beach.

"I thought you were taking me out for dinner," said Laura.

"Well, actually, you have come out for dinner, but it is me that is cooking," he said as he came around and opened her door. Then he put out the crook of his arm and invited Laura to walk with him arm in arm up the stairs to his second-floor apartment.

It was a surprisingly spacious apartment, with a small kitchenette. Aris poured them both a glass of wine and as Laura sat on the couch and surveyed the room, Aris set to work making dinner.

"That was a wonderful meal. You really are a decent cook," complimented Laura.

"*Efharisto*, Laura, I am glad you enjoyed it. So, are you ready for home?"

"I am and I am not. I feel in many ways I am torn. So many emotions… finding my grandfather alive is truly wonderful, but I am still not quite sure how I feel. There are so many loose ends now."

"In what way?" said Aris, frowning and topping up Laura's wine glass.

"I now have to tell my mother that her father is still alive. How will she take it? I wonder. Will she want to see him, and what about Victoria? Do I tell her that Dennis, her husband, is still alive and has been living with a Greek lady for fifty years?"

"I see, you have a dilemma, Laura. As you share this information, you are affecting people's lives. I think you have to decide how this will make them feel. We have a Greek proverb, 'You must keep quiet or say only things that improve silence.'"

Leaving Laura cogitating on that somewhat profound thought, Aris rose from the table and placed an LP on the turntable. He took Laura's hand and brought her into an embrace as they slow-danced cheek to cheek to Nana Mouskouri's *White Rose of Athens*.

Laura did not resist as she laid her head on Aris' shoulder. Rhythmically, they slowly moved around the room, the warmth of their bodies and his tender touch felt comforting to her as the haunting melody washed over them.

"Til the white rose blooms again
You must leave me, leave me lonely
So goodbye my love 'til then
'Til the white rose blooms again
The cotton leaves are falling in the valley
And soon the winter snow will lie on the ground
But like the rose that comes back with the springtime
You will return to me when springtime comes around'

Twenty-Three

Traveller's tales

A few days later, Laura had returned to Arisaig House to recommence work. She had managed to get the photographs she had taken on her Greek odyssey express printed in Fort William and at the first opportunity drove to Comrie. She could not wait to share her experiences with her mother. She was tired but the adrenaline was coursing through her veins; partly excitement, partly trepidation.

"Well, this is a pleasant surprise. I thought you had run away to sea," said Elise, hugging Laura.

"How was Greece? I didn't even get a postcard from you," she said sarcastically.

"Sorry, Mam. I was so busy and discovered so much, I didn't get the chance to send one. Besides, I would probably have arrived home before any postcard I was to mail if the pace of Greek life is anything to go by!"

They settled around the kitchen table, that familiar meeting place of home comfort. Laura asked, "How have you been, Mam?" and then proceeded to present her mother with a bottle of *tsipouro* as she excitedly began sharing with her the astonishing events of her adventure into history.

Elise was saddened by the pain of the Kalavryta story, and pleased she had made new friends in Euthymia, Aris and their family, and so pleased Eleni and her husband had proved such good hosts.

"Did you find out anything about your grandfather and his fate?"

Fixing her mother with a smile, she replied, "I did, Mam." She took the wallets of photographs from her bag and opened the first folder. She showed Elise a few photographs of the beach and Kalavryta and especially the memorial and the clock tower of the cathedral, stopped at 2.34pm.

Then a photograph of Aris, and of her with a couple of older people.

"He is a very handsome boy, what does he do?" enquired Elise.

"He had been at university but helps with his family taverna business. He is a smart fellow, Mam."

"Are the couple with you his parents?"

Laura beamed. "No, Mam, prepare yourself for the most incredible revelations. You may find them incredulous, almost surreal."

Laura was bursting with excitement as she paused theatrically, her mother intrigued.

"We went to find a house in a small village called Kerpini, not that far from Kalavryta. We thought it belonged to an old lady related to a girl and boy we had learned about who used to live in this vicinity during the war. We were looking for them, thinking if they were still alive, they would now have been in their sixties. We hoped they might know something about Captain Dennis Greaves, your father. When we arrived, this lady greeted us and we found out this was the right house, but the older lady we sought had died, but amazingly this was her niece, the girl we were seeking."

"So, the older man is her brother?" guessed Elise.

Laura hesitated then replied, "No, Mam, this is your father, Captain Dennis Greaves."

Elise's eyes widened. Speechless, she went white then her face reddened as her tears flowed. She wiped her eyes with her handkerchief as she stared at the image with blurred vision. She tried to study the photograph as Laura put her arm around her.

"My father, this is my real father?" Elise trembled as she was overcome with emotion. It was difficult to assimilate this astonishing information; she could not quite comprehend what she was being told.

For a few moments, they both sat in quietness as Elise regained her composure, holding the photograph tightly.

"He is handsome," said Elise, breaking the silence.

"He certainly is, he is very philosophical about life, Mam. He wants you to know he knew nothing about you being born or that your mother was even pregnant with their baby."

Elise nodded as Laura proceeded to tell her the rest of his story, from the war right up to the modern day!

Elise took it all in, never letting go of the photograph and glancing at it from time to time.

"I understand wartime was a strange and difficult time for men," she said finally, then kissed Dennis' image in the photograph.

"Do you think you would like to meet him, Mam?"

Elise looked towards the window and thought for a short while. "I am not sure after all these years that I might not be unsettling to him. Did he say he would like to meet me?"

"We didn't have that conversation, Mam, but I am sure he would."

"I have been thinking, Laura, since you have been away. I have missed you so much, and I am so sorry for the pain I caused you in not telling you about Hans, your real father."

"As you say, Mam, life can be difficult and tricky decisions have to be made at times. You made the best ones you felt were right for me at the time."

Elise nodded, her facial expression acknowledging and agreeing with Laura.

"I have been thinking about the past a lot. Until you began this search for your roots, I had always wanted to forget and move on. Indeed, I was frightened, perhaps even a little ashamed to share the story of my life back then, but I remember what a special man your real father was.

"Yes! He was older than me and some might say he was taking advantage, but if they had really known the full true story, that I did care for him greatly, I am sure they would have understood. It was my feeling of shame caused by society at the time that meant I was unable to share my true feelings with neighbours and friends and why it led to me breaking up with him and the stigma you would have carried too if people found out you were illegitimate. I have carried that guilt all these years until now, but right now I feel strangely liberated.

"Laura, I would like to go and find your real father, just so you can meet him and round this rather convoluted circle of life. Would you come with me?"

Now it was Laura's dilemma to ponder.

"We don't have to, Mam. Do not feel you have to prove anything to me. I love you!"

"I love you more than words can express, sweetheart, but I think we should."

Laura paused and finally said, "If it makes you happy, I am happy, but it will have to be a short visit. I don't have much vacation time left. Do we know where we might even find him, though?"

Elise stood and went through to the writing bureau in the lounge and returned with a letter.

"This is the last communication I had from Hans. It is postmarked Munich in 1970 and there is an address. We could start here, even though we are talking a quarter of a century ago.

"I had replied to an earlier letter from him and explained that I was now happily married and had a little girl called Laura. I told him to forget me and never contact me again. He wrote a few more times but I tore all these letters up. For some reason, I kept this one.

"As you see, he apologises once again for not being there for you and me and asks for a photograph of you. He says he wants to help in any way he can. He explains he had gone back to Germany to care for his ailing mother but she had since died.

"To my shame, I never replied. I thought it would be unfair on Reggie, who as we know was a great dad to you. I never heard from him again. Even this was still addressed like all the others to *Elise Macrae, Comrie c/o Royal Hotel*. It was only because I had kept in touch with Marjorie the cook there that I had the letters forwarded to me.

"It's twenty-five years on now. He must be late seventies at least. He may not even be alive, but I would like to see where he was from at the very least."

"Let's do it, Mam. Wow, this is some year of finding out who we really are," she said, laughing and hugging her mother.

Twenty-Four

Mission reunion

It was early afternoon one December day as they reached their hotel in Munich. There was snow on the ground and it was bitterly cold.

This historic, 4-star Torbrau Hotel was situated in the Old Town, just a five-minute walk away from the Marienplatz, and just 100 yards from the nearest S-Bahn station.

Dropping their bags in their room, they decided to wander out for an hour or two to stretch their legs after the day's journey and to get their bearings, soon reaching the Marienplatz with the Neues Rathaus (the New City Hall) dominating one side of the square.

As they arrived, a small crowd gathered, looking up at the centrepiece, the rather colourful 'Glockenspiel'. It was very busy, with pedestrians everywhere scurrying like ants on a mission to get home out of the cold. A Christmas market was attracting tourists and residents alike, and the delicious scent of red wine, brandy orange and assorted spices in the aromatic *Glühwein* on sale was the perfect temptation to warm them up on this wintry day as Christmas music played, filling the Marienplatz with seasonal joy!

Standing behind the small group, Elise and Laura listened with them for a few minutes to the city guide.

"It chimes and re-enacts two stories from the 16th century. It consists of forty-three bells and thirty-two life-sized figures. The top half of the Glockenspiel tells the story of the marriage of the local Duke Wilheim the fifth, but sadly we have missed it for today, as in the winter it is only at eleven and midday the Glockenspiel rings out its story." A sigh of disappointment accompanied by acceptance of the guide's explanation murmured through the group, but Laura and Elise made a mental note to come back at those times in the next day or so!

Returning to their hotel, they entered the small café, warming themselves up with a delicious hot chocolate. Both sat warming their hands on the mugs, as two plates of *Apfelstrudel* arrived at the table, and their eyes lit up in anticipation of consuming this Bavarian delight.

"Shall we get a taxi to this address we have tomorrow, or perhaps the train, the S-Bahn?" said Laura, alluding to Hans Lautenbach's last known residence.

"Perhaps we ought to find out whereabouts it is first," said Elise, sensibly planning as always.

Laura stood and took the letter to the front desk. "Can you please tell us where this address is located and the best way of getting there? Could we walk?"

"Let me see," said the smartly turned-out grey-suited gentleman behind reception. "Ah yes, Laimerstrasse, this is near the Nymphenburg Palace, too far to walk, Madam." With typical Teutonic delivery, he said, "Take the S-Bahn to Laim. It is efficient, not expensive and very quick, and then just a minute or two's walk to number 40. Train every six minutes and about a twenty-minute journey."

*

Sure enough, next morning, after a good night's sleep and fortified by a hearty Bavarian breakfast, Elise and Laura took the short walk to the S-Bahn station and in no time, they were disembarking at Laim Station. Stepping onto the street, they asked a passer-by for directions, who typically spoke English and told them the way. Within a minute, they were standing in front of a rather grand turreted property, painted in lemon. The three-storey property with its garret rooms beside the turrets was impressive. It looked like a mini-chateau.

Most astonishing, though, was the fact that this was not just a superb piece of architecture but it was a hotel.

As they approached the entrance, Laura said, "I think we might have the wrong address." She checked the letter again, but it just confirmed this was the right place.

When they entered the small reception area, a young lady was busy behind the curved semi-circular desk in the corner.

"*Guten Tag, wie geht's?*" came the greeting with a smile.

"Hello, do you speak English?"

"Yes, I do, how can I help you? Do you have a reservation?"

"Er... no," hesitated Laura.

"We were looking for Hans Lautenbach. Does he live here?"

"I know no one of that name, I am afraid. What is it in connection with?" Laura produced the letter and asked if she had the right place.

"Yes, this is our address. I have only been here for six months. Excuse me, can I just check with the owner if they have heard of this gentleman?"

A few minutes later, a rather rotund middle-aged lady appeared.

"Hello, I am Margarethe Erdmann. I believe you are looking for Hans Lautenbach."

Elise and Laura nodded in unison.

"Hans used to own this hotel, but he sold it to my husband and I about ten years ago. It had become a little too much for him. I think his health was not so good and I believe he retired to the mountains around Königssee in Southern Bavaria near the Austrian border, a beautiful location."

"Thank you, might you have an address or a telephone number?" said Laura.

"Let me see," said Margarethe. "I do believe I did

have a contact for Hans." Disappearing into her office momentarily, she returned with a slip of paper. "There we are, address and telephone number. It was ten years ago, so hopefully he is still there. How do you know Hans?"

Laura smiled. "I am his daughter, Laura, and this is my mother, Elise," she said, without hesitation.

"Pleased to meet you. I didn't realise Hans had any family. That is a coincidence but maybe not – this hotel used to be called the Gasthof Elise before we changed it to Hotel Erdmann Hof."

Stuck for words, they looked at one another, thanked Frau Erdmann and took their leave as they headed back into the Old Town by S-Bahn, neither saying anything for a while.

Both knew, though, what the other was thinking. Gasthof Elise, after Laura's mum, and was Hans still alive?

Standing in the Marienplatz, they had made it back in time to see the wonder of the Glockenspiel in full action at midday, then walked the short distance to their hotel. They had two more nights booked but knew now was the time to go to Königssee if they were ever going to.

Calling from the hotel room, they accessed an outside line and listened as the phone dial clicked and purred away, then the ringing tone, repeating time after time before finally someone answered. '*You have reached the home of Hans Lautenbach. I cannot come to the phone at the moment. Please leave a message after the beep.*' Laura looked at her mother and hung up.

The rail route was too complicated, so Laura decided to hire a car. She was told it was a four-hour journey.

It was dark by the time they arrived in Königssee. They managed to get a room right by the lake at Schönau on the Königssee in a splendid establishment called the Schiffmeister Hotel. It seemed to be closing down for the winter, as there were not many guests in evidence, and a middle-aged man seemed somewhat grouchy. They had clearly disturbed his evening, but he warmed up and became friendlier. He was resplendent in his green embroidered waistcoat and lederhosen. He very kindly carried their bags to a first-floor room, the old wooden staircase and hallway floorboards creaking to announce their arrival and progress on the first floor.

They were shown to a very large room with two single beds and an ornate walnut wardrobe, then advised breakfast would be served between 7.30 and 9.30am and wished by their host a good night's sleep.

Laura went to close the heavy curtains and noticed the close proximity of the Königssee, as she could make out the twinkling of lights below them near the lake edge and around the small boat dock, just across from their small balcony.

Exhausted from the journey and driving in unfamiliar country, they slept soundly and were only disturbed by the sound of people outside. Laura reached for her wrist watch on the bedside table; it was 8.30am.

She looked over at her mother still sound asleep. Laura walked over to the window to see the source of the sounds that had woken her. A number of people were lining up to board a small attractive white-topped wooden-built lake cruiser; some people were sitting on tables in front of the hotel, awaiting their turn to board whilst finishing a coffee.

Elise stirred and before long they were enjoying a rather satisfying buffet breakfast.

In the light of day, the hotel oozed history and was in a perfect location. Over lunch, they learned that it was ninety-five years old and had always been family run.

Armed with the address of Hans Lautenbach, they checked its location with the hotel desk. Both wrapped up warm and stepped out into the cool but sunny morning air as a brisk breeze blew up off the lake into Schönau am Königssee. A dusting of snow lay on the surrounding peaks, making rather an idyllic winter vista.

"Mam, it's so beautiful, it almost takes your breath away."

Elise could only nod. They set off on the main road out of Schönau and sure enough, as per their instructions, a left turn near Berchesgarten Railway Station took them onto Oberschönauer Strasse, and as the road steadily climbed, they were surrounded by spectacular mountain views.

"We are so fortunate that the day is clear and sunny, even if it is a little cold," said Elise, absolutely enthralled with the scenery.

Laura was rightly cautious, suspecting the road was a little treacherous from black ice in places. Before long, they reached a small but distinct sign on their left which told them they had arrived at 'Berge Blick Oberschönau'. Steadily and cautiously, the car was guided up the narrow but well-laid track until a large old traditional chalet-type house came into view. Its long sloping roof and carved wooden balconies were quintessentially Alpine.

Feeling somewhat as if they were part of a fairy tale, Elise and Laura stood in silence as they surveyed this beautiful old structure. Snow lay on the roof, and icicles hanging from the guttering twinkled in the morning sun, dropping their meltwater drilling holes into the snowy ground below.

A bench sat outside, up against a whitewashed exterior wall, below a shuttered window to the side of a small door. Around the corner, an arch of stone seemed to be the main entrance as they approached the solid-looking metal-studded wooden door. They were full of trepidation as Laura raised the heavy door knocker and announced their presence.

Stepping back, they scanned the dark wood upper storey for signs of life and gazed through the rather small downstairs windows.

There didn't seem to be anyone stirring. They noted there was another vehicle parked outside, a pale blue Audi station wagon. After no response, they started to walk around the outside of the house; they could see an animal-like figure on one gable and a very attractive mural or painting on the side.

It was cool in the shade until they reached the back of the property, where the sun warmed them again.

A man came into view on a narrow terrace. He was slumped in a wheelchair, his lap covered in a colourful heavy woollen blanket, his homburg hat keeping his head warm. A light breeze ruffled the blue and green feather in the hatband. As they approached, he seemed to be dozing.

Just as they reached the table, a small stocky woman came through the door.

"Who are you?" she forcefully blurted out in a harsh guttural German. "What are you doing here?"

Her outburst awoke the elderly man. His eyes focused, his mind adjusted and he looked at Elise and Laura.

Ignoring the lady's questions, Elise spoke first. "Hans, is that you? It's Elise." She knelt beside him, took his hand and looked into his light blue eyes, and his bemusement turned to recognition.

"Elise, can that really be you, Elise? *Mein liebling, mein schatz.*" They hugged each other. Laura felt a tear on her cheek and the older lady looked on, bewildered.

Twenty-Five

Bittersweet

The startled lady, now realising the interlopers were friends, offered to bring a pot of coffee.

"*Ja bitte! Kaffee, sehr gut,* Frau Winkelmann."

Settling themselves around the rectangular wooden table, Elise sat beside Hans, holding his hand, and Laura opposite as Frau Winkelmann returned with a pot of steaming hot coffee and a plate of home-made stollen.

Elise patted Hans' cold hands and rubbed them to warm them up.

"You always did have a sweet tooth, Hans."

Hans smiled. "What a wonderful surprise, Elise. *Wunderbar, ausgezeichnet,* Frau Winkelmann."

Frau Winkelmann, not quite understanding the gravity of the situation, said, "Don't be out here long, Herr Lautenbach, you will get cold," before she departed for the warmth of the chalet's interior.

"Do you want to go in?" said Laura.

"No! I am fine. I love the fresh air," he said, breathing in deeply before lapsing into a coughing fit, as Elise massaged his back, settling him down. He looked at Laura then Elise.

"Is this…" and then hesitated. "Is this by any chance Laura?"

"It is indeed, Hans," said Elise proudly, a big grin on her face.

Hans looked at Laura and said, "You are beautiful, like your mother. I never ever thought I would get to meet you. I am humbled and blessed all at once," as he beamed benevolently and Laura shyly inclined her head without reply, just kneeling beside him and taking his left hand between her palms.

"At last, I meet you, Father."

For an hour, they shared their stories and their adventures, barely scraping the surface of the last thirty years.

"You must stay for lunch. Mrs Winkelmann is a wonderful nurse and housekeeper, if a little strict," he said, winking and smiling at Laura whilst squeezing Elise's hand.

Laura wheeled the chair towards the door and a little ramp before entering a large lounge. The dark varnished wooden floor arrayed with superb Persian carpets and two old-fashioned ornate carver chairs besides an armchair and settee were in perfect keeping with the old property. A white marble fireplace was surrounded by a fireguard, its mantelpiece adorned with candles. A large gilded framed landscape filled the wall between the two windows above the settee.

"This way," said Hans. Frau Winkelmann met them in the doorway to the next room, wiping her hands on her pinafore. "Ah! Frau Winkelmann, there you are, please prepare lunch for us all."

"Herr Lautenbach, I have already anticipated this. Will soup and some cold dishes of meat and cheese suffice?"

As Elise was about to interject not to go to any trouble, Mrs Winkelmann, not waiting for a reply, made a sharp exit to fulfil her duty.

Hans shouted after Frau Winkelmann, "*Herrlich,* Frau Winkelmann. *Herrlich und ein flasche rote wein bitte, nein, champagne.* We must celebrate," he said, turning his head towards Elise.

Over their long lunch, whatever fears Laura and Elise had that it might be tense or difficult, perhaps uncomfortable, disappeared completely. It was as if Laura had known Hans all her life; he didn't seem like her father but more like a kind old uncle or grandfather. His thinning grey hair framed a tired and colourless face. He would eat a little and cough a little.

"How long are you here for?" asked Hans hopefully.

Laura looked at Elise. "We must go back tomorrow. Laura has to be back at work. We hadn't planned to make this journey until we met Frau Erdmann at your old home."

Hans nodded, clearly melancholy at the thought that this meeting was only fleeting.

"But we can visit again," consoled Laura, trying to offer hope. Elise nodded agreement.

"That would be nice, but let's just enjoy what time we have together."

"Hans, do you remember you used to sing to me? One song I remember and which was very special was *Auf Wiedersehen*," said Elise, squeezing his hand.

Hans smiled and looked out of the window then in an amazing tenor voice, he began singing.

"Auf wiedersehen, auf wiedersehen.
We'll meet again, sweetheart.
This lovely day has flown away.
The time has come to part.
We'll kiss again, like this again.
Don't let the teardrops start.
With love that's true,
I'll wait for you.
Auf wiedersehen, sweetheart."

Hans started another fit of coughing and put his handkerchief to his mouth. Elise held his hand and tried to calm him, seeing a tear in his eye. He squeezed Elise's hand tightly.

"Frau Winkelmann," shouted Hans, and the obedient and loyal Frau Winkelmann appeared in a trice, albeit with that look of someone being disturbed from their work.

"Can you help me?" said Hans.

Frau Winkelmann, understanding, wiped her hands on a cloth she was holding and wheeled him out of the room. Hans called out, "Back in a moment."

Sure enough, Hans returned after a short while. "Sorry about that, call of nature." Hans' voice trailed off as he started coughing once more and, putting his handkerchief to his mouth once more, he became a little distressed.

"I think Herr Lautenbach should rest for a short while now," said Frau Winkelmann, not waiting for a response, as she manoeuvred his wheelchair out of the room.

Elise rose with Laura and followed them towards a room which had clearly been turned into a bedroom. Elise could see some oxygen cylinder apparatus beside the bed.

Hans put his hand up and Frau Winkelmann turned the wheelchair slightly towards Elise and Laura. A sense of futility could be seen in his misted eyes. With cracking voice, he said, "Perhaps you can call back in the morning before you leave." Elise stepped forward and kissed him on the forehead. He wearily produced a half-smile and Frau Winkelmann closed the door.

Laura felt it was best they leave and collected their coats before walking out across the sun terrace into the cold afternoon. The sun had disappeared and grey foreboding clouds promised more snow. As they returned to their car, the front door opened and the gravel crunched under Frau Winkelmann's ample weight.

"Herr Lautenbach wishes to apologise. He has been so pleased to see you. I have not seen him so happy ever, he is just a little overcome and needs some rest."

"What is wrong with him?" asked Elise.

After a little hesitation, she said with surprising emotion, "He has lung cancer, I am afraid it is incurable. He refuses to go to hospital. I do not know how he has lasted so long. I have been with him almost the entire time he has lived here, he is a fine man!"

Even the redoubtable Frau Winkelmann looked as though she might cry.

"Thank you for all you do for Hans, Frau Winkelmann. I can see he is very thankful for your kindness."

Frau Winkelmann smiled, nodded, turned and returned to the house.

That evening was spent having a pleasant meal at the hotel and talking about the day and discovering Hans but, most of all, accepting he may not be here for long.

"I think my biological father is a very pleasant and charming man, Mam. I am not sure what I was expecting. I almost didn't want to like him, but I do!"

Elise looked affectionately at Laura. "I see him when I look at you, Laura. I always have and I have never until now been able to share that with you! I am so glad we made this journey."

"It was meant to be," said Laura.

*

Next morning, having paid their bill, they left after breakfast and returned to Han's house on the hill.

Over coffee, they chatted. It was like coming home already.

"Before you go, you must give me your address, Elise. I would like to write to you if I may." Before Elise could answer, he looked at Laura. "Would you mind if I wrote to you also, Laura?"

Laura, sitting beside him, this time put her hand on his. "Please do, I would love to get to know you."

Hans inclined his head as if accepting he knew he might never see her again.

As they left, Hans was wheeled to the doorway by Frau Winkelmann. Elise and Laura gave Hans a big hug and Laura pecked Hans on the cheek. "May God bless you, *Vater*."

Hans filled up; his strong façade melted. Elise kissed his hands and looked him in the eye. "Thank you so much for Laura. She is wonderful and with her, I always have you."

Returning to their car, they exchanged waves and before long they were on their journey home.

*

For the next two months, they exchanged correspondence and Christmas cards with Hans. Their world now seemed at ease whenever they were together. Elise and Laura laughed and told stories just like old times. The tensions of the past year had all disappeared, and now they seemed closer than ever.

Hans wanted them to return in the spring. '*I have so much to show you,*' he wrote. '*Cable car up Jenner Mountain, if you can bear it. Berchtesgaden and the Eagle's Nest. You didn't have time to take the boat across the lake to St Bartholomew's Church, lots to return for,'* he pleaded.

Both Elise and Laura said they would be back, hopefully in the summer.

One day, Elise and Laura were returning from a leisurely walk along the River Earn, where they had been chatting about their holiday plans to travel back to Königssee and perhaps fly to Salzburg and stay a couple of nights there first. It was a bright, sunny winter's day; a little frost had melted and the weak winter sun sparkled on the water, giving them hope of impending spring.

Elise needed to pop into Hansen's and pick up some cheese. "Nice day today, Mrs Dewar. Nice to see you, Laura. Thank you so much. See you soon," said the assistant. Elise placed the cheese into her wicker basket besides the sourdough bread she had picked up earlier.

"Shall we pop into the Café Comrie for a coffee and a treat?"

"Why not?" said Laura, her arm locked in her mother's.

This delightful old café, once the granary, still sported its old wooden counter. Elise thought back to her younger days and reflected on the last year and all she now knew about her real parents and what had happened to them.

"Penny for them," said Laura as she stirred her coffee and took a bite of a pain au chocolat.

"Just thinking, I wonder what would have happened if I had never met Hans."

Laura raised her eyebrows. "Well, I suspect I might not be here now." They both laughed and felt blessed. Life was back to normal but enriched.

*

"Hello, Mrs Dewar, how are you today?" said the postman as they arrived at the gate to their home at the same time.

"Very good, Hamish, and you?"

"Fine and dandy," he said, shuffling the mail in his hands and giving Elise a couple of letters. "Another airmail one for you, Mrs Dewar."

"Thank you, Hamish, have a good day."

Dropping the letters on the table, Elise took off her coat, hung it on the coat rack in the hall and returned to put the kettle on.

"Another letter from Hans, eh, Mam?" said Laura, teasing.

"Aye, he writes regularly."

Placing the teapot and cups on the tray, she rattled the cake tin. "I made some scones yesterday. I knew you were coming and you love my fruit and cheese scones," she said, turning and placing a plate of her creations on the table.

"Wow, Mam, I will have to get some exercise done. I have just had a pain au chocolat."

"So, you don't want one then?"

Laura gave her mother a winsome smile and took a scone before lathering it with a thick layer of butter.

Settling down to enjoy a hot cup of tea, Elise used

her trusty letter opener, which had been a gift from her Aunt Janet, and sliced open the first letter, a bill from British Telecom, before tossing that aside. She deftly opened the delicate paper of the Par Avion airmail letter, unfolded it and started to read.

As she did so, her eyes filled up. Her hands shook.

"What is wrong, Mam?"

"He's passed away, Laura."

"Oh no, not Hans! I am so sorry, Mam," she said, standing and skirting the table to embrace her mother. "I am so sorry. We were so lucky to meet him, Mam – so glad you took me too."

Through misty eyes, Elise continued reading. "Mrs Winkelmann says the funeral is on the 31st of March."

She looked at Laura. "That was yesterday."

"The letter must have been delayed. We have missed the funeral, Mam."

Elise started to sob, releasing the years of tension and emotion all rolled into one. She was so relieved to finally have had hope, joy and happiness and, over the moon, she had begun to accept and understand her life's trials and tribulations and the benefits it had brought, as she hugged Laura. But no sooner was there joy than it was being taken away, but at least some closure had been achieved. But she had learned a tough lesson: never delay doing something it may become too late to achieve!

Twenty-Six

At the crossroads

Elise had kept busy and tried not to think about what might have been for Laura and her real father, if only she had told her earlier.

Elise pondered the future not just for herself but also for Laura, as they came to terms with Hans passing.

In the couple of weeks that had passed since hearing of her biological father's death, Laura had continued to work hard but was more unsettled than ever; she had little social life, as she was always busy.

"Hi, Mam," said Laura, making her weekly call home.

"Hi, Laura, are you okay? You sound a little tired and sad if you don't mind me saying."

"I am tired, Mam, but I am also a little irritable. I

cannot settle to do anything, somehow. I am uncertain about my life path."

"In what way?"

"I don't know. Perhaps it's just a phase but when I finish work, I am too exhausted to do anything, too tired to even think about the future. I feel emotionally drained. Occasionally, I will go out for a drink in Arisaig with a couple of colleagues from work but somehow, well, I don't feel I know what I want out of life. I love my job but this last year has unsettled me. I feel I need to spread my wings."

"Do you mean you should be looking for a new challenge, seeking a new job, love?"

"Maybe, but putting my cards on the table, Mam, I have been thinking hard about going to live in Greece, perhaps getting a hotel job there, changing direction and reinventing myself."

"But you don't speak Greek, Laura, and their lifestyle is totally different to anything you are used to," said Elise dismissively.

"If it was in one of the popular resorts the British go to, I could be useful, especially with my experience, and I could learn Greek, and I feel I need a total change!"

"I would miss you so much," said Elise in a soft but melancholy tone.

"I know, Mam, but I am into my thirties, and no family, no house, no husband and, well, I have not travelled much. I feel I need to take a risk or two and explore whilst I have no real ties."

There was a silence on the other end of the phone.

Then "I understand, Laura. It's selfish of me making you feel bad just because I would miss you."

"Why don't you come with me?"

Elise spluttered a little then laughed.

"You must be joking. This old woman in Greece? Who do you think I am, Shirley Valentine?" She followed it with a chuckle.

"Mam, you are only in your early fifties, you are young. I know you still do a bit of cleaning for people but why not give it a go?"

"Laura, I have to be practical. Where would I live? How could I afford it and where would my income come from? This house is rented and it's home. Everything I know and feel comfortable with is here, lots of fond memories."

"I have some savings," said Laura, realising it might be a pipe dream for her mother to join her.

"Even with our joint meagre savings, it would be hard. It's clear to me you must go and find yourself and enjoy life, sweetheart."

Accepting defeat, Laura changed her tack. "I received a letter from Dennis today, Mam, your pa."

"Is it him that has put this idea in your head?"

"No, Mam, really it has been on my mind for a while."

"How are Dennis and Maria?" she said, trying not to sound sarcastic.

"Dennis said he would like to meet you one day but totally understands if you do not want to. After all, who knows what time there is left for all of us? There is a letter here for you, Mam, from Dennis. I will send it to you."

Laura posted the small sealed envelope that had come enclosed with Laura's to her mother.

*

The next day, Elise received the letter. She propped it against the toaster and left it there for an hour or so before curiosity got the better of her. Pouring herself a cup of tea, she sat at the kitchen table, turning the letter in her hands then finally opening it.

> *Dear Elise,*
>
> *I don't really know how to start this letter other than to say I wish I had known about you all these years.*
>
> *I want to share with you the last time I was with your mother, it is important to me.*
>
> *It was late summer, 1943. I never thought I would see Martha again but I had been in Scotland doing some training attached to a Commando group at Inverailort. We were given a weekend pass before returning to base in Aldershot.*
>
> *I had borrowed, well, unofficially, anyway, an old Triumph Dolomite Roadster and driven myself and a couple of pals into Fort William. It seemed to take us ages. The other chaps went for a beer but I just wanted to relax and watch a film.*
>
> *So, I headed to a local cinema called the Playhouse in the High Street for the matinee.*

Actually, there was not much in Fort William at all. The guys had already fallen into the first pub they came to.

In the cinema foyer, I was suddenly transfixed. I thought I was imagining it. I had heard Martha's voice. She was with a couple of French army chaps and another FANY colleague.

She had her back to me. As I put my hand on her shoulder, she turned for one moment. We just stood, incredulous. Our eyes met, then we just melted into each other's arms. All I heard from her companions as we walked out of the cinema was "Mon dieu."

We jumped into the little Triumph, its roof down. It was a surprisingly warm afternoon and we drove alongside the loch towards Glencoe, your mother's auburn hair blowing in the wind. We didn't know where we were going. We just knew we were together. We drove along the A82 and stopped to witness a fabulous small waterfall, the meeting of three waters. It felt like our emotions were gushing just as wildly as nature's bounty.

Before long, we saw a small road to the right and decided to follow the river, which was pounding seawards to our left, and a narrow track with the occasional passing place took us to a splendid sea loch. There was not a soul around.

It was by now late afternoon. Bracken, ferns and fallen trees festooned the landscape. It was desolate but beautiful. It was clear this was a forested area but no logger in sight, and I spread a red tartan blanket on the side of the loch and we just gazed at each other like it was all a dream.

I cannot explain the feeling I had. I loved your mother so much! We talked and laughed and held each other. It started to get dusk and the midges were starting to be bothersome, so we jumped back in the little roadster and the darn vehicle would not start. It just wheezed and turned over but the spark plugs would just not start. Martha was laughing as I tried to dry the spark plugs and try again but no luck. Then it started to rain. I grabbed the blanket and wrapped it around us and we walked back to a small bothy we had seen about half a mile back up the track, hoping to get some assistance.

A powerful burn thundered its way off the mountain towards the river beside the bothy. I knocked but there was no reply. Walking around the outside, there was no one around. The rain was heavier. I tried the door and leaned against it with some pressure and the door burst open and we fell into the cool and musty interior. It was rather dark. I struck up my lighter and found some wood and soon had a fire going in the fireplace. An oil lamp gave us some light and a further search resulted in a treasure find of a half-empty bottle of Scotch and a basket with a small batch of neeps and tatties.

What a wonderful night we had. It was really cold and damp but we cuddled up, our two hearts *beating as one. We did not want the night to end!*

Of course, it did. We both went back to duty and I was posted overseas, not at all where I thought I would be but to the Middle East.

I never saw Martha again, although I did receive a letter or two. Sadly, I no longer have those.

Listening to Laura's determined efforts to find out who her grandmother and grandfather were was wonderful, yet so sad to hear Martha is not with us anymore. I cannot thank her enough and, of course, what means so much to me is knowing I have a daughter and granddaughter who both look so much like Martha.

One thing stays in my mind: Martha took the code name 'Etive'. I can only think and want to believe it is because of our last night in a bothy together beside the loch. The loch we spent our last hours of loving union on was Loch Etive. It sounds such a French name, and I guess that is how it became part of her identity.

One more thing... when we parted, I serenaded your wonderful mother with a popular song we enjoyed together called We'll Meet Again. I guess we never had the opportunity.

But I do hope one day I might meet you, Elise, and be able to hold you, but I totally understand if you do not want to do that.

Your father,
Love, Dennis XXX

In that moment, Elise understood and had to admit to

herself she would never feel whole until she met her father. Perhaps that would be the right thing to do or she would always wonder exactly what the experience would be like, to actually meet someone of your blood for the first time.

Reaching for the phone, Elise called Laura.

"Mam, great to hear from you. Are you all right?"

"Would it make you happy if I did come to Greece?" Elise probed.

"Ecstatic, Ma, absolutely made up."

"Laura, you have a way with you, and I love you so much. I will make sure I have some cover for my little part-time job. When were you thinking?"

"A month's time if that suits you"

"That soon? Won't it be too cold?"

"No! It can be warm in Greece, even hot in May, Mam."

*

And so it was, on a warm windless Greek day in Mid-May 1996, the year of the coolest May temperatures in the United Kingdom since 1902, Elise and Laura disembarked at Athens Airport.

Collecting their bags, they passed into the terminal arrivals area and there they were greeted by a whole reception committee consisting of Dennis, Maria and Aris.

Elise looked at Dennis then at Laura. Dennis hesitated, then stepped forward, hugged Laura and hesitantly turned to Elise.

Putting out his hand, he held hers. "I never knew about you, Elise. I just wish I had. I loved your mother. She was a treasure, and I can see her in your eyes." He hugged Elise, who melted into his arms. Her heart thumped and she felt secure. Dennis took her bag and Elise put her arm through his, as with Maria, and they headed out into the warm afternoon sun.

Aris looked at Laura. Both said nothing, just gazed into one another's eyes, then Aris produced a white rose from behind his back. "Like the white rose which has bloomed again, I knew you would be back!"

EPILOGUE

The word *epilogue* comes from the Greek *epilogos*,
which means '*conclusion word*'.

Laura was sad to learn later in life that Vera Atkins had passed away. She was cremated in the year 2000 and her ashes went to her sister-in-law, Phoebe Atkins, wife of Vera's brother, Guy, who lived in Cornwall. Vera's ashes were scattered amongst the memorial stones of Vera and Guy in Zennor Churchyard near St Ives.

Vicky Greaves sadly developed dementia and is in a care home in Ludlow but still enjoys a glass of red wine.

Laura keeps in touch with Cathy Arvieux and still hopes to take her grandchildren and husband to meet her one day in Toulouse!

In the autumn of 1996, a letter arrived in Comrie addressed to Elise and Laura. It was from a lawyer in Munich. It announced that following the settling of the estate of Hans Lautenbach, it transpired that he had bequeathed a substantial inheritance of money to Laura and a small amount of money to Elise, along with some artefacts, including his gramophone and record collection, one of which was a long-playing record of Beethoven featuring *Für Elise*.

Thanks to the bequest from her biological father, Hans, Laura is now the proud proprietor of her very own hotel.

ACKNOWLEDGEMENTS

Sincere thanks once more to my editor at Matador Publishing who has been as constructive, understanding and patient as ever, also my cover designer at Matador, who has created a brilliant cover design. Dianne and Pauline for their preview read of *Etive*, giving thoughts and advice, and the wonderful copy editor at Matador.

Henrik Chart, who gave up his time to give Dianne and I a splendid in-depth S.O.E.-themed tour of Arisaig and its neighbouring coastal environs. His knowledge and keen search for the minutiae of the S.O.E. in this area have been very important in my understanding of life and use of locations in the S.O.E. during WWII in this beautiful area of Scotland.

Although this book is a work of fiction and its story and characters imaginary, I was anonymously told the tale of a lady who was found deceased on liberation of a concentration camp in Germany in the closing stages of WWII. These awful circumstances were discovered by an Allied Army officer who knew her. My recreation of this event has been altered and dramatised considerably.

Noreen Riols, former S.O.E., provided a fabulous insight into the machinations of this secret organisation in her book *Secret Ministry of Ag and Fish,* whilst *A Life in Secrets,* Sarah Helm, was invaluable for understanding the life and character of Vera Atkins.

Moondrop to Gascony by Anne-Marie Walters inspired and informed me through her own experiences in wartime France.

Flames in the fields – Rita Kramer was helpful, and continual factual information and correction from Steve Kippax, Bernard O'Connor, Alan 'Fred' Judge, Martin Briscoe and many others of the Specialoperationsexecutive closed email group proved invaluable.

Not forgetting Tania Szabo and the wonderful insight she gave us over lunch with her recollections as a child of her mother, Violette, as well as discussing the splendid book Tania wrote about her mother's missions in the Special Operations Executive, *Young, Brave and Beautiful.* Sharing such personal memories was invaluable in my understanding of the world of S.O.E. agents.

A really long chat with Tony Thomson, nephew of Pearl Witherington, who was the only woman to lead an S.O.E. network in France during WWII, was fascinating, as Tony had a personal insight into her life and shared experiences with her, such as the dedication of the Valençay Memorial. Pearl and I share the same birth date: 24th June!

Veronica Garman, whose splendid insight into wartime Cairo, which she portrayed in her diaries, was a terrific boon in setting the scenes there.

Vera Lynn's inspiring and heart-warming songs of the era gave real life hope and support to many through the tough days of war, as my characters would have drawn strength from them too.

I could not resist referencing a childhood favourite song by Nana Mouskouri, *The White Rose of Athens*. which evokes the joy of that splendid country, its people and of course love!

DON'T BRING ME FLOWERS

RONALD D MORGAN

In 1995, following the death of his father, Billy meets Gwen, an old friend of his parents, and so begins an odyssey into their mysterious wartime past, bringing surprising consequences.

Billy's quest for the truth leads him to Wales, Scotland, Myanmar, Singapore, Australia and Japan, where he unearths heart-wrenching stories of bravery, sacrifice, love and survival during World War II in Southeast Asia.

Will the roller coaster of discovery, new relationships and unexpected changes in his life bring Billy the contentment and fulfilment he craves?

REVIEWS

An intriguing story which unravels to reveal the horrors of war through personal hardships. Twists and turns right to the end to keep the reader fully engaged. A thoroughly good read!
Pauline T

A wonderfully poignant first novel, written with the panache of a seasoned author. Having all the ingredients of a best-seller, its cleverly interwoven story and memorable characters linger long after the final page is turned. Brilliantly researched and beautifully descriptive, this book will take you on an unforgettable journey.
Isobel S

I purchased the kindle edition of this book after it was recommended to me; I actually had no idea what the book was going to be about, but boy, I'm so pleased I did buy it. The story twists and turns with quite a few 'I didn't see that coming' twists in the tale. The book is moving, and in some parts sad, however it too is an uplifting book and certainly one I found hard to put down. Highly recommended.
Emma H

This was a very informative read, I learnt a lot about the Far East and the War. The story gripped me and I kept reading all day as I wanted to find out what happened! There were also parts of the story that were based in familiar territory I recognised – Shrewsbury and the Welsh coast. I recommend this book.
Deborah S

RONALD D MORGAN

MORGAN
✈ THE ✈
TRAVEL

FROM THE TOPIC OF CANCER...

...TO THE TROPIC OF CAPRICORN

Morgan the Travel is an autobiographical travel memoir tracing over fifty years of globetrotting, much of the time as a Tour Manager escorting groups of adventurous souls around the world. The anecdotes related reflect the myriad of adventures, cultures and colourful people who have crossed Ron's path and enriched his knowledge and life.

This is also a story of the wonderful influence his family plays on this journey; of the parents, partners, children, grandchildren and friends who shared many of Ron's escapades. It reflects the highs and lows of life and the importance of never giving in.

It helps us understand that we learn every day and it is the journey not the destination that educates us, makes us wiser and ultimately comforts and sustains us.

To accept we are always learning allows us to have an open heart and mind and to be a more contented person, always prepared to listen!

More than anything, *Morgan the Travel* strives to give us hope that we can triumph over adversity whilst having the desire to leave a positive legacy and make the world a better place! Remember: every day, we all have a choice. Better times will come!

REVIEWS

Inspiring, informative, funny, entertaining and at times brutally honest. I loved Morgan the Travel. Ron Morgan's sheer vitality and determination to follow his dreams and make the most of his life is a revelation. If you want to be inspired, plan a holiday or just have a good read, this book is a must.
David Taylor

Ron shares his personal back-catalogue of incredible journeys to far-flung places and through life itself. Descriptive, evocative, and always authentic, he has a knack of taking you with him whether soaking up the smells and sounds of his beloved Indian subcontinent, or navigating his way through the more sobering challenges of his health.

A Christmas Miracle

By Ronald D. Morgan

In these times of doom and gloom, this is a perfect gift to lift the spirits, an opportunity to get this heart-warming festive tale for your children and grandchildren! It is a short children's book set in the 1930s in a South Walian hill village and tells the tale of a heroic act and the wonderful community-spirited efforts of two small boys, Dennis and Roy, and their faithful dog, Lucky! Full of adventure, excitement and the feel-good factor.

REVIEWS

It's a heartwarming tale… we loved it.
Rhian T

Absolutely beautiful story, my grandchildren loved it.
Gill P

Eve and Mia are really enjoying this book and I love reading it to them every night.
Sally B

THE **ADVENTURES** OF
TOGGLE AND **TARKA**

RONALD D MORGAN

JUST RELEASED!

A charming book with a strong Shropshire setting, this has the feel of a Beatrix Potter meets Dr Seuss with wonderful colour illustrations supporting the rhythmic prose.

It's Toggle and Tarka to the rescue!

Toggle and Tarka live in an old Georgian house in the Shropshire countryside as adorable companions to the venerable Mrs Parker. Toggle is a sensible black Labrador. Tarka, is an adventurous cocker spaniel who is full of life.

Join the duo as they embark on many adventures together, as they help those around them, make life better for people and animals alike while getting into scrapes and having a lot of fun along the way.

FUTURE BOOKS

Mrs Martin
The biography of an amazing lady who served in the S.O.E. in Cairo during WWII. A fabulous artist and painter, Mrs Martin was multi-talented and lived an extraordinary life, meeting many interesting characters and blessed with three fabulous husbands in her ninety-five years.

Contact us on:
https://www.facebook.com/ronmorgan11

Website: www.ronalddmorgan.wordpress.com

Email: ronmorg@gmail.com

RONALD D MORGAN

Ron was born in Shrewsbury, Shropshire, England and has lived and worked there most of his life, with stints in the USA and Canada. Ron has travelled extensively, tour managing groups worldwide and running his own travel company, Ron Morgan Travel, until 2001.

He was a teacher of travel, tourism and business for over twenty years and a Green Badge guide to tourists around the medieval town of Shrewsbury.

Since 1995, Ron and his wife, Dianne, have also devoted time to the charitable fund they founded, Dreamcatcher Children, which brightens the lives of children and their families who suffer from chronic and life-limiting illnesses.

Ron and Dianne continue to live in Shrewsbury, and he has been dealing with his own terminal diagnosis since 2015. Ron has found writing such a cathartic distraction from dancing with cancer whilst still travelling and watching his beloved local football team, Shrewsbury Town, and of course reading books whenever he can.

This book is printed on paper from sustainable sources managed under the Forest Stewardship Council (FSC) scheme.

It has been printed in the UK to reduce transportation miles and their impact upon the environment.

For every new title that Matador publishes, we plant a tree to offset CO_2, partnering with the More Trees scheme.

For more about how Matador offsets its environmental impact, see www.troubador.co.uk/about/